NOWEVER

Nowever

by Kristina Bak

LUMINARE PRESS
WWW.LUMINAREPRESS.COM

Printed in the United States of America

Cover Design: by Claire Flint Last
Illustrations by Kristina Bak

Luminare Press
438 Charnelton St., Suite 101
Eugene, OR 97401
www.luminarepress.com

LCCN: 2018966747
ISBN: 978-1-64388-035-8

Remembering Anna Purdes Bak and Florence Strand
for their precious gifts of love, light and wisdom.

Table of Contents

Part One:

The Island, 2025

CHAPTER I

I was Stevie The Mouse, an unpopular kid, unremarkable, then I turned sixteen and everything changed. Over that summer I grew taller than my mom, taller than my best friend, Winter, with longer legs. My zits cleared up overnight, my breasts swelled, and I grew cheekbones, like I was digitally enhanced in 3D. *Thank you, DNA.* I started our junior year high on hormones and on the way guys' glances skipped past Winter and widened in surprise at the new me. I was as surprised as they were.

I didn't handle the new admiration and envy that came my way with a lot of grace. I'd never had any practice. I'd done a stellar job of being No One since my first day of kindergarten, when I was so shy I peed my pants rather than ask to use the toilet. I'd started school on the wrong foot and never recovered my balance. From the beginning, I hid behind Winter. I relied on her offhand acceptance, never challenged her starring role. Our moms worked together in real estate; they were the ones who'd declared us "best friends."

When we were little and cute, people mistook us for sisters, because we both had white-blond hair, but Winter was the pretty one, round pink cheeks, round china-blue eyes. My eyes were maple syrup brown and soon my hair turned brown, too, like my mom's. After preschool I grew skinny and sallow. Winter mocked me for my clumsy cartwheels at recess and for using big words, which meant any she didn't know. By third grade, I proved to be a numbers geek and, on into high school, as long as I let her copy my math homework, she let me orbit her like the farthest out planet. In the girl solar system, whether the other girls loved her or feared her, she was the sun. Without her I'd have spun off into deep space alone.

The first Wednesday after Labor Day, three boys who'd scarcely spoken to me all the years we'd shared classrooms and soccer fields cornered me at my locker. Nearly six feet now, I could look them straight in the eye. They seemed friendly, but Winter's shoulders stiffened; she barged in between us. "Leave her alone!"

The boys looked amused. She turned to me. "I'm protecting you, Stevie, because I care. You're naive and gullible. I *know* those guys. You want to stay away from them."

The boys sniggered and automatically, to be a good sport, I laughed, too. You could say I laughed in Winter's face, but I hadn't meant to. I'd learned from her to get along by going along and that was what I was trying to do. For the rest of the week, Winter refused to sit with me in the cafeteria or walk with me between classes. I pretended to ignore her coldness, hoping it would pass, and I avoided the boys, partly to show Winter I'd listened to her warning and partly because I didn't know what to say to them.

The fad for teens of all genders that season was to shave off our eyebrows and grow our hair long. We girls wove fine programmable LED threads through our hair, setting the

Kristina Bak

miniscule lights to brighten and twinkle in the presence of friends and dim near those outside our circles, signaling cliques and alliances. On Monday, Winter flounced by in the hall as though I were invisible, my lights twinkling frantically, hers remaining stubbornly dull. The two girls with her smirked as I called out. "Winter!"

Winter sped up. I chased her and yanked her arm hard. Her feet skidded out from under her and she landed on her butt on the tiled floor. "Ow! What the shit, Stevie?"

The other girls stood back, aghast. I hadn't meant for that to happen. I was shocked, too—shocked at how good it felt, revenge for years of put-downs so subtle no one else caught them, or everyone did, secretly laughing at me. I'd swallowed my hurt as the price of Winter's friendship.

"Sorry, Winter." I offered to help her up.

She batted away my hand. "You knocked me down on purpose! You think you're cool? You've always been weird, Stevie. Now you're big and dangerous, too."

A crowd was gathering, jeering and goading us into a fight. My vengeance didn't feel so rich with Winter playing the pathetic victim, me looming over her. "I didn't do it on purpose."

I'd kept my voice down, but hers rose, melodramatic, to recapture center stage. Oh yeah, that was Winter through and through. "You did! You've been stalking me forever!"

"Stalking?" *What?*

"And copying me!"

"So not fair! You …"

Winter shouted up at me with a mean twist to her lips. "I don't feel *sorry* for you anymore, so *fuck off!*"

My ears rang, everything turned red. I grabbed fistfuls

of Winter's flossy hair. She screeched. I clawed out her light threads, ground them into the tile under my heels and fled.

I'd show Winter my contempt for her crappy popularity games! I hid in the gym locker room and chopped my light threads out of my hair with tiny manicure scissors from my makeup bag. The school security officer nabbed me there. She "disarmed" me and frogmarched me through my gawking classmates, guaranteeing my brief popularity dead.

How invisible had I been? Our high school wasn't large, but the counselor had to look up my name. "Wales... Stevie? Class of 2027? Your mother is Elizabeth Cruz Wales?"

A wide metal desk separated us. I knew the mirrored wall was see-through from the other side. I saw the two of us in it, me wild-eyed, my hair sticking up where I'd cut out chunks with the lights, her all blow-dried and office-appropriate. I looked scary, or scared. She looked coolly efficient. She generally got the worst of the worst in her office. In our privileged Puget Sound island community the *worst* usually involved pharmaceuticals stolen from a parent's stash, sexual misbehavior, or failing grades. My greatest crime until now had been introversion. Honestly, I only knew the counselor's name from her name tag: Ms. Ortega. She hardly looked older than me, but she put on an attitude and said "Hmm" and "Mhmm" as she brought up my records on her screen.

She typed, read, typed, wrote something on a card and gave it to me, meeting my eyes for the first time. "I've made you a crisis appointment with a therapist, Stevie. You're a good student with a clean record. Normally we'd suspend you for this kind of assault, but we're giving you another chance."

Assault! And was someone watching through that mirror glass to protect the counselor from *me*?

She was all no-nonsense, ready for me to leave, no warm and fuzzy facade. "We've called your mom. She's coming. See the therapist on this card and, depending on her risk assessment, you *may* be allowed into your classes tomorrow."

In the car I had a screaming fight with my mom. I did the screaming. I refused to tell her what had happened. She didn't say I'd humiliated us both, but it was true and I knew she was thinking it. She was dressed in her realtor clothes—island business casual and high-heels—so I'd taken her away from something important at work. She clamped her lips in a tight line and clenched her jaw as we drove through a storm. Rain threw itself at the car windows, fir trees shook their branches at us. At home my little dog Hero ran to meet me. I shoved him aside, grabbed the kitchen shears from a drawer, and locked myself in the bathroom with them. I hacked off more hair to fix the damage I'd done at school; I went on cutting for the satisfying crunch of the sharp blades. My hair fell in well-conditioned skeins, leaving clownish patches bunched behind my ears. They wanted weird, I'd give them weird. I slathered peppermint shave creme onto my scalp and shaved it bare with my pink plastic razor, erasing myself like a bad drawing, while Hero whined and scratched at the door to come in.

As I made my last stroke, the light over the sink flickered off. Outside, lightning zigzagged blue-white, thunder cracked and boomed. Suddenly dizzy, I dropped the razor and clung to the granite counter. It dissolved into a jillion pixels, then my fingers and arms and the walls did, too, and …

Sunlight poured into me through stained-glass windows every color of the rainbow, yet I saw myself, too, as an elfin child. My eyes, clear the way only a young child's can be, caught the glass colors; my face beamed bright. My hair, a pale cloud, spiderweb fine, tickled my cheeks. My tiny fingers settled floaty as flower petals toward …

Our lights came back on, revealing the plain old bathroom and me, the new bald me, solid and bleak in the mirror, eyes dilated like I'd seen a ghost. Had I, or was I going psycho? Mom rapped on the door. She gaped like a landed fish when I opened it. I gave her a look that dared her to take me on about my hair; I hadn't used up my fury and hurt. I wanted someone to yell at, but her voice held less anger than pity. "You have an appointment."

Her restraint frightened me. I wanted her to believe I could handle anything she said. If she didn't think I was strong enough, maybe I wasn't. Mom soft-pedaled when another parent might have taken me head-on, but I didn't have another parent, not since my dad sailed away on his "once-in-a-lifetime adventure." I remembered him, or thought I did. I kept our last photo on my dresser. I wanted it to be alive to me, but it was flat, a picture of a blond man in a kitschy Hawaiian shirt, a white-haired preschooler on

Kristina Bak

his lap, both looking surprised over a birthday cake with three candles.

He'd vanished off the coast of Australia. For years, when my mom and I took the ferry across Elliott Bay to Seattle, I'd choose a distant sail. *That's Dad, he's coming home!* I'd look for him among the sailboats tied up on the island's docks. I knew he'd turn, his face ablaze with joy, when I called his name and ran to throw myself into his arms. I was nine or ten when I told myself to stop watching for him. It was like keeping the Santa Claus myth alive after I knew it was bogus, leaving notes with milk and cookies on Christmas Eve, for Mom's sake.

But Dad lived on in my nightmares. He hauled down thrashing sails, his hands scraped bloody from rigging ropes, his teeth bared against the howling wind. The deck tipped up and up beneath his feet, waves tore him off and hurled him overboard. As he sank, his boat creaked, flotsam above him; cold-eyed sharks rose from below, scenting his blood.

The dream recurred with its deadly violence. I never told Mom. Eventually, we got an official-looking letter from Australia. Pieces of my dad's boat, the *Stevie*, corroded by sand and tides but identifiable, had washed up on a beach near Darwin, the last place anyone reported having seen him.

Mom did the best she could to give me everything I needed growing up, but she couldn't bring back my dad. For my twelfth birthday, she gave me watercolor paints. Until then, my artwork involved intricate doodles at school, when I faked working on math problems I'd already figured out. With the watercolors, I spent hours in my room with Hero, part terrier, part who-knew-what, who had been my friend as long as I could remember. I painted portraits of him and pictures of imaginary oceans, undulating blue and green, a tiny boat bobbing in the distance.

I papered my walls with the dog portraits, but hid the seascapes from Mom to not make her sad. She encouraged my art and bought me more paints whenever I ran out. As Hero grew old and slow, I painted him obsessively—chasing balls or cats, digging in the forbidden flowerbed, jumping high in tall grass, as though I could bring back his youth through his image.

Nothing was far from anything on the island. Gena, the therapist, worked in a private clinic a block from the ferry. The storm had passed; I could have walked there in ten minutes, but Mom drove me, to make sure I went. Gena looked familiar, like half the middle-aged people I saw on the ferry or in the local shops did without my really knowing them. She was slim, as tall as I was. She had unusually white skin and sad gray eyes surrounded by crinkles that lifted with her broad smile. I didn't notice what she wore, which may have been why she wore it. I was afraid she was the kind of person who hugged everybody and relieved she didn't try to hug me. I saw recognition in her greeting, but she shifted into professional neutrality and I might have been mistaken.

I didn't belong in her office; the kitten and puppy posters with their sappy *Hang In There!* clichés didn't warm me to her; I wasn't tempted to snuggle her Teddy bears. I vowed to say nothing, whatever platitudes she fed me when she probed my psyche. But she didn't probe. After a few sentences of

Kristina Bak

explanation I didn't listen to and a couple of general questions I didn't answer, she fell silent, too. We sat in matching cushioned armchairs, facing each other across the small room. An antique clock ticked the seconds on a shelf beside a bubbling aquarium, where iridescent gold and blue and orange fish slow-danced through the water. Neon tetras darted among them; a brownish muck-eater bumbled below. However forceful Gena's silence was, I wouldn't talk. Gena watched me watch the fish while the minutes passed. I was mesmerized by the reflected light flashing off their sides. Our hour was nearly over, I was winning, when I thought I heard a man's voice, syrupy, wheedling:

"I smelled her mother's perfume, they passed so close. I could've reached out and touched her, but I didn't, not then. I followed them."

Gena didn't react. Did she hear it? The voice creeped me out like caterpillars down my back. The room disappeared bit by bit around me. Not this again!

My heart hammered. I was buckled tightly into the backseat of a car speeding through the night. My feet didn't reach the floor. It was like watching a movie and being in it at the same time. The man's voice I'd heard came from the driver. He was talking to a woman in the passenger seat. I smelled lilacs and lilies she wore woven into a crown on her head. She said nothing. He went on.

"If you'd seen the light choose that child, so pure, she shone with it. I had to take her."

I kicked at his seat. I couldn't reach that either.

The woman was turning to look at me. I panicked—I didn't care that we were moving, I struggled to get out, but I couldn't undo my seat belt.

"I can't!"

Gena repeated what I'd said aloud. "Can't?"

I rubbed my eyes to refocus. The afterimage of the strange woman's face faded into Gena's, like a forgotten dream.

If I told her what I'd seen and heard, *she'd* label me psycho for sure. I blurted a different answer. "I can't be like the other girls. I don't care about the things they care about, but I fake it, so they'll be my friends. And now they won't be. I've ruined it with Winter and she'll ruin it for me with all the others."

She gave me an intent gaze. "How do you feel about that?"

As therapist-trite as her question was, it hit me in my gut. "Kind of relieved." I laughed, then sobs strangled my laughter. Where did *that* come from?

Gena waited until I'd exhausted my tears and sat hiccuping and wiping my nose. "What *do* you care about, Stevie, when you're not pretending?"

"I like animals. And I like art and …" I stopped. She'd got me to show too much of myself. No way would I say anything about my dad. "I don't know—lots of things."

We watched the fish; my breathing slowed with their tranquil circling. They didn't seem to mind living in a prison safer than the ocean they came from.

The school let me return. My naked skull unnerved the boys who'd loitered around me before. To the popular girls, I'd become an untouchable. I wouldn't show them how much

Kristina Bak

they hurt me. I strode the halls from class to class, head held high, speaking only when called on by teachers. Ms. Ortega summoned me, concerned. I told her I was training to be a Buddhist nun. Banned from questioning religious beliefs, she gave me a skeptical look and let me go.

At home I rarely left my room. I told myself I didn't need friends, I had Hero. He drowsed in my lap as I read nothing in particular, anything to distract myself. Or, he'd limp to the kitchen door and go reluctantly into the yard in the rain, then return to rest his eyes on me while I painted another portrait of him. With my paintbrush, I tried to capture every hair, every glint in his eyes, his pink tongue. I conjured him younger on paper as his flesh and blood body declined.

Until the worst day came. Mom tapped on my door and opened it without waiting, her face drawn and unsmiling. She knelt where Hero lay on his cushion and offered him a treat. He refused it. He licked her hand in apology and gave his stubby tail one feeble wag. Mom fondled his ears. "Stevie, sweetheart, we have to call the vet. She makes house calls. Hero can be right here at home where he's comfortable."

I stared at her, willfully puzzled. "Hero's not sick. Why should we call the vet?"

"Because he's suffering. He's very old, we need to let him go."

I threw down my paintbrush. "Get out! No way, *NO WAY!*" I shoved Mom into the hall and kicked my door shut. I heard her talking on her phone.

I lifted Hero and cuddled him. He whimpered *please make it end.* He looked up at me and I lost myself in his eyes, spiraling into their dark depths.

My breath rasped. I was a little girl again, running behind him through a forest; we were two white blurs in the night. Moss

and fir needles gave beneath my sequined slippers. Brambles
snagged my nightgown, twigs reached out and tangled in my
streaming hair. Fear slithered across the nape of my neck. A
stitch stabbed my side and my short legs faltered. "Puppy, wait!"
I sank to my knees.

We were back in my room, on my bed. In my arms, Hero closed his eyes for the last time. I wailed. Mom rushed in. When she hesitantly reached to hold me, I let her, still partly the little girl lost in the forest. She rocked me while tears streamed down my face, dropping onto Hero's still body.

I wrapped him in an old baby blanket of mine he liked to sleep on. Later, when I was ready, Mom brought a shovel from the garden shed. She dug a hole in her flower border, where daffodils would bloom in springtime, and I lined it with dry fir needles and cedar branches. We buried my heart's companion. His grave was by the fence in the backyard, where I could see it from my bedroom window.

Kristina Bak

CHAPTER 2

I depilated my head until it gleamed, wore the same oversized baggy sweater with torn tights under a thrift store trench coat every day for weeks, and let my eyebrows grow uncontrolled in mourning for Hero. I didn't look like anyone's first choice as a friend, not even my own.

Few others defied techno-chic peer pressure at school. Some who did were labeled Fur People. Imitating rebels and idealists in the urban districts across the bay, they wore hemp and wool, and repurposed vintage leather and fur from species that survived primarily in zoos. They disdained electronic accessories and took pride in their eyebrows, refusing to shave them, drawing them in more heavily, or even getting thick eyebrow weaves. The Fur People paid me some regard; they liked my eyebrows, but the rest of my appearance mystified them.

On a drizzly morning at the end of September, I found a note taped to my school locker. It was written with pencil on paper, in cursive—a style I hadn't seen since my grandmother wrote me letters. I crumpled it and threw it into a recycling bin in case the person who'd written it was watching, but the disused medium intrigued me and, frankly, I'd become about as lonely as I could stand to be. When the hallway emptied, I groped in the bin until I retrieved the scrap. *Please meet me after classes at the Harborside cafe,* unsigned. The handwriting slanted backwards, the writer probably left-handed. It looked harmless, but it could be someone setting me up for a nasty trick.

The historic old coffee shop, intact over three generations, was popular with the wrinkly and nostalgic among islanders and tourists, generally shunned by high school kids. That afternoon, I sidled cautiously into its perpetual coffee and chocolate dusk and relentlessly un-ironic retro music, past framed pages of the last-ever paper *Seattle Times* issue. A boy waved from a banquette in a window niche, the only place in the room touched by cold blue daylight. I knew him. He had level eyebrows, black, like his hair that snaked around his shoulders in multiple thin braids.

I approached, alert for some cruel prank. He stood to greet me, a gesture so anachronistically chivalrous I'd seen it only in movies. He was shorter by three or four inches and not strongly built, but by this one act he claimed ownership of all that was to occur between us. I'd been in third grade and he'd been the new boy in fourth, all dark, watchful eyes, when he'd moved from Singapore with his family. My mom was the realtor when they bought their sprawling house at the south end of the island. His mom, Belinda, had become part of a gym trio with her and Winter's mom.

"Hi, Stevie."

"Nate Wu." I could have left then. I slapped the note onto the table. "Why the mystery?"

"I was afraid you wouldn't come if you knew it was me."

I might not have. We'd never been friends, or enemies,

either. We'd last talked in middle school. He'd gone over to the scruffy Fur People fringes; now I was at least as outlandish as he was. I slid into the banquette. "True, but I'm here. You can buy me an almond cream mocha."

When he came back with our drinks, we lifted our cups and sipped, involuntarily mirroring each other. Nate wore a hemp shirt over scuffed leather pants, an old-fashioned tweed jacket, and laced canvas boots. His clothes gave the impression they'd been worn climbing mountains in 1949, rinsed in rivers and left to dry in the sun—a look that took effort and expense. A fur square was pinned to his left lapel like a badge.

"Is that leopard skin?"

"Ocelot, only about three hundred left in North America. This bit's from a coat that belonged to my late great aunt in Vancouver. After she died, I cut it into three hundred pieces. We wear them in solidarity."

"With the ocelots?"

"For what it's worth. I doubt if the ocelots care."

"But *you* do. Have you seen one?"

"In Woodland Park Zoo."

"That's sad."

Nate's earrings, silver loops, caught the light. No one cool had piercings. Most of the oldies had let theirs grow closed. Either Nate didn't care about coolness, or he had a different definition. He cradled his cup in both hands. "I'm sorry about Hero."

"What? How do you know about him?"

"Our moms talk at the gym."

"I never tell my mom anything important."

"Me neither, but it's not exactly a state secret when your dog dies. You've been looking glum. I get that."

You don't get anything, I was thinking. Hero was embedded in my soul. Nate touched the fur patch over his heart. He leaned forward and spoke with great gentleness.

"Our companion animals share our souls."

My eyes burned with tears I refused to shed. Nate *saw* me, exposed and defenseless. Had he heard my thoughts, too?

He reached inside his jacket. "I brought you something. Hold out your hand."

It was a palm-sized square of grayish animal pelt, warm from Nate's body heat. "What's this?"

"Coyote. He gave his life to a hunter, but his spirit will visit you through this."

"His spirit... I suppose you think you're a *shaman*." I put scorn in my voice while my fingers closed on their own around Nate's gift.

"You don't have to believe me. Keep it with you for when you need it."

"When would that be?" I wanted to argue with him. He didn't take the bait. I stuck the coyote fur into my coat pocket, where it flexed like a living animal in my hand. I grew lightheaded. *Whoa, don't faint, don't faint!:*

The space between us swarmed with stars so countless I couldn't see Nate's face. I heard coyotes' yip and howl call-and-response echo across a desert I was sure I'd never seen, through sage-perfumed air I breathed like a memory.

"Stevie, you okay?"

The stars evaporated with the desert. "Of course."

"Your mom says you paint dogs, you're an artist."

I'd never dared think of myself that way. I tapped my boot heels on the floor. "My mom talks too much."

CHAPTER 3

*I*t was a measure of my loneliness that I let Nate come home with me to see my artwork; I hadn't invited anyone into my room since Winter and I outgrew dolls. My paintings and drawings coated the walls in chronological layers. Nate lifted pages to see the ones beneath. The earliest ones featured Hero with me and my family, happy and whole, from when I believed I could magic my dad home if I wished it hard enough. I'd gained skill with the pencil and brush as I'd lost that illusion.

Nate gave a low whistle. "They're like stills from some mysterious movie. You're good."

I resented his invasion, ashamed that I blushed, furious with myself for giving this boy the power to move me with praise. "You've seen them, you should go." I switched off the lights to let him know the show was over. The colors grayed, Nate became a darker shape against my window. I didn't like facing the dying day, exposing my turmoil to him.

Nate made no move to leave. "You're beautiful, too—feral. I love your look."

No, my strength lay in my ability to be repellant. "What do you want?"

Nate took two steps closer. "A tattoo. I want you to tattoo a wolf face on my shoulder."

"You're a lunatic! Why would you want a tattoo?"

My mom's tattoos hadn't aged well. The climbing roses that wound around her upper arm sagged and drooped like autumn vines on a rotting lattice. No one my age wanted that mark of our parent's 1980's generation, except apparently Nate and his reactionary ilk. He never gave me a good explanation. It was the craziness of his request that convinced me to agree, and the prospect of having him at my mercy.

We researched techniques and equipment like the world depended on it. I made sketches. Nate bought the ink and tools. We met secretly in an old beach house his family owned, but rarely used, climate change having brought king tides lapping in beneath the front door. I didn't find the technical parts of creating the tattoo that difficult. I was perversely fascinated by the blood spots blooming on Nate's smooth boy skin beneath the needle point. Nate cringed and exclaimed, which made my work harder. My hands vibrated with an odd urge to soothe him, as though I could make the pain go away, but that was absurd; I didn't try. I wasn't sure I wanted to. Instead, I made up a mystical story: "You need to suffer if you want this wolf to be your ally. It's your blood sacrifice that summons him." Nate liked the concept and adopted it as the yellow-eyed wolf face grew on the back of his left shoulder. I refined the wolf bit-by-bit, adding more detail once the swelling went down from each session.

I counted the days separating my tattooing rendezvous with Nate. We took care these went unnoticed by anyone, without remarking on the several reasons his parents or my mom might stop us. He trusted me with his body. I didn't tell him that sometimes his blood called up inexplicable mirages of other blood that blocked my view of what I was doing. I'd have to lift the needle until they dwindled. When the wolf was finished, Nate tried to pay me for my artwork. That mortified me. I'd believed we were on an adventure together, not that he had hired me to do a job and the job was done.

After that, I barely acknowledged him when we crossed paths, but I itched to see the tattoo beneath his clothes. It was as surely mine as his. On a chilly evening crossing I ran into him in the ferry stairwell and led him up to the empty sun deck. He let me pull his jacket and shirt aside. The tattoo had healed perfectly. By moonlight the wolf glared at me, so real he seemed to breathe. I licked Nate's shoulder to bring out the colors.

Nate shivered. "I feel him there, like he's alive."

I settled Nate's shirt and jacket into place, his sweet-spicy taste on my tongue. I had nothing more to say. We *knew* each other too intimately to need words.

My teachers encouraged my proficiency in math and I indulged them, blasting through the algebra and calculus they offered. They knew nothing about my artwork. I'd always kept that to myself at home, a separate, parallel life painted on paper. In both lives I solved problems based on patterns, one set made of numbers and signs, the other, lines and colors. While I pursued the comfort of order and beauty through both, all the adults seemed to worry about me.

The island's many eyes crawled like spiders on my skin. Some afternoons, I escaped to Seattle on the ferry. Mom thought I was staying late at school, blinded by her hope that I was joining a club, making new friends. In the city, I felt less anxious, anonymous, yet not alone. I prowled parks and plazas where groups of apparently homeless teens hung out. Their uncritical acceptance of me was fleetingly comforting, but ultimately pointless. I felt their drug cravings and hunger pangs in my hands so strongly I expected my palms to turn red. I didn't know what the sensation meant or what to do with it. I found myself watching for a familiar face without knowing whose it might be.

Mom tried to shelter me and I tried to protect her from worry about my aloneness. That left a lot we couldn't talk about. Our unspoken distance was unbridgeable, but other people talked. Gossip about my eccentricities pushed her beyond embarrassed to desperate. She dredged up the money to send me to Gena again.

I resisted, but as before, Gena drew out my words by leaving space empty of my mom's fearful love for me, or my teachers' judgement:

Kristina Bak

"You know, Stevie, whatever you tell me stays here. Nobody else gets to hear it."

Gena learned I was unmoored, without direction or definition, but not about my inexplicable visions, or the strange vibrations in my hands, or about Nate. It was none of her business that I kept my fingers anchored in Nate's coyote fur in my pocket.

CHAPTER 4

ecrecy had become my default mode; it took constant vigilance to protect myself from me, the anxious, angry me who might emerge at any time. I honed my awareness so nothing would catch me by surprise. Of course I didn't tell Gena this, but she picked up more than I said aloud. What Gena got right was that my anxiety around other people made friendship more fraught than loneliness for me, but my loneliness was terrible, too. I'd been to see her three or four times when, in her stuffy, overheated office, she broke one of our aquarium-viewing silences. "Do you like horses, Stevie?"

Her question was so irrelevant I had to stop and think. "I don't know. Yeah, I guess so. They're beautiful."

"I have a friend who needs help at her rescue stables. She'll pay you to give her a hand."

"I can't. I don't know anything about horses. I've got no experience."

"How do you imagine people *get* experience? She'll train you on the job."

Money of my own, a new degree of personal power, sounded appealing. Being outdoors in the fresh air sounded good, too. From the eager way Gena was looking at me, I knew she wanted me to say yes, so, despite my total equine ignorance, I did.

———————

My days took on new structure. My teachers allowed me early dismissal, removing my unsettling presence from their classrooms. Weekday afternoons, I caught a bus up the island highway and walked a quarter mile from the stop to the stables.

Gena's friend Sierra was petite and perky, the kind of person who in high school would have been a cheerleader and volunteered for committees, and I would have avoided like the plague. In middle age she channeled all that energy into caring for abused and unwanted horses, her red ponytail swinging beneath her Stetson. She appeared to be living out a fantasy of the Old West and Universal Mom combined and loving it. She took for granted I shared her keenness for her four-legged family. On my first day she led me into the horse barn, a long space divided into stalls and smelling not unpleasantly of horse dung and hay. "I'm *so happy* you've come, Stevie!"

I understood why after two hours of feeding and brushing and cleanup, settling the animals for the night. Sierra had bought the stables with an inheritance. She supported the operation with donations and with income from her equine therapy groups. Of her rescued horses, five were fit to be therapy horses, seven others were too old, traumatized, or sick. Some would recover their strength and health, some simply live out their last years beloved.

"They'd all be canned meat and dog food if they didn't live here, Stevie. It's every evening for me and every morning, too. The animals' needs don't take a day off, so I don't either. I have volunteers who help, but I need someone steady and predictable, somebody who works hard like I see you doing."

Sierra saw me flushed and bedraggled from shoveling and hauling manure. She couldn't see the joy coursing through my entire being. The horses' size, their formidable teeth, their ponderous hooves, had frightened me until Sierra introduced me to each one and I recognized in them a quality I'd loved in Hero: they were the same inside and out. They lived their integrity, walking in beauty with no pretense, true to themselves. Intuitively, without intending to, I touched hurts I sensed in them. When I did, I felt a river of energy, like light and heat, that seemed to pour through the top of my head out through my hands, to them. The horses leaned into it, their muscles relaxed beneath my touch. My burning palms cooled and my fingers relaxed, too. I'd been, at least metaphorically, holding my breath for a decade without realizing it and here I began my long exhale. Sierra noticed that the animals I touched turned their heads and followed me with their eyes.

"If these guys could smile, they'd be smiling at you. I've never seen them take to anyone like this." Her praise felt good, too.

My job wasn't easy. In a book about Greek mythology, I'd read about Heracles in the Augean Stables; now I identified with his plight. The task was endless. After my shifts helping Sierra I strained to keep my eyes open over my homework. I slept like the dead, undisturbed by nightmares. I didn't have energy to perseverate on my anxiousness or depilate my scalp. I stopped going to Gena and went to the stables instead. I loved the horses' soft nickers greeting me, their salty smell when I leaned my face against their necks. And there was something else.

My body was discovering (or was it *remembering?*) a gift that baffled my mind. It seemed ... no, I *knew,* I eased the animals' discomfort with my touch; my hands went toward their pain without my trying. Pain passed like an electric charge through me and away—a slight charge, no more than a tingle, for a slight pain, stronger jolts for more acute ones. In my amazement, I congratulated myself as a healer, but a sixth sense warned me to beware. If I *could* take away the horses' pain with my touch, that was a healing of sorts, but treacherous, too. Pain was a message and I soon realized I couldn't heal the wounds and illnesses it announced. Of course, what I was doing had to stay secret. No one would believe me, *Weird Stevie* raving. I'd lose the meager credibility I'd regained and I'd have nowhere to hide from danger. That last part was a funny thought, not funny *ha-ha,* funny strange, disturbing that I'd thought it, like someone else had thought it through me. I didn't know what danger it warned against, but it made me cautious.

As I learned more about them from Sierra, the horses became my best friends. Weeks passed and she gave me more responsibility. Life wasn't perfect, but it was better than I'd known it since the day my dad set sail.

CHAPTER 5

My hair grew back in a feathery 'do that looked deliberate. I wore jeans and shirts, practical for working with the horses. My new look pleased Mom. She saw it as a sign that my "rebellious phase," as she put it, was ending. With renewed holiday season optimism, visions of my future danced in her head.

For years, Mom had dragged me to Mass, until she broke with the Church over one doctrinal stupidity or another. I'd fought going, especially when I got into middle school, but I missed the liturgy around Advent—the four candles and caroling, "Oh come, oh come Emmanuel"—left behind with my childhood. Improbably, my faith in a Compassionate One remained and my dresser top had grown to resemble an altar. Mom forbade real candles in the house; battery-driven flame shapes winked in votives around a ten-inch-tall ceramic figure, to me part Mary, Mother of God, part Quan Yin. I didn't recall where she'd come from. She'd always been there, everything else gathered incrementally around her. Nate's coyote fur patch rested at her feet at night next to Dad's photo, Hero's collar and tags, my old ballerina jewel box, seashells, a dried autumn maple leaf, and wave-

Kristina Bak

buffed agates. I couldn't describe it, but my spiritual center lived there. I didn't pray anymore, or I didn't call it praying.

On December twenty-third, I came home from the stables to find my mom on her knees in the living room amidst boxes spilling our Christmas ornaments.

She greeted me with a glass dove of peace in one hand and a Mexican tin angel in the other. "Oh, good, you can help me decorate." A naked evergreen, not quite straight in its stand, reached toward our eight foot ceiling, crowding our small living room.

I stared with my rain parka dripping onto the carpet. We hadn't had a tree taller than me since I was in fifth grade. "Mom, what's going on?"

"I'm putting up our tree. What does it look like?"

"It looks crooked." It did, but did that matter? The tree meant Mom was in a mood for us to celebrate. I hadn't seen her this cheerful for a long time. My getting good grades and a job had made her happy. It was gratifying; lately I'd felt like a burden to her.

Mom stood up for a better view. "Oh my God, you're right. I'll have to call the tree guy back to adjust it."

"We can fix it ourselves, it's not *that* crooked. I don't

mind if it's off."

Mom retrieved a half-finished drink from the mantel where she'd left it. "Stevie, sweetheart, it's not going to be just us this year."

It had been just us on Christmas Eve since my dad left. Every year I hung a stocking for him, believing against all logic in the possibility of a Christmas miracle. Now, for one eternal second, I was filled with joy. Was the miracle finally happening, Dad coming home at last?

Mom read my expression and looked away. "A friend is coming for dinner tomorrow night."

My joy died. I wrapped my arms around my stomach and braced myself against whatever she was about to say. "What friend? Whose friend?"

Through my adolescence Christmas Eve had been our time to put aside conflict, me with hot chocolate, Mom with her bourbon, the aromas of both mingling with the fir branches' pungent scent. We'd open one gift each, the smallest or the most irresistible, then lower the lights and sit side by side, entranced by our Christmas tree. One night of harmony.

Mom waved her glass. "You'll like James."

"Who the *hell* is *James*?" I wouldn't like him, I knew I wouldn't, not on Christmas Eve!

"I've talked about him, if you'd been paying attention. He's a retired veterinarian from California. I sold him that house on Battle Point."

"Retired, you mean he's old?"

"Not that old, he retired early. I'm forty-one, Stevie, and I haven't met a decent man in years. I'm worn down. Don't spoil this for me."

She didn't look "worn down" to me; she looked like my mom, thicker in the waist and hips than she used to be, but flat-bellied and strong, her shoulder-length hair dyed darker, nothing wrong with her face she couldn't fix with a little blusher and mascara whenever she wanted to. Mom didn't raise her voice; she didn't retreat or plead. That was how I knew she was serious and implacable, that I could argue forever and she wouldn't change her mind.

"But, Dad …"

Mom raised her voice. "You have to grow up! Your father was lost at sea. They found pieces of his boat!"

"But never a body!" I was perilously close to hollering at her. Mom's lightness had disappeared. She tossed back the rest of her drink and took a deliberate breath.

"They said sharks, Stevie, *sharks*. Please don't do this to yourself."

Each reminder hurt like hearing it fresh. How had I kept him alive, ever young, out there sailing, or coming up the walk, to toss me into the air and catch me, laughing? Now, when I was grown and knew, why didn't he die for me?

I hung my parka on a chair and helped straighten the tree. Though we did a grim job of decorating, it looked good with our lifetime collection of shiny ornaments reflecting lights like rainbow-colored stars. Mom slipped her arm around my waist and I let her hug me.

———

I suppose to a visitor our household could seem normal enough. James arrived acceptably early and I was first to the door to confront the interloper. He held an extravagant red poinsettia in his arms like a florist's delivery man. It hid his face. All I could see clearly of him were his broad brown hands clutching the gold-foil-wrapped plant pot. I blocked the doorway, saying nothing. He spoke to me through the plant. "You must be Stevie."

Of course I must be.

"I hope you don't have a cat. Poinsettias are poisonous to cats, so naturally they love them."

I let him in. "No cats."

My mom bustled up behind me. "Merry Christmas!" She puckered to give James a welcoming kiss, but she collided with the poinsettia any way they turned. Finally, she took it from him."Come in, come in."

Mom found a place for the plant and I took James's coat. He didn't ask me fatuous questions about school, or try to play jolly. He accepted the glass of wine Mom offered and smiled at the tree, the gas fire with its realistic imitation logs, carols in the background, a setting for the perfect Night Before Christmas. To me, James was the only discordant element. I wondered what he'd heard about me. I helped arrange dinner on the table around the monster poinsettia, sneaking looks at him. At least he wasn't Mom's usual bland, glad-handing, white-bread type. He stayed where he'd been placed, in the recliner close to the fire. He didn't look as old as I'd expected, given away only by his fuzzy gray hair thinning on the back of his head and a negligible paunch stretching his green cashmere sweater. He made no effort to conceal either, resting his drink on his belly, half-turned away, not watching us. He was a sizable man, filling the chair.

Mom had gone all out with polished silver, fancy napkins, crystal goblets we never used. In defiance of her

Kristina Bak

own rule, she'd lit white candles flanking the poinsettia that obviously took up more table space than she'd planned.

At dinner, the plant was a lifesaver for me; I slouched behind it so I could eat in peace. James had a rumbling laugh he exercised as Mom prattled on about island history and gossip, leaving out years around my dad's disappearance. What, she didn't think that mattered? Over dessert, she played Hero as our animal-loving card in the so-much-we-have-in-common game when James brought up how he missed his late corgi. I didn't like Hero used that way, but James was respectful. My mom had dated far worse men and her relationships didn't last. I ate my chocolate mousse without comment.

When we regrouped around the tree, I couldn't stop remembering how Dad would dance around in his funny red jester's hat with jingling bells and make us sing "Deck the Halls" and "Here Comes Santa Claus." James crooned "White Christmas." I had to admit he had a good warm baritone voice. He acted surprised when Mom laid a package on his knees. He opened it carefully, folding the gift wrap and setting it aside. Mom had chosen well for her purposes, a coffee table book of island scenes by a local photographer, not too personal, but attractive for James to display in his living room, with her name and fond wishes inscribed on the first page. I'd never seen it before, but she told him it was from me, too. It wasn't. I felt sick seeing my mom sitting close to this man not my father, giving his arm a pat, the two of them exchanging smiles with secret messages in their eyes.

James couldn't miss Mom's disappointment at his present to her, red insulated ski gloves, neither glamorous nor practical in our region, where glaciers were melting away in the Cascades and Olympic mountains and snow had become rare. He let her hang long enough to tease without being heartless.

"The whole gift wouldn't go in a package. I have a timeshare in Banff. I'm hoping you'll come for a ski week in January. To be honest, it would be a gift to me." He caught me watching more unspoken messages fly between them. "You're welcome too, Stevie. There's plenty of room in the lodge." He sounded sincere.

I was about to refuse when Mom answered. "Oh, it's too bad Stevie has work and school, but January's a dead season for real estate here, too dark, too wet."

A dead season. A mountainside roared over my mom in my mind, an avalanche scoured her off her skis, one new red glove marking her tomb beneath the snow.

"*No*, Mom, you don't know how to ski!"

I'd spoken louder than I'd meant to, but James was unfazed. "I'll teach her. I went from skateboards to snowboards when I was your age. I worked as a ski instructor in Colorado to pay for veterinary school."

A thousand years ago. Mom patted my knee, but I saw that rare steely look in her eyes. She was determined to orphan me. James handed me a small flat box in gold paper with a matching bow. Not more ski gloves, I hoped. I ripped off the wrapping. Inside was a set of watercolor brushes, professional quality, expensive. He was either thoughtful and perceptive, or awfully good at manipulating people. Mom stared at me until I thanked him. With exquisite timing and delicacy, James said his goodnights.

After he'd gone, Mom poured herself a bourbon and made me hot chocolate in my chipped Santa mug. We sat side by side on the sofa sipping our drinks. The burnt down candles guttered on the table amidst the remains of our feast. I tried not to notice Mom held her red gloves on her lap. The Christmas lights glittered and looking up at the tree made me feel small as a child. I closed my eyes.

Evergreen trees lit from below by streetlights towered over the quiet sidewalk. Hero and I trudged uphill from the ferry dock. I hadn't learned to read the street names yet, but I knew my way home in my bones. There on Towhee Lane was our house! The grass was a relief to my bare feet as I raced across our lawn. The front door was locked, but the porch light on. I pushed the bell button and kept pushing it. What if my mom was gone?

She opened the door. I couldn't move, couldn't swallow, couldn't smile. She didn't smile, either. She tilted her head the way Hero would when he was trying hard to understand me. Then she crouched and touched my hair. She whispered, "Stevie?"

"Mommy!" I threw myself at her and held on with all my might. She clutched me to her, rocking me like a baby.

"Stevie?" Mom took the empty mug out of my hands. "I think you fell asleep. It's bedtime for both of us."

CHAPTER 6

I have to say James made a good try to include me as he spent more time with my mom the week after Christmas, but I wasn't convinced he liked me. I was an inconvenient part of the package. He was laughable as a substitute father. A grandfather maybe; I recollected vaguely having one of those.

Mom's parents I knew only from photos. Her stories about them sounded more like the thrillers she read than a family history. They'd been journalists covering the Afghanistan war. They'd died in a bombing in Kabul while Mom was in college, before I was born. I wished I'd gotten to meet them.

Dad's parents were very different, original old hippies eking out a living on a derelict commune in northern Vermont. I'd last seen them when they drove their rattletrap van cross-country to wish their son *Bon Voyage* as he embarked on his ill-fated sailing endeavor. Grandma held me on her lap and let me play with her long silvery braids. Later, she wrote me letters from Vermont, in longhand, "so someday you can read these and remember us." My gray-bearded grandpa soon died of a stroke and the letters

Kristina Bak

Grandma sent became scrawls, then stopped. I never saw Grandma again, but I saved her letters.

On New Year's Eve I refused Mom's and James's invitation to a party Nate's parents were giving. *Nate* hadn't invited me. What if I went and he was with someone else? So what, why should I care? But I did. Sulky and bored, I padded around the house in fluffy socks and flannel pajamas Mom had given me for Christmas. I scorched the popcorn I tried to make, opted for cereal and found the milk carton empty. I tried Mom's bourbon, but gagged at the taste. Was I the only teen in the world who hated alcohol? Another example of my freakishness. *Poor me!*

Tired of feeling sorry for myself, I opened a book, couldn't concentrate. I tried a movie. It turned out to be all sex and romance—the last thing I wanted to watch alone this one night of the year when *everybody* else partied. I hungered for something new to look forward to. I sifted through the mess on my desk with a half-assed intention to organize my life. In the supernatural way the universe, or whatever, answers questions you don't know you've asked, I found a loose page from one of my grandma's long letters.

She wrote with with pride about *her* mother, who had worked as a Red Cross volunteer in a Brooklyn hospital during World War II and had a reputation for being able to soothe wounded soldiers' agony. I'd read this before without much thought, but now I wondered, had my great-grandmother passed this pain-healing gift down to me?

I'd always envied kids with close aunts, uncles, grandparents, cousins. My three cousins lived in faraway Massachusetts, my aunt and uncle estranged from my mom, reduced to Christmas cards and names in harmless anecdotes like folklore. Sometimes, Mom told me, without much explanation, it was better that way. What Grandma's letter hinted was that family can't be shed like old clothes. Some traits always remain. I folded the page into an origami bird shape, closed it in my ballerina jewel box on my dresser top, then watched replays of New Year's Eve fireworks in New Zealand and Australia and on around the world.

I tried to lose myself in the celebrations, so lavish they had to be projecting a different future for the world than I could, but that made me think about the past and the past sucked at my thoughts like quicksand. My bizarre dreams and visions seemed real when I was in them; how could I know where memory crossed over into delusion? How could I know I wasn't *crazy*? One sequence repeated in my mind with such undramatic detail I was certain it was a genuine remembered fragment:

Was it when I was ten, six years ago? Mom served me a blue bowl of vanilla ice cream dribbled with chocolate sauce and sat beside me at the kitchen table. "Sweetheart, remember when you were little I fractured my wrist?" Her voice was more casual than if she was asking if I wanted another scoop. I stirred the chocolate sauce, making swirls in the ice cream. She persisted; "It hurt so bad I couldn't stop crying, but you touched it and the pain went away?"

I put on my best puzzled face. I didn't want to lie to her and I wasn't sure of the answer. Something about the question chilled me.

"You don't remember doing that?"

"*What* did I do?"

"Never mind. I must have imagined it."

She got up and left me at the table, too agitated to finish

my ice cream—instead, I jittered around the house pouncing on things that struck a strange chord and correcting them. Mom had moved a chair closer to the fireplace; it had to go back where it belonged. A lamp in a new corner had to return to the old one. I didn't want anything in our house to change until my dad came home.

That was where the memory ended. I determined I would ask Mom about it. She generally avoided talking about the past, especially about my dad, and I tried to protect her from more sadness. I watched a million drunken people cheer the falling ball in Times Square.

———————————

On New Year's Day, while I unloaded the dishwasher and Mom measured coffee beans into the grinder, I approached the subject obliquely. "What was I like when I was a kid?"

"You're still a kid, aren't you?" She sounded jokey and upbeat, if a little hung over. *Her* New Year's Eve must have been good.

I waited out the noise while the coffee grinder whirred. "Oh, *Mom*, I mean when I was *little*."

She tamped the fresh grounds into the holder. "You were brave when you had to start kindergarten. You didn't want to go, but you did it without any fuss."

I liked that—for a change, a story about my doing something that made Mom's life easier.

She went on over the espresso machine's hiss, watching her cup until it filled. "But when you got home from school you were like a two-year-old, wanting to keep me in sight." Her laugh sounded forced. "You wouldn't go alone any farther than the deck. You'd teeter there with your toes over the edge while Hero ran and pooped in my flowers. I couldn't blame you." Mom peered into the fridge. "Damn! No milk."

Her phone sounded then, James calling, of course.

———————

In January Mom packed her ski clothes and left our soggy green island for Canadian snow with James. They made a good-looking couple despite the age disparity and Mom being eight inches shorter. They were both robust, sturdy and wholesome-looking. Mom had never been glamorous, but her eyes were brighter since she'd met James. She'd been on the school swim team when she was my age and her weekly workouts with Winter's and Nate's moms at the pool kept her fit. I guessed that could count as glamor for a man fifteen years older than she was. Besides her goodbye kiss drying on my cheek, I had a contact list, her itinerary, her passport number, and written instructions for every eventuality. I looked forward to my first ever week at home on my own.

———————

Between school and the stables, my days were full, but my solitary evenings left me fretful. I'd always feared the ruthless virtual world and social media's anonymous cruelty. Since the incident with Winter I avoided it completely. Every online network I belonged to, she did, too. I was abnormally alone.

Kristina Bak

I lay on my bed listening to night rain on the roof, watching the battery candles' artificial dance over Mother Mary Quan Yin's face. I caressed my cheek with the coyote fur. This couldn't go on; I craved someone's touch, *Nate's* touch, the taste of his skin, his voice praising me and my art the way no one else had. My past susurrated on the walls with the furnace fan's breeze through my tacked-up paintings, like whispering voices mocking me. *Time to grow up!* Too quickly to lose my nerve, I messaged Nate to come over, then I rose and stripped my walls layer by layer, excavating my hopeful childish dream scenes.

I slipped my bare feet into rain boots and squelched down the lawn to the garden shed where I disentangled my dad's portable charcoal barbecue grill from among Mom's shovels and rakes. It had remained in the shed unused since Dad left, first through inertia, then unutterable sorrow. I dragged it on its two wheels to the covered kitchen deck. I found the matches Mom had bought for our Christmas Eve dinner candles, crumpled my first painting, and lit it over the grill. The heat from my paintings as I fed them to the flames warmed my face. I watched them flare, send sparks up into the windless night, writhe and blacken on a growing pile of ash.

The side gate clicked and my stomach jumped. Nate came around the corner of the house. He had cut off his snaky braids and wore no earrings. That worried me. "You look different." I saw a new Nate in the intense expression in his eyes, in the soldierly way he held his body.

He smoothed his hair. "So do you."

He'd found me beautiful bald; I wondered if he did now, with my hair growing back. "Everything's changed." I knew I sounded defensive.

"Not everything." Nate unwound a wooly striped scarf from around his neck and pulled his jacket and sweater off his shoulder. The wolf's eyes shone by the firelight, its teeth bared more fiercely than I recalled creating.

"The tat looks so good! I had no idea what I was doing."

"Do you now?" Nate readjusted his clothes to cover his tattoo as I burned the final paintings.

"This is the past. It has to go."

"Then what happens?"

"We'll see." We were talking coldly, like acquaintances, when I wanted to throw my arms around him. Where was the Nate I'd imagined coming to me? "What's up with you?"

He faced me over the last flames. "My parents are sending me to my uncle in Singapore. He's a surgeon with influential friends. He got me into a prep program for med school there."

"Singapore! What, abandoning the Fur People, your wolves and ocelots?" *And me, when I need you?*

"I'm not! This is a long-term strategy. I'll be more useful from inside the machine."

"The oldest excuse."

"I mean it."

"You mean it *now*."

"What difference does it make to you? Since when do you care about anything besides yourself?"

That was a conversation stopper. The fire died. I decided not to be peeved. What did he know? "It's cold out here. Come inside and I'll make us cocoa."

In a parody of my childhood, we took the hot chocolate I made into the living room and sat on the carpet beside the Christmas tree my mom hadn't taken down before she left. I thought of the romcoms I'd watched, the romantic novels I'd read. I was a beginner at this; I tried to be candid, but blasé. "I need a friend, Nate, a more-than-friend, and lacking one I'm conscripting you. Consider it payment for my artwork."

Nate scooted closer. "Reporting for duty."

"This isn't a joke, Nate."

The Christmas lights twinkled in Nate's eyes. He set down his mug, put his arms around me and drew me close. "I'm not joking."

I kissed Nate. His lips tasted hot and sugary. We kissed more, tentatively, experimentally, learning each other's feel.

After Nate left, my room oppressed me with its thumb-tack-hole-pocked walls, its suffocating vacancy. I took my pillow to the sofa and watched the parched evergreen drop a needle now and then until I drifted off.

The next evening I made a half-hearted effort to dismantle the tree. I fetched ornament boxes from the garage, tucked fragile glass balls and a ceramic snowman in protective tissue, but all the time I was reliving being in Nate's arms, feeling his hands and mouth. How ironic that I'd once dissed his obsession with the radical Fur People's animal-saving cause; here I was working for a horse rescuer, while he joined the conservative medical establishment! Even as we were growing closer, we were moving apart. The doorbell rang. I ran to answer it. Nate stood hatless, rain like tears on his face.

"I have to leave for the airport in an hour. I came to say goodbye."

I pulled him into the house. "What, tonight? I'll never see you again!"

"Jesus, Stevie, worst case!" Nate grabbed me roughly. His wet jacket fell open and I pressed myself against him. He was still shorter than I was, but already more substantial, less boy than man.

"Singapore's too far!"

"Just a plane ride." His breath tickled my ear. "I lived there when I was little."

I ran my hands up Nate's spine inside his shirt. His skin was hot. "I can't imagine." I couldn't; growing up I'd fastened myself like a limpet to the island. I'd refused bribes of Disneyland and broken out in hives at the thought of the school's eighth grade trip to DC. Mom never forced me to go. Now I wondered, why not? What skulked out there beyond my fear? Why this constant dread? My pulse pumped faster. I kissed Nate and this time was different.

Kristina Bak

CHAPTER 7

idweek, an Arctic front brought a rare freezing day to the island, everything magically frosted white, the way I hadn't seen it since my childhood. The air was soundless and silvery, but I felt like a walking scream. I'd simultaneously drawn Nate deeper into my life and said goodbye to him. I couldn't name my chaotic emotions. If this was falling in love, I wanted none of it. Or I wanted more. Pretending to be attentive in class was torture. I left school for the afternoon like making a jailbreak.

At the stables I discovered a welcome distraction—a rangy pinto mare, white with gray splotches on her cheeks and flanks. Her body was carved with neglect. Her mane and tail were matted, her hooves untrimmed. Her previous owner's sadism or ignorance left open sores around her mouth where he'd sawn the bridle bit. She stood quivering in the corral, watching Sierra and me with her eyes rolled back.

Sierra leaned on the corral fence. "Are you up for this one, Stevie? She'll be a challenge."

"What's her name?"

"*Paint*, of course." Sierra laughed.

I climbed up and sat on the top pole beside her. "She's beautiful!"

"She will be when she's fed and groomed."

"Will she be okay to ride?"

"Someday far from now. She's awfully spooked. She practically kicked out the trailer sides when the rescuers brought her. Give her food and water, but don't go nearer." Sierra gave me a look just short of severe. Her cheeks and nose were red from the cold. "We'll leave her alone out here and let her get used to her new home."

A therapy group waited in the riding ring, so Sierra left me to feed the horse. I rubbed my hands together, wishing for gloves. I brought an armful of timothy hay and a bucket of water, set them at a distance safe for me and not too startling for the pinto, then I sat on the corral fence and talked to her—nonsense reassurances and soothing sounds. She must have known some kindness in her past because she took hesitating steps forward, dipped her nose into the water bucket. She sniffed at the hay, hungry enough to investigate the possibilities, but not eating. The mouth sores would make eating painful for her.

Paint had to eat to heal. I'd never disobeyed Sierra before. I looked around; she was nowhere in sight. She'd never need to know. I climbed down the fence rails into the corral. Paint watched, stiff-legged. I eased toward her, hand outstretched, closer, closer, until her head lowered to me, our white breaths rising and combining in the frigid air. I reached to touch her sores the way I'd furtively done with other horses, but for this poor creature no touch had been benign. She huffed and reared. One heavy hoof struck my face and knocked me backwards. I rolled and covered my head with my arms. The pinto's hoofbeats shook the ground beneath my cheek as she galloped around the corral. I moaned through explosions in my head until something moth-wing wispy brushed my brow and my agony melted, but I lay frozen, my bones turned to ice. The pinto didn't come close, neither did anyone else for an eternity.

I couldn't move, my mouth couldn't form words. Why couldn't I open my eyes? Sierra held my hand. She told me we were at the ER and my mom was on her way. I couldn't ask how many hours it would take for Mom to come from Canada. Someone who said she was a doctor cleaned grit from the wound on my head. I heard every whisper and mechanical beep. She said fluid was building up inside my skull. She didn't find it heartening that I showed no sign of pain. As she worked, incoming messages began breaking up in my mind, into sound blips and hollowness. Radiance burst behind my closed eyelids, my body shattered into a trillion trillion fractals of light, spinning like a galaxy, small as a quark—*I* was going, nearly gone, so easy, yes!

Crystalline message ringing music or... ? *Not yet,*

Stevie Wales, not yet. And the dazzling void around me, that *was* me, gradually re-formed in my shape. I felt my blood whoosh-whooshing through my veins, my solidity, my separateness from that perfect beauty I'd glimpsed, and the precious imperfection of my unfinished life.

CHAPTER 8

Winter fog engulfed the island, like the fog in my bruised brain that made familiar things phantoms to me. At first I couldn't distinguish my mind's elaborate productions from the rehab center's wallpaper pattern, or find meaning in either. As my awareness grew, the disorientation maddened me. The first time I pounded my pillow in frustration, everyone celebrated; I could move.

When insipid February sun finally burned through to Puget Sound, unveiling the city and mountains, and I was mobile enough to go home, I clung to the world my brain created from transient memory shards. In it my dad and I sailed on a timeless, luminous ocean. I grieved leaving that voyage. I didn't like what I saw in my lucid intervals, least of all, the semi-circular scar that marred my left cheekbone and pulled up the corner of my eye so I looked slightly distorted seen from the front.

Speech returned to me. I relearned how to feed myself, dress myself, take showers alone, practicing in rehab sessions, fast-forwarding progress from infant to toddler to child to teen. My mom, beset by self-reproach, suffered most. James's reminders to her became a mantra. "Liz, darling, leave your daughter alone. Stevie can do that for herself now."

My body recovered and in the fourth month my sixteen-year-old self rushed back in a torrential data dump. *Dump* was the right word for it, too—more trash than valuable information, I thought. Sometimes I pretended to be lost in oblivion, but now Mom saw through it instantly. By my seventeenth birthday in May, the old Stevie had returned, or at least, with any luck, the best parts of me. The doctors warned my recovery might have gaps and ragged edges.

Usually, I seemed normal again, but it shook me to discover that numbers had become strangers to me and mathematical formulas gibberish; I missed the comforting security of their predictable behavior. Nightmares erupted and perplexing things that seemed neither memories nor not-memories. Sometimes "normal" was a moving target and innocent thoughts took on lurid tones when I said them aloud in social situations. I could be embarrassing to myself and others. So, back to Gena, to regain acceptable behavioral control.

Gena's face was soft and sad as we talked. She knew what normal was supposed to look like, but through our sessions she let me sort that out for myself. In her office I reconstructed the ordinariness that had made me a safe nonentity from kindergarten to adolescence. I proved to her satisfaction I could contain my emotions and opinions. At the beginning of June she signed the release that said I matched the healthy diagnostic template. As her clock ticked the last minutes of our fifty-minute hour that would end in my being free, I finally told her about my dad. "… and I never believed he died in that shipwreck."

Gena controlled her expressions well, but I saw one eyebrow twitch.

I went on. "I'm going to Australia to find him."

Gena raised both eyebrows. I'd surprised her.

"I've saved the money I earned working with the horses, round-trip airfare to Sydney and on to Darwin, the last place anybody saw my father alive. I've done my research; seventeen-year-olds can travel there solo. I'll need a passport. I need you to help me convince my mom; she'll listen to *you*. No matter what it takes, I'm going to find my dad."

Gena stood and laid her notebook and pen on her desk. "I'm sorry, Stevie, it's time to end this session."

"But, Gena!"

"You're my last client of the day. I need some exercise; I'll walk you home." She gathered her jacket and handbag. I had no choice. I let her coax me through her empty waiting room into the dying afternoon.

In the outdoor light, silver strands traced through Gena's short reddish-brown hair. She didn't hurry. I matched her steps, trying to think how to get her to do what I wanted. We ambled uphill from the island's compact main street, past gardens overflowing with pink rhododendrons, blue stocks, roses. She talked to me in a way she never had in her office.

"Something different is going on with you, Stevie; I can feel it. What is it? It's not an illness, or a syndrome I can diagnose. I know a lot about you, but not that. If you want to tell me …"

And risk being retagged not-normal? Not a chance. "No, I can't." I recognized my mistake immediately.

Gena paused and stared at me, her gray eyes bright with curiosity and triumph. "Then there *is* something. One day you might change your mind. I'll be here when you need me."

"I need you *now*, to help me find my dad."

Gena walked on. I stuck close. We turned left onto Towhee Lane before she spoke again. "You understand, a therapist is *never* supposed to get involved in a client's personal life." I kept pace with her while she argued with herself. "But the island is small and it used to be smaller. I've known your mom for years."

"What!" I grabbed her arm and made her face me. "Have you been telling my mom stuff I say all this time?"

Gena calmly detached my fingers from her sleeve. "I've told you before, whatever you say to me stays with me. She doesn't get to hear it unless you say so." She gave me a sharp look. "You have to be straight now, no lies."

"Yes, absolutely!" I'd guarantee anything to get her on my side and I'd never been able to lie to her effectively anyhow.

We'd stopped in front of our worn cottage. Even with its DIY improvements intended to make it look richer, it was a dull-looking place, not somewhere I would live by choice, but it was home. As I had that thought, my conceptual world kaleidoscoped, filling in another blank: Hero's grave was under the hedge in back. How could I have forgotten? How much more of me was missing?

We watched a hummingbird bury its head in a red and purple fuchsia, then zip off to another one. Gena announced her decision. "Here's my deal: I have a dear Australian friend, Fiona, from when we were young. She has an art gallery in Sydney. If I help you persuade your mother to let you go, you have to let Fiona help you there. You can't be on your own."

"I don't need a *babysitter!*"

Did Gena roll her eyes? Was a therapist allowed to do that? I couldn't lose it in front of her now. *Breathe, slow down, think, speak softly.* "I'm well, you said so yourself, and I'm practically an adult, not some irresponsible party kid. Why does everybody judge a person by their age?" The last thing I wanted was some stranger riding herd on me, controlling me, holding me back; I needed freedom to act. Gena did me the honor of not laughing at my petulant pout.

"I'm not suggesting you're a child. With Fiona you'd be more like an exchange student. Any lovely young woman alone asking questions in a foreign country can get into trouble. It's hard to know who to trust when you're an outsider. And if you're determined to find your dad, why do it the hard way? You think Australia's just an exotic version of the US with kangaroos, but it's not. It's a place of its own, with its own ways. You need to have an Aussie friend to watch your back, especially if you're going into the North. Bottom line, if you won't agree to go to my friend, I won't help smooth things with your mom. In fact, I'll warn her against it if she asks me."

I didn't want to admit how terrified I was at the whole idea of going. My dad would make everything all right; I'd be safe once I found him, but I didn't know how I would do that. One thing at a time. First, I had to get there.

"Okay, I understand. I'll do it."

The deal was done.

I parted my hair on the right and brushed it forward. It wasn't quite long enough yet to cover the mark left by the pinto's hoof. The scar on the side of my face looked red and angry, like me inside. Not angry with the horse—I was angry with Nate for going, with everyone who tried to keep me from being myself, whoever that was. I was angry with my body, sculpted with muscles when I worked at the stables, gone scrawny from disuse. I'd lost interest in food and looked like an emaciated six-foot pre-adolescent, all bony knees and elbows and cheekbones.

Our first taste of summer came the Saturday after my pact with Gena. We'd agreed that I would talk to my mom first. If that went well, Mom and I would talk with her together. I suspected Gena thought Mom would say absolutely no and that would be the end of it, at least until I turned eighteen.

On the island, especially since our climate had grown wetter, a sunny day brought everyone outdoors. People used to joke that in our region, we had the rainy season and August. Over the past five years even August had become iffy and the rain more persistent than ever, so Mom was celebrating this improbable June weather event with a picnic lunch surrounded by her overgrown flower garden. She'd invited James, or he'd invited himself. He'd become a fixture in our lives, like he thought he was part of the family. I wanted to tell him he wasn't—our family was Mom and me, and Dad once I found him and brought him home. There'd be no room for James then.

Since my accident, Mom had been lucky to find time to mow the lawn. Now I detected in her eyes the avid expression she always got when she saw weeds to pull and plants to prune. She had her gardening gloves and clippers handy for after lunch.

She'd produced the ideal summer tableau: blue-checked tablecloth on our slivery old picnic table, matching napkins, china plates. The stemmed glasses for wine were purely symbolic for me; I wasn't to be drinking and didn't like wine anyway. Mom was well into her second or third glass of Chardonnay before she presented the quinoa salad and smoked salmon.

James dug in. "Delicious, Liz!"

I held out my plate. "Give me extra, would you, Mom? I'm hungry." A harmless lie.

"That's a blessing! Look at you." She served me a heap of quinoa.

"I *was* looking. I could trick-or-treat as a skeleton without a mask or costume."

"Oh, no, honey, you're not that bad." She added more salmon and a buttered whole-grain roll and sat down beside James, across the table from me.

Not that bad. Damning with faint praise. "I mean it— that looks scrumptious." I didn't mean it. Was a lie a lie if I wanted it to be true? While James and Mom ate, I poked at my lunch with my fork, distracted by two tiger swallowtail butterflies pirouetting over the table. Mom noticed.

"Moving the food around on your plate isn't going to put any meat on you. It has to go into your stomach."

That she was right didn't keep me from resenting being told what to do, but this wasn't a moment to revisit old battle lines. I had a fight to face and James was handy to keep things calm. I ate a bite of salty salmon before I began. "You know, Gena signed off on my behavioral assessment yesterday. I'm officially as fit and normal as I've ever been." I hadn't meant to sound snide.

Mom refilled her wine glass and lifted it, but not without a concerned glance my way. "Congratulations! We're so proud of you, sweetie; you've worked incredibly hard."

James hoisted his glass, too. "So what do you intend to do with your freedom this summer?" My accident had complicated the potential for his peaceful retirement with Liz at his side. He'd rolled with it, but he might be relieved to get rid of me now. Time for my announcement, while rapport reigned.

"I want to travel."

Mom choked on her wine, coughed and dabbed her lips with her napkin. "Travel?"

"To Australia, to find Dad."

James stood and collected empty dishes. "I'll take these inside." He left Mom and me facing off over the pretty tablecloth.

Mom's eyes drilled into mine. "Your mind's not right yet, Stevie. Your father died."

Could she really believe that? I dropped my fork and my pretense of eating my unfinished meal. "I don't *care* what they told us. Without a body there's a chance and if there's a chance, he's not dead to me. *I* almost died, but here I am. I *know* I can find him."

Mom covered her face with the cheery blue and white napkin to hide the tears I could hear in her voice. "Oh, baby girl, we have to let go of the past, some things don't have answers. Some answers you don't want to know."

"You're wrong! I'll never give up." I'd made her cry too often. I swallowed hard, softened my voice. "Ten days, that's all I ask. So I'm only seventeen, does that make me an idiot? I need to see where he was, even if it's hopeless he's still there. I've saved my money, I can pay."

Mom wiped her tears with the napkin. "The money's not important, it's that I've come so close to losing *you*, too. I couldn't bear it."

That brought me up short: she needed me. I'd thought I was the one who needed her—my mom and me, hostage to our love. She shoved aside glasses and plates and clasped my hand, forcing me to meet her eyes.

"When your father disappeared I researched ways to die in far north Australia, Ross River virus, venomous snakes and jellyfish, crocodiles, sharks, malaria, food poisoning, a mosquito bite, anything to explain why he didn't come home. So many reasons, I had to accept what they were telling me, that he was dead. I couldn't believe that he didn't want to come back to me, to us."

I wouldn't believe it either; it had to be her fault. I snatched my hand from hers. "So you gave up on him. You took the easy way."

My mom hissed her answer. "You think it's been *easy*? You haven't understood anything." She picked up her gardening gloves and clippers from the picnic bench and stomped away across the lawn.

That hurt. My anger boiled. I wanted to break the china and shout at her. She furiously pulled weeds, elbow-deep among her cloying lilies. I detested her, knowing she was right.

Knowing and accepting were two different things. Mom's motives weren't unmixed. How would her picture-perfect world with James change if I discovered my father alive? And my mom was ignorant. I'd kept her that way, ignorant of my pain-healing gift and the visions that haunted me, to maintain my disguise as Normal Girl in the world. I'd never suited her comfortable idea of how things ought to be. She'd been too preoccupied by her own distress to recognize the depth of mine. I told myself she'd been selfish and careless and weak, but it cut my heart to hurt her. I would come back. She wouldn't have to wonder where I'd gone, or why. I had waited for my dad as long as I could endure.

Part Two:

Sydney

CHAPTER 9

I t took a miserable week of unrelenting begging, shouting, threatening, rational and irrational argument—not behavior I would ever brag about, but it worked. In the end, convinced I wouldn't give up, Mom agreed to see Gena with me. Gena's assurance of a guardian in Sydney, and pure burnout, persuaded her. By the end of July, I had my passport and ticket. I was ready to go.

While James waited in the car at SeaTac, Mom shepherded me to Departures through hordes of purposeful travelers. They all looked more sure of themselves than I was. Everything was noisy and in motion. Digital reader boards and video ads changed continually; planes lifted into the sodden sky outside huge windows; important-sounding announcements rang out in multiple languages and utility carts whirred by on rubber tires, beeping to clear their paths.

When my turn came in the security check line, Mom hugged me tightly. "Be careful." She wore her sunglasses, so I didn't have to see the look in her eyes.

Leaving her was harder than I'd imagined it would be. "I promise I'll be home soon."

A TSA guard impatiently waved me forward. I extricated myself from Mom's arms. She watched while I went through the checks, reclaimed my backpack and rolling carry-on, and headed down the concourse. My ears rang with her *goodbye, be safe, love you.* I didn't turn to wave; I didn't want Mom to read the apprehension in *my* face, either. A recorded voice directed me onto an underground train to my boarding gate.

I was cool with the takeoff, the sensation of speed pressing me into my seat, the smooth lift off the tarmac and climb into the air, the swing west. I was congratulating myself on traveling like I did this all the time, when the captain announced we'd reached cruising altitude at 30,000 feet, a spot of minor turbulence here. I felt the thin floor beneath my sneakers dip, abruptly aware it was all that supported me flying through empty air above the bottomless Pacific. The engine sound changed—was it failing, were we about to nosedive, screaming and praying not to die? In rising panic I wanted to scramble over the knees of the nonchalant couple between me and the aisle. *Let me out!* I forced myself to breathe into my belly. What was wrong with me? There's no way to get halfway around the world from home without crossing an ocean. I was being carried across in a padded reclining seat; my father had done it on his own in a sailboat. I couldn't see where he'd been, only billowing cloud tops that seemed to go on forever. The airplane icon crept across the map on my screen. Thirteen more hours before this flight would end.

Kristina Bak

As the plane tilted and circled into our landing approach, I pressed my forehead against my window. Below, Sydney Harbor dazzled turquoise blue. Long inlets like tentacles meandered among red roofs and greenery and towers glistened in the sunrise. I'd slept little, haunting the plane's aisles with other bleary insomniacs among the blessed sleepers since takeoff, day-before-yesterday considering the time change, but now I vibrated with anticipation, fully awake, at arriving.

Whole areas of Arrivals were curtained off with dusty plastic sheeting and yellow tape, barricaded with plywood. It all looked temporary. Signs blazoned with a completion date already a year past suggested a default into semi-permanence. I was funneled with other dazed, travel-smelling passengers through one-way corridors to Customs and Immigration. The process was quicker than I expected and I got through the passport queue, out the ground transportation exit, and into a taxi before I was ready with the address Fiona had sent me.

The driver waited while I brought up my hostel's directions. He was a turbaned Sikh, an older man with gentle eyes, his taxi impeccably clean, the steering wheel on the right. "Ah, yes, to Balmain."

He pulled into traffic so jammed I didn't realize we'd left the parking lot. Walled in by freight trucks on two sides and a bus in front, I was antsy to see out. "Is it always this bad?"

"Your first time in Sydney? No, this is good, we are moving. Often we don't. Someday, if the Chinese complete their project, we'll have more tunnels and trains and good streets. The company that won the bid began, but came the Beijing financial collapse, they went out of business. All works ceased."

Our movement had ceased, too; the taxi was at a stand-still. "But I saw construction in the terminal."

The driver turned and smiled at me around his seat back. "Work going on? No. Perhaps someday. No worries, I love Sydney. I've journeyed many places, have family all over the world. Thirty years ago I came here, I stayed. I love Sydney Harbor. I go to the Botanical Gardens and sit beside the water, in the shade beneath the ancient fig trees. Some of them have died since I first came, the droughts I think …" His voice trailed off.

The truck on our left moved. My driver snapped to attention, honked and nipped into the gap. He laughed. "Those self-driving cars behind us can't think as fast as me. We still need humans to drive taxis!" We picked up speed past industrial buildings and multicolored mid-rises catching the morning sun. As we neared the city center, I strained to see the harbor, but the towers I'd spotted from the air blocked my view. We bore left onto a bridge with a tantalizing harbor glimpse. The driver's commentary revived as our progress slowed.

"Anzac Bridge to the Balmain Peninsula. From Balmain you can take a passenger ferry to Circular Quay and walk to the Gardens. The newer ferries are fast, but the old wooden ones are better. Costs heaps to ride either kind now." He turned on a sports broadcast. When I asked what sport it was, he threw me an incredulous look in his rearview mirror.

"The cricket!"

He attended to traffic and the cricket match, which sounded equally slow. At last we pulled up on a street lined with three- and four-story 20th century buildings, small shops, and cafes with outdoor tables. "This is Darling Street and here is your hostel. Be careful stepping off into traffic you're expecting from the other way. The danger when we change countries."

As I paid, the driver had one last admonition. "You will love Sydney, too, but better if you learn about the cricket."

He left me on the sidewalk with my luggage, alone on an island continent 8,000 miles from home.

———

They say the best remedy for jet lag is to stay up until bedtime your first day at your destination. I couldn't count how many hours I'd been traveling. My body and mind demanded sleep, but I determined to get in synch with Sydney time. I checked into the hostel, my room cramped but clean: single bed, night stand, lamp. I blasted myself with cold water in the shower down the hall, dressed in a fresh tank top, cotton skirt and cardigan, slung my tote bag over my shoulder, and ventured out into Darling Street's morning bustle for a caffeine fix. I'd promised everyone at home to meet Gena's friend, Fiona, the day I arrived. She'd arranged my lodging. It was a ten-minute walk to her Lyre-bird Gallery and she'd known the hostel owner since school. I found a cafe and, restored by the best double espresso I ever had tasted, I set out to keep my promise.

CHAPTER 10

Winter in Sydney was like the best summer day at home. I stuffed my sweater into my bag as I walked. I'd never spoken to Fiona Faelly, but we'd exchanged messages. She sounded amiable and nonintrusive, taking me at my word that I wouldn't want hand-holding or touring around. I found her gallery in a neighborhood of gentrified pastel-colored row houses, far enough downhill from Darling Street to dampen traffic sounds. The house beside her building had a wrought iron balcony above a pocket-sized garden lush with banana plants, orchids, and tropical flowers I couldn't name. I didn't recognize the bird calls that owned the air, either. I envisioned myself in a different life, on a balcony, barefoot and languid, wearing a sarong, one of those orchids in my hair.

The same sun shone here as at home, but with more substance. It scraped across the gallery's façade, high-lighting Lyrebird House etched into the golden sandstone wall. Several steps led up to a tiled porch and a substantial wooden door. A Closed sign hung in the window.

I knocked. Inside, heels clicked on a hard floor. The door was flung open and I was swept into an embrace in a cloud of perfume before I could see the woman behind it.

Kristina Bak

"Stevie! Exactly the way dear Gena described you."

How was that? Fiona held me at arms' length to get another look. Somewhere in her fifties, voluptuous on the edge of plump, her style was Nineteen-Eighties-Retro-Revival motherly glam. Her makeup was just this side of too much, lipliner and gloss, lashes that didn't pretend to be real, but she obviously hadn't bothered with fillers or botox and her wrinkles were progressing along good-natured lines. With stiletto heels, she came to my chin. Her blond curls piled on another several inches.

"Come in, come in! Welcome to Lyrebird." Fiona flipped the sign in the window to Open and led me inside. Her voice was high and melodic, but she spoke emphatically, like someone accustomed to making decisions. Every accent I'd heard in Sydney so far had been different. I might have thought Fiona's was English if we weren't in Australia.

"This building is Heritage listed, well over a century old when we bought it. The name was already there in the wall, so I adopted it when we started the gallery twenty years ago. We would've needed an act of God to get Council to let us change anything on the outside. But I've quite liked it. Lyrebirds are splendid and they can imitate any sound—chainsaws, ringtones—incredible performance artists! Now I'm about to retire, going out with one last exhibition, a grand finale. You *do* like art?"

Another breathtaking download of my reintegrating self: my paintings exploded like fireworks in my memory. I hadn't touched a paintbrush since my accident. "Yes, art, *love* it!"

I'd spoken too fervently to seem wholly sane, but Fiona squeezed my arm, pulled me close, and half-whispered, as though imparting a great secret, "Me, too, darling!"

She ushered me through the gallery's three high-ceilinged rooms. The first was bright with sun from the front windows reflecting off the shiny wood floors, the middle one windowless and lit to dramatic effect by spotlights on the paintings, a wide oak bench in the center. The third, with Fiona's desk and two side chairs, caught ambient daylight from sliding glass doors opening into a small rear courtyard. The courtyard was surrounded by high walls and occupied by a leafless tree. The tree was twice my height, with swollen, scaly green limbs. "That's a frangipani out there, the aroma's utterly lewd when it blossoms." She waited for my response, which was slow in coming.

"Sorry, I'm kind of overwhelmed."

"Oh, that vile jet lag! Did Gena tell you my hubby Graham flew twenty-five years for Qantas? Back and forth across the big pond. He was always very blasé, but I never got used to it, however many trips I made. Two things Aussies are good at, swimming and flying overseas. Well, not this Aussie, except, naturally, the swimming part. Do sit down and I'll make you a coffee."

Fiona opened one of the cabinets behind her desk, revealing a kitchenette. She busied herself with an espresso machine as she talked. "I've told them at the hostel you're my special guest. So sorry we can't have you stay with us! Grahammie and I downsized last year, bought a flat in Lavender Bay, one bedroom. I normally take the ferry here to work."

"The hostel's fine." It would have been rude to refuse the coffee; I owed her. My opportunity to at least partially repay my debt came as she handed me the cup.

"Milk? Sugar? It's a blessing you arrived today. I chipped a tooth last night on a piece of macadamia shell. If you'll mind the place while I dash out to the dentist, I won't have to close."

"Of course." What else could I say to Fiona, if I could get a word in?

"When I get back, we'll sort out what we might do to help your search. First, you'll need to recover from the jet lag and let us show you around a bit." She checked the time and gathered her handbag and phone. "Now look, you needn't to do anything but *be* here and if someone comes in, give them a brochure. Any questions, call me. My dentist's just in Rozelle, shouldn't be more than an hour."

So, I was in charge. I rinsed my coffee down the sink as soon as Fiona left. The gallery was between shows, only the middle room properly hung. There, in grand spotlit landscapes—*skyscapes,* really—clouds ascended to infinity, seas or cities dematerializing at the horizons, each painting like a giant window to a different world. I was amazed to learn from the gallery brochure that these were by Fiona. There was more to her than first impressions revealed; she was an artist, too, a fine one. I imagined her balancing on the top rung of a ladder in her stilettos to reach the paintings' tops with her brush.

Smaller canvases leaned against bare walls in the front room waiting to be hung or taken away; oil paintings that, from an angle, were all blurred wings, fearsome beaks and eyes, bloodied claws. Straight on and closer, I wasn't so sure. Perhaps my warped imagination had drawn those images from the paint's strokes and smears. Either way, I was transfixed by the combined threat and beauty. I stifled my startled squeal when the door swung open behind me.

"G'day!" The figure silhouetted in the doorway loomed like an outsized stick insect. He stepped inside, a tall, lanky, youngish guy in super skinny red pants and a tight yellow tee. He carried a battered messenger bag. "Pity my exhibit's ended. Fiona can show you what's unsold."

"You're the artist?"

He came nearer and smiled down at me. "Waleed Tanoos, delighted to meet you." His smile was childlike in its sweetness and so, to my ear, was his slightly lisping, drawling accent, yet another form of Aussie. His hazel eyes emanated warmth. He offered me his hand; his fingers were tapered and stained with paint. His hair was dyed orange, shaved on the sides, high and thick on top. Silver cuffs jeweled with citrines clasped the rims of both ears.

"I'm Stevie Wales." Did he hold my hand a beat longer than simple courtesy? How did they do things here? I swallowed hard. "I love your work, scary fierce."

"Meant to be. About a bloke murdered by a magpie in Melbourne."

"Murdered by a *bird*?"

"True! Pedaling his bloody bike, lost to the world, looked up and got the beak through one eye, right to his brain, that bird the last thing he saw, I reckon."

"A beautiful death."

Waleed studied my face. "Good on you! You see the beauty, like I do. Not everybody can. Fiona does. Where is she?" He peered over my head into the next room. "*Cooee,* Fiona!"

"She's gone to the dentist. I'm a visitor, gallery sitting."

"Lucky me I stopped in! I'll wait a bit, in good company."

His delight struck me as sincere. Neither of us spoke for a few moments; Waleed hummed a cheerful tune, covering the silence that, for me at least, was juicy with potential. I stood close to him, but not as close as I wanted to, both of us studying a murderous magpie painting.

I'd never met anyone I considered a *real* artist and here I'd met two already. My life was changing. "I have to ask, you seem so lighthearted. I thought the person who painted those killer birds would be, I don't know, like, brooding."

"Going through a rough patch when I did them. That's what you see. I got my troubles out of my head and onto canvas. I've changed now." Waleed pulled a tablet from his bag and flicked through its files. He moved so we could both see the screen; our forearms touched; he smelled of soap and sunlight. "Here's my new series."

The blackness was gone for sure. His new paintings blazed with more hues than I could name, writhed with shapes in shades of scarlet, gold, magenta, chartreuse, ultramarine that couldn't quite be caught before transforming into something else—the passage of time into space, or energy into matter. I couldn't explain to myself what I was seeing. My blood was zinging, my mind gyrating with a million questions. How did he do it? I wanted to create like this, not the same imagery, my own, but with Waleed's skill and passion and confidence.

"Waleed, these are awesome, totally amazing, beyond brilliant! Are they oils?"

Waleed closed the file and refolded the tablet like he didn't need my praise, sure of his own worth. "Too right, six of them, tremendous ones, bigger than this." He reached his arms up, then out as far as they could go. "Completely different from anything I've done before. No one's seen these yet, not even Fiona. I don't mean to come the tall poppy, but I wanted to tell her in person: I'm showing these photos to the exhibition director at the MCA this morning."

"MCA?"

"Museum of Contemporary Art, tons of prestige. Lucky break, I met the director at a party last night! If I get a show there, I'll owe Fiona. She was the first person who believed in me. For now, it's all hush-hush, so forget what you've seen, or I'll have to kidnap you."

I laughed. How long had it been since I'd done that? I'd forgotten I had a sense of humor. "I wouldn't mind, but I'm good at secrets. I'll keep yours. I'm honored you showed me your work."

"Ah, well, a discerning Yank, not mired in the local scene. I've been psyched to show *someone*." I covered my scarred cheek with one hand when Waleed paused, that sweet smile playing around the corners of his mouth. "Want to come with me for good luck? Lunch at the MCA cafe after? I'll tour you through the place. Largely rubbish, but you never know, you might enjoy it. If I triumph with the director, we'll have something to celebrate; I'll take you dancing. If I don't, you can pat me on the head so I feel better."

I imagined patting his orange hair, its give and spring beneath my hand. "I love dancing." I didn't, but I could learn to with him. "I have to stay here until Fiona gets back. It shouldn't be long. I could meet you."

Waleed's eyes, clear green-gold, looked into mine, sparkling like he'd discovered a wonderful surprise. "Excellent! Got to catch the ferry now. One every forty minutes to Circular Quay from the dock at the end of

Louisa Road." We exchanged contact info. "See you soon and we shall dance!" He kissed me on my good cheek and pirouetted out the door.

———————

Sexy. I hadn't thought about anyone as **sexy** since Nate left me, but I felt aroused and enlivened by Waleed in more ways than one and guilty about it. His kiss burned on my cheek; how would it feel on my mouth? When Fiona returned, mumbling her thanks through numbed lips, I told her he'd dropped by to see her and invited me to lunch, loyal to my pledge to say no more. Fiona approved and sent me on my way.

As I followed her directions through the neighborhood and across a grassy soccer field to Louisa Road, I fought thoughts about what Nate might be doing in Singapore. I'd heard nothing from him, no get-well message after my accident, not a word. He wasn't exactly my *boyfriend*. My guilt wasn't about him, but about being sidetracked from my mission to find my father.

Everything had been hard for so long, could it be bad to allow myself this one pleasure, an afternoon of Waleed's creativity and passion. Or *more* than an afternoon? Waleed was an artist and I was an artist. Okay, in a small way, but we shared that and with someone like him, I could be more. This didn't feel like a crush; I'd had crushes before. This felt like fate. Was Waleed my soulmate? Could this be a serendipitous opening to a new life? *Whoa, slow down!*

My dad wouldn't begrudge me one day's delay now that I was here. I was probably the only one who believed I wasn't on a fool's errand, everyone else indulging my stubborn illusions until I gave them up. I didn't want to admit I had no idea how to go about my search, but it was a comfort being on the same continent where Dad might be. Tomorrow I'd figure out what to do next.

Getting lost on Louisa Road was impossible. It ran down a narrow finger of land reaching into the harbor. In some places, houses were built right to the street, sandstone walls so close on both sides two cars could scarcely pass. But no cars came, the street was empty. Evidently, life on Louisa Road took place facing the water and every house was exclusive harborside property. I was an intruder, conspicuous until a gaggle of middle-school girls in plaid uniforms and straw hats chattered past me. The hats looked like a good idea in this sun-washed, stone-paved channel.

The street dead-ended at a small park overlooking the water, with shrubs and shade trees and a token monument to the displaced Aboriginal owners. I trailed the schoolgirls down mossy stone steps to a floating passenger dock, less than an hour behind Waleed, but his ferry had apparently come and gone, because the girls and I were the only people in sight. I seized the not-quite-waist-high metal bar that symbolized protective railing and imitated their nonchalance when the dock bobbed underfoot with waves from an approaching ferry.

It was one of the older boats the taxi driver had recommended, painted green and cream, puttering along, so like a jolly character from a kids' cartoon I expected it to have eyes. It bumped to a stop against the dock, roiling the water. A deck hand looped a rope around a piling and pulled it taut; another slung a precarious gangway across the gap between us and the rocking boat and called out something in incomprehensible Aussie English. The schoolgirls giggled aboard and I followed them, almost as giddy. They flocked to the upper deck. I stayed on the lower deck near the water, a rich indigo now.

Sydney's sun warmed my unaccustomed skin. From this side, the Louisa Road houses looked romantic, the water so high up their protective seawalls, the flowering plants spilling over them gave the illusion that they rested in floating gardens. The flowers' fragrance mingled with salt air. This city's sensuality thrilled me. Anything could happen here. The ferry gave a jaunty toot and pulled away from shore. Beneath the dock behind us I saw something long and red, then something yellow, half obscured by churning water— some plant or, no, some creature. The ferry began to turn and the creature swept out in its wake, a pale hand waving like five-fingered kelp. I screamed.

"Stop! Stop! Help! Stop the boat!"

I pointed. My mind was frozen at *No, no, no, no ...!* A crewman tried to subdue me until the schoolgirls on the upper deck saw what I'd seen and set up a collective cry. The captain reversed engines and held steady. Someone threw a flotation ring. Passengers who'd gathered to watch groaned, seeing the person in the water was past reaching for it. One deck hand used a grappling hook to keep him from being sucked under the hull, while another dove in for a rescue. People around me raised their phones to capture ghoulish videos. Reflexively, I prayed, *God, don't let this be Waleed!* It looked like him floating there, but how could it be? Impossible. Wasn't it?

The would-be rescuers wrestled the body, streaming water, onto the deck, forced us spectators back, and closed around it. The captain came running heavy-footed with a first aid case. On my toes, I strained to see through the crowd, saw only the captain's tensed back as he set about CPR. A doctor taking the ferry with her grandchildren pushed into the huddle. She returned, too soon, meeting no one's eyes. Someone fetched a tarp. The captain stood, took off his cap, and wiped sweat off his face with one arm. When he put his cap back on, the brim cast a shadow over his eyes from the sun almost straight overhead. He addressed the passengers, most with their phones lowered now.

"Anyone here think they know this bloke?"

I spoke, sounding muddled and incoherent. "Me … I think I do." Everyone turned to stare at me. I stumbled forward, unbalanced on the rolling deck as another boat passed. "Show me."

The captain barred my way. "He's not a pretty sight for a young lady."

"Show me or I'll look for myself!" I tried to push past him.

He held me back. "All right, calm down."

He slowly lifted a corner of the tarp. I recognized the citrines first, tiny gemstones sparkling in the sun, and the orange hair, wet and flattened. At first I thought the face was blue from light passing through the plastic tarp. The mouth twisted in a grotesque rictus. The eyes bulged; the forehead was scraped raw, the nose pulped. My legs went weak, bile rose in my throat. The captain dropped the tarp back, but I couldn't un-see what it covered no matter how despairingly I wanted to. I whispered his name: "Waleed…" The captain leaned in and asked me to repeat it, louder. "Waleed Tanoos."

Kristina Bak

CHAPTER 11

The cup of tea Fiona passed me across her desk rattled on its saucer. Her spoon clinked erratically against china as she stirred sugar and milk into hers. "So horrible for you, dear. I feel it's my fault." She looked ten years older than she had that morning, an interminable few hours ago, owl-eyed from migrating mascara and tears. The spoon slipped from her grip and clanged onto the floor. She held her head in her hands, elbows on the desk, and massaged her scalp hard with her fingers. Her blond curls stuck out every which way, like they were trying to escape. She'd come to pick me up at the park when I'd called her. The ferry passengers had been offloaded there. Police had taken witness names and numbers and let us go.

"How could it be your fault? You weren't here." My tongue seemed to move in slow-motion; I heard myself like a bad recording. "It's more horrible for you. Waleed was your friend, I'd just met him." Impossible Fiona could feel more horrible than I did, but I couldn't let her carry blame I knew was mine. Whatever had happened to Waleed wouldn't have happened if I'd persuaded him to wait until Fiona got back, or just locked the door and gone with him when he'd asked me to. Why, *why*, hadn't I? One simple "yes" and he would be alive right now. Right this very second his hand could be warm around mine. Instead he was cold and blue and dead, naked and alone in the morgue. An unthinking, unforgivable mistake, the worst I'd made in my entire life full of mistakes and Waleed had died for it. Now Fiona was afflicted, too.

She took a quavery breath. "Waleed had an extraordinary talent for art and for friendship. I'm gutted losing him." She managed a sip of her tea, spilling some down her front. "I've rung Graham. He should be here soon."

We sat together, increasingly desolate, until Graham bounded in like an old golden retriever—large, warm, affectionate. With his tousled sandy hair, soft mustache, and kind eyes, he embodied reassurance. I felt brutally alone watching Graham's tenderness toward his wife when she went to him. I imagined how it would be if he were my father and would hold me, too, or if Waleed were here to share grief, not be the object of it.

Fiona sobbed out the news. "The police are calling him a suicide. They thought robbery, the way some characters lurk around that park, but his phone was in his pocket, jewelry on his ears."

Could it have been *suicide*? Had I seen anyone "lurking" in the park? Had I caught movement among the trees? I was sure no one had passed me on the street. All I saw when

I closed my eyes was Waleed's dead face. "But he'd been beaten, that's not from drowning himself."

"Oh, Stevie, this is Graham. Graham, this is Stevie, Gena's friend from America. She found…she found the… she found him." By the time Fiona had collected me, Waleed was zipped into a body bag and the area taped off and guarded by the police, but her persistence had pried information out of a uniform. "They told me with the tide rising Waleed came up under the dock. Maybe he'd changed his mind, panicked at not being able to get his head above water, thrashed around until he passed out and drowned and…"

Graham kissed the top of Fiona's head. "Shush, love, that doesn't help."

Fiona moaned against his chest. "I can't bear thinking that's what happened to him." She stepped away, wringing her hands. "Or, they said, he might have swum out a ways before he let himself drown, then washed in dead with the tide and got bashed on the rocks and the rubbish under there then. God knows that's bad enough."

I slammed my hand flat on the desktop. "Someone should have been there!" Like me if I hadn't dawdled, reveling in the sunshine. "Someone should've seen him, or heard him struggling if he tried to get out."

Graham shook his head. "It's likely no one was there. Not many people use that little dock except at commuting time. He would have done it when he was alone."

I saw a different scenario. "If someone pushed him, they would have made sure there were no witnesses."

Fiona stared at me. Graham applied the voice of reason. "But Stevie, you're talking murder. What would be the motive? And besides, he could have swum off a ways and climbed out."

"Duh! They knocked him out first!" I shouted at Graham. His reasonableness grated—in a rational world Waleed wouldn't be dead. "I might have been the last person he talked to before he died. If it *was* suicide I should have seen it coming, should've kept him here, should've gone with him, said something to keep him alive!"

Graham stroked my hair. His kindness was more than I thought I deserved.

CHAPTER 12

omeone banged on the locked front door, ignoring Fiona's Closed sign. "Bloody hell, what now? Whoever it is, Grahammie, get rid of them, will you?"

Graham tromped off, jaw set. We heard voices, then he came back, shrugging. "It's his mates, I had to let them in."

Four young people trooped behind Graham, their agitation filling the gallery. The larger of the two girls, her face splotched red and wet, hurled herself into Fiona's arms, nearly knocking her over, keening. "It's my fault, my fault!"

A hunky blond, my stereotypical Aussie surfer boy, peeled her off Fiona. "Yair, Nikki's been this way since we heard. Can't talk her down."

Graham threw Fiona an apologetic look. "You lot, go in the other room. We'll bring tea."

The surfer boy led Nikki aside. "Ta, Graham, and a bikkie or two? We've had bugger-all to eat."

Making more tea calmed Fiona. She served it from a tray, with a package of cookies, in the middle room where her landscapes offered us their tranquility, a surreal contrast to the situation. Graham added some extra chairs.

I covered my scarred cheek with my hand as Fiona did

the introductions. "This is Stevie, visiting from the States. Nikki, Col, Lala, Raven." The pack of intruders seemed too distressed to be curious about me.

Col, the surfer with freckled good looks, helped himself to a handful of cookies. Nikki filled most of the center bench, curled miserably with her knees drawn up, her skirt barely covering her abundant backside. She hid her face in Lala's lap. Lala was slight, South Asian, with hair bleached like dandelion fluff. She wore fluorescent lipstick so you saw her mouth and hair first, like a blind she watched you from behind. Raven sat cross-legged on the floor apart from the others. He was watching, too, but with an air of being in charge. His black hair swung partly over one eye; his features, suntanned, strong-jawed, straight-nosed, didn't quite add up to handsome. He wore paint-splattered jeans and a white shirt with sleeves rolled up, exposing brawny forearms.

Nikki whimpered. Col spoke through a mouthful of cookie. "Nikki thinks it's her fault Waleed topped himself."

Lala corrected him. "She thinks it's *our* fault."

Nikki heaved out of Lala's lap. "It *is* our fault, I know it! When I left him he fell off the perch. He wasn't worth the skin he was in, nattered about 'my depression' like it was a pet."

Raven cut in, declamatory. "Always the center of the bloody universe, Nikki. He was in the sulks before you dumped him. He'd whinge to Col and me at the pub, that he had the Black Dog at his throat, then later say it was the piss talking. You saw how he'd lock himself in his room for days, without food, to drink and paint. Trust me, it wasn't about you."

"How would you understand, you macho empathy-voids?" Nikki turned her scowl full force on Raven and Col, her lashes wet, dark brows drawn together, long auburn hair in snarls.

Col blinked. Raven met her glare. "I understand because in the country town where I grew up every second person down the road was medicated—the men, but women, too. They blamed the drought, or their neighbor, or the government. You wondered, is this bloke depressed, or just a surly bastard with a bad attitude, next thing you'd find he'd hung himself in the shearing shed."

This earned him a sour smirk from Nikki. "Awfully Tim Winton, Raven, reflecting your superior literary education and humble beginnings ad nauseam, but you're nothing compared to Waleed, so don't go judging him."

I squirmed at the give-and-take I didn't fully understand. Some score was being settled for old hurts, something beyond Waleed's death.

Lala patted Nikki's thigh.

Nikki pushed her hand away. "So did you and Col know we were planning to be married, Waleed and me?"

Raven frowned, thrown off track, as she went on:

"We were, before Lala. Nobody gets married, but if you live with some bloke for six months he thinks you're the wife. I don't believe that Happy Families crap, grins and cuddles for the photo. I want to rip their eyes out. Who do they think they are? Children shouldn't be trusted to those people. But Waleed wanted to marry me. I couldn't imagine life without him, so I said yes. The next day Lala moved into the co-op. That's when Waleed started his magpie death paintings and now we've lost him. It's our fault, mine and Lala's, for falling in love."

Lala wrapped her arms around Nikki, either in affection or as restraint. Whichever it was, Nikki slumped against her.

Raven sneered. "Stuff your fantasies, Nikki. They can't hurt Waleed anymore, but leave Lala out of it. She doesn't need to eat that guilt."

Nikki lurched in Lala's arms, Col half stood then sat back down as Lala put one finger over Nikki's lips and Nikki collapsed against her.

Graham cleared his throat. "Look, we feel ratshit about what's happened to Waleed. He was brilliant, a lovely young man, and his death makes no sense. He wouldn't want you at each others' throats this way. Go home now. Make peace." The four gaped at him like wild animals caught by surprise.

Fiona protested weakly, passing the cookies. Col took another handful.

Raven stood. "No, Graham's right, Fiona, we should go. Sorry to be so snarky." He directed this last in a general way toward Nikki. She grunted with what might have been apology.

They left with embraces all around, including me. I took comfort from the body contact. They had no idea I'd met Waleed, alive or dead.

From a front window Fiona watched them go. "That's been brewing. Raven was Waleed's best mate; they started the co-op in a condemned warehouse, a *collective* they called it, where they'd live and work and get famous together instead of being in competition, practically blood brothers. Col's part of it, too. He's a Sydney Uni dropout, traded law for sculpture, he'd have you believe. I haven't seen the evidence. More like traded uni for the beach."

While Graham swept up cookie crumbs, Fiona and I

gathered tea cups from the middle room and took them to the kitchenette sink. She went on as she washed them. "Nikki moved in two years ago, when she turned sixteen, taking classes at TAFE to get into film school overseas. The inevitable ensued. One way or another, she and Waleed paired up and Waleed had a lot less time for his old mate, Raven. I got to know them well. They kept coming to me to get a show. I wanted to help, took a piece or two sometimes to exhibit. Then came Lala, Nikki and Waleed broke up and, coincidentally or otherwise, Waleed's work … well, you've seen it."

"Yeah, he's … he was …" I broke off. This would have been the time to tell her about his new work, but I couldn't talk without bursting into tears. I crumpled the empty cookie package and threw it in the trash. Fiona dried the cups and saucers.

"Lala's an artist, too, costume design. She runs a clothing booth at the Saturday Market in Rozelle. Does quite well at it. Nikki fell in love with Lala, or so she says. Nikki switches partners pretty regularly and she's so young. I didn't think Waleed was devastated, more relieved. Raven should have been, too. I'm glad they came here today. When something dire happens, it's good to touch one another." She put the last cup in the drainer. "There, love, will you be all right if we drive you to your hostel? You'll need some sleep by now."

CHAPTER 13

I wanted to call home, to claim comfort from my mom, but I couldn't calculate the time difference and I didn't trust myself to talk to her without crying. I messaged my safe arrival, which I should have done hours ago, then lapsed into what was more unconsciousness than sleep. My dreams had me falling out of airplanes, being pecked to death by birds, bound in crime-scene tape. My bed sheets were wrapped around my legs when I woke. I'd slept from afternoon to morning and yesterday's real nightmare rushed in. Waking or dreams, neither a good option. My phone sounded.

I answered through a yawn. "Yeah, it's me."

"This grief, it stuffs you. I'm a wreck." Fiona sounded harried. "I'm on my way to work. Did you sleep? Can you manage on your own this morning?"

"Yes, sure."

"I'd hired a van for today, to deliver Waleed's paintings and get them hung in their new homes. I can't cancel; the buyers are expecting me. It breaks my heart these are his last."

I took a breath to tell her about what Waleed had shown

me, but it turned into another yawn too enormous to control.

"Graham's dropping me off at the gallery. We'll talk later, Stevie."

"Wait, I ..." But Fiona was gone.

I envied Fiona's busyness. I felt lost when I got out of bed, not from being in a foreign land, but from not knowing what to do next. This day stretched ahead filled with black holes. I assigned myself tasks. First, shower. I was back in my room dressing when someone knocked on my door and told me I had a visitor.

The man waiting in the poky lounge off the lobby was baby-faced, with round cheeks and flyaway hair needing a trim. I pegged him as over forty from the slight slump in his shoulders and his weary eyes. I seldom met men wearing suits and this man clearly wished he wasn't one of them. He flashed an official holographic photo, himself in what looked like the same suit. "Detective Inspector Richard Morgan, Leichhardt Region. Stevie ...?"

"Stevie Wales."

"The American witness. Fair enough, we need to have a chat. About Waleed Tanoos." He caught the skinny boy on desk duty watching us. "You have something else to do, mate?"

The boy put on headphones and slouched over the office computer.

"Shall we?" The detective waved me to a vinyl-covered sofa before I could say yes or no. It wasn't merely a request; I wasn't sure if by Australian law I had a choice. He maintained the dominant position, standing over me, typically male, or a ploy he'd learned in police school. His eyes moved around, taking in details, especially of me. He looked restless, like he'd be more comfortable outdoors. "So, yesterday."

His brusqueness triggered my hostility. The police had judged Waleed a suicide. I didn't buy it. "I won't believe Waleed drowned himself."

"I'm not interested in what you believe. I want to know exactly what happened, from your meeting Waleed to finding him dead."

He softened his demand with a manipulative smile, good cop and bad cop in one. The way Richard Morgan observed me would have been intimate in other circumstances. He watched my mouth and the nervous hand gestures I made as I unreeled my account. He looked at my legs and feet when I talked about walking. I did well until the part about seeing Waleed's face under the tarp. It came out wheezy. "I know Waleed wouldn't have drowned himself."

"You *know?*" He raised his eyebrows almost comically.

That pissed me off. "He was excited about his *future*, about his new paintings."

"And you say he hadn't shown them to anyone else?"

"Not even to Fiona. I was the first."

"And as you say, apparently the only. We haven't recovered the tablet you describe. Of course, if we suspect any foul play, we'll send a diver."

I wanted to slap the condescension off his face. "I'm not inventing this."

"Why would you be?"

Was that a question or an accusation? "When he left the gallery, he had his tablet with him. I didn't see him alive again." My voice went a pitch higher. I was sounding suspicious and hysterical to myself. How did I sound to the detective? What could he suspect me of? "You can go to his studio and *see* the paintings."

"You're sure about that."

"Yes, I…" Of course I was, wasn't I?

"If we need to, we'll search there, too."

"Then do it! What are you waiting for?"

A trio of girls with backpacks hurried through the lobby. Noise from the street came in as they left, then was muffled again as the door swung shut. The vinyl squeaked as Richard Morgan sat next to me. I felt his body heat and noted the weave of the not-quite-nice synthetic fabric of his jacket sleeve brushing my arm. Closer than I'd expect from a detective on official business. Did Aussies have a different sense of social distance? I didn't want to offend him by shifting as he patiently answered me:

"You don't grasp the situation. My investigative resources are bloody thin. In this state we police more than ten million people, those not one atop the other here in Sydney strewn over an area twice the size of England, Scotland, and Wales. Add thirty-plus different languages, ethnic and family loyalties, enmities and misunderstandings, terrorist threats—you get the picture. Heaps of these people live within *cooee* of the sea, an hour or less on a good traffic day. We don't all carry guns like you Yanks, so suicide by drowning is a popular option. I admit, young men usually prefer it more dramatic, in the surf off a cliff rather than a ferry dock." He waited until I met his eyes. "Young men can be such fools."

We sat that way a moment longer, my body misreading cues from his, or not. To my great relief, the detective sighed, stood, and straightened his tie. "Thank you for your help.

Oh, and welcome to Australia."

After he left I texted my mom: Gena's friends were kind, Sydney as beautiful as everyone said. That was all she needed to know. I tried to drag my mind off Waleed's death. I was here to find my dad. No official data suggested he was alive somewhere on this continent, only that he had been and almost certainly died in a typhoon off the far north coast. We'd known this before I came, so now that I was here, how could I prove it was wrong? I had to figure that out for myself.

CHAPTER 14

When Graham called, I was wandering down Darling Street in a listless daze, attempting to work up appetite for a late breakfast, queasy at the sight of meals on other people's plates at the outdoor tables. He'd been the calming influence yesterday, now he barked, indignant. "That bloody detective, Richard Inspector Hoo-Haw, caught up with us at the gallery. He said he'd been to see you. He's wanting Fiona to *confess* she saw suicidal depression in Waleed's art, so he can draw a line under his case!"

So, the detective wasn't after answers; he'd come to his conclusion, another piece in the blame game. "I think that's how he operates. He made it pretty obvious he didn't believe what *I* said."

"As may be." Graham shifted emotional gears. "Where are you? I'll take you to lunch at the yacht club. Hotbed of geriatric reactionaries, but the food's good and the living have to eat, or who will be left to remember the dead? One stop to make first. I'll explain on the way."

I'd told Fiona I'd be all right alone, but I wasn't, not really, not today. Thankful for Graham's invitation, I bought myself a takeaway espresso and drank it waiting on the street corner where he said he would meet me.

Minutes later, he pulled up in a classic pre-electric Mercedes. We drove toward the city center, turned off before the Anzac Bridge and wound beneath it to a bay. Lining the shore, luxury residential towers crowded older, smaller maritime enterprises that looked to have insecure futures on the costly waterfront real estate. Graham parked in front of a large corrugated metal building barnacled with add-ons and sheds. Three tall masts rose from a dockyard behind it.

"I first came here as a favor to a pilot mate of mine. 'Now that you're retired, mate,' he says, 'what are you going to do?' Ah, take up my old hobby flying antique Tiger Moths, I tell him, sail to Tasmania, take Fiona on an Antarctic cruise, grow some roses. 'Very good,' he says, 'Meanwhile, we need your assistance fundraising to restore the *Mary Murchie.*' She stole my heart. It happens with ships."

I followed Graham into the workshop that clamored with hammering, sawing, drilling. Every bang and shrill whine reverberated inside my head as we picked our way over metal scraps and lengths of lumber, heavy-duty electrical cords and hoses trailing from roaring equipment.

Men in overalls, most of them gray-haired, some with welding masks, bent to tasks amid an alarming combination of sparks and sawdust. I saw one man nudge another who prodded the next in a domino effect of genial leers at the sight of a female person. I remembered what Mom always said: "Boys never grow up, only old."

It was quieter once we passed through the building to the dry dock outside where the elegant curve of the *Mary Murchie's* bow loomed over us. I shielded my eyes with my hands and squinted up into the sun to see the tops of the masts.

Graham opened his arms in royal proclamation. "There she is, masthead taller than a ten-story building. A wind-jammer launched in England,1874, carried cargo around the globe for thirty years with a seventeen-man crew. Epic gales rounding the Horn, iceberg collisions, fires in her hold—she survived everything the sea threw at her, even when not all her crew did." Graham's enthusiasm as he described the hazardous voyages made the ship sound like a dauntless living thing.

"She could have sailed another hundred years, but technology did her in; steamships made her obsolete. She was stripped and used as a coal hulk until she became a floating hazard. The owners sank her in a Tasmanian backwater, by good fortune, on a sandy bottom in still water. That preserved her hull from salt air corrosion. When our restoration team brought her up a century later, everything below the waterline was whole."

Graham's fervor grew. "Someday soon she'll put out to sea past the Heads, all twenty-one sails raised to catch the wind. I intend to be on board, like traveling back in a time machine. Look at her beautiful lines. And see that mermaid figurehead, hand-carved and gilded? Cost a bloody fortune to recreate."

I admired the mermaid propped on the dock. She was waiting to be mounted on the front of the ship, larger than life-size, if mermaids were the size of humans, shoulders back, chest forward, her expression intrepid to inspire the sailors' courage.

Graham lowered his voice. "You know the saying, a sailboat's a hole in the ocean you pour money down?"

"Yeah, my mom said that about my dad's boat." She'd

said it often, loudly, when the bills came in.

"Well, a windjammer like this is a *colossal* hole. That's why we're here right now, summoned by our major donor, and here he comes."

A wizened man in a perfect blue double-breasted suit approached us, his eyes gleaming with the passion I saw in Graham's. I couldn't say the same for the two burly boys flanking him like dull bookends. They were near my age, but wore matching gray slacks and tailored jackets, outfits a young person would be unlikely to choose for a sunny day on the waterfront.

"Graham, thank you for coming on short notice." The donor turned to me. "And will you introduce me to your lovely companion?" He didn't politely not look at my scarred cheekbone, the way most people pretended to do, but neither did he stare. Easily a foot shorter than me, he had the poise of a big man.

Graham obliged. "Stevie Wales, our American friend. Stevie, meet Marco de Torino Blandis."

Marco took my hand in his, a papery-skinned grip, firm like his voice, yet tender, showing he no longer had to try to impress, that his name alone was sufficient.

"I am enchanted to meet you. These," he nodded left and right, "are my sons, Tony and Lucco." The two were twins, identical. They looked nothing like their father. I speculated their mom must be large-jawed, dark eyed, substantial, and considerably younger than her husband. Did *she* choose their clothes?

Marco released my hand. "If you will please excuse us, Ms. Wales, Graham and I need a private word together, concerning business." He pinned his sons in place with one pointing finger and gestured Graham up the gangway to the ship's deck with him, controlling the scene like an orchestra conductor.

Without their father, the twins seemed unsure what to do with their bodies. One opted for casually leaning on a black metal barrel that proved too low. They both settled for hands in their jacket pockets and positioned themselves on either side of me, so I could speak to one only by turning my back on the other. I was primed to be sociable, but the twin introduced as Lucco took me by surprise. "We hear you met Waleed Tanoos."

I pivoted to face him. "You know … *knew* Waleed?"

Tony answered from behind me. "An old friendship, our father and his. Waleed's family's in a bad way over his death." I backed away to get both sons in view, but they moved with me. Tony went on, speaking in an undertone, so I had to turn to hear him. "Sydney Harbor's a tricky place—easy to slip off a dock, or a boat. All kinds of accidents happen here. Sometimes we have sharks in the water. Or people fall and bash their heads, like Waleed did." He stretched out his words as though he liked their taste and curved his lips in a smile that didn't reach his eyes.

The sun-warmed pier gave off a tarry smell; a gull perched on a shed roof gave one raucous cry that sounded like a warning. I nervously looked for Graham. I could see him and the boys' father up on the far end of the ship's deck, deep in their own conversation. I doubted he'd brought me here for this on purpose. "I don't want to talk about it." I wasn't sure the twins intended the threatening, conspiratorial atmosphere they created, but I wasn't sure they *didn't*. I didn't want to be alone with them, either. They seemed dumb enough to be dangerous, but why?

Lucco pushed Tony aside. "Ignore him. My brother's a dill, no feel for sensitive women. He's only saying you don't understand how things work here. Forget Waleed; let everybody get past what's happened. It's nothing to do with you. Get out of Sydney and have a good time. Go up the Gold Coast. Take a tour to Uluru, see the red desert." He stepped back as Graham and his donor descended from the ship and rejoined them.

Marco de Torino Blandis, beamed benevolently. "My sons enjoy a beautiful young woman's company, but we're due in Elizabeth Bay for lunch with their mum and she is a lady who hates delay." The twins went to their father like iron filings to a magnet. They left without looking back.

On our way out through the workshop, we paused so Graham could talk with a scrawny old man supervising the activity from a high stool. They had to shout to hear each other over a circular saw blade shrieking through wood and a hammer pounding on metal. I plugged my ears with my fingers and wondered how the men could stand the din.

Graham started the car. "Puzzling, that. When Marco rang, I told him I was taking you to lunch. He said we needed to meet and I should bring you to see the ship. Then we went aboard and rehashed something we'd settled last week. I can't suss out what he was on about."

"His sons told me they knew Waleed."

"Did they? I suppose they would. Same pricey schools."

Kristina Bak

We headed toward Balmain. "The old salt I spoke to as we were leaving? He's lived his life on the sea and around northern Australia. I asked him if he'd heard about your father, either by name, or as a Yank who'd survived a typhoon and a shipwreck. They all knew one another up there back in the day. He said he'd give it a think."

"That's *all*? A *think*? He didn't know my dad?" I whined and despised myself for it. They weren't my parents; they didn't have to be patient with me. My chagrin ricocheted around inside me.

Graham grinned as he drove. "You sound like our daughter twenty years ago, makes me almost nostalgic." He glanced over and caught me wiping angry tears from my eyes. "Sorry, I know it's nothing to joke about. Never mind, don't lose heart; he'll ask around."

Further on, he grumbled as traffic in our lane ground more or less to a halt. "Some bridge mishap ahead, puts paid to my lunch idea. The yacht club's on the other side of the harbor." He inched forward and made a sharp turn down an alley. "We're stuck in Balmain, so let's see if Fiona's at the gallery. I'm determined to get you fed before lunch turns into dinner."

We bought takeaway from a Vietnamese restaurant on a side street. It smelled alluringly of fat and spices, but when we got to Lyrebird, being back where I'd met Waleed knotted my stomach.

Fiona rose from her desk to greet us. She gave me a quick kiss on the cheek. "I had to send Waleed's magpie paintings to be delivered without me. I've got an unholy migraine. I couldn't eat a thing."

Graham set the food containers on her desk. "Right now, you'd be stopped somewhere on Victoria Road, anyway. Why don't you go on home and take something for the headache? I'll mind the gallery." He began opening the cartons. "You can help me, can't you, Stevie?"

I felt the flutter in my palms I'd forgotten during my convalescence. I clamped my hands together to stop their reaching for Fiona's pain. My *knowing* dimension moved toward her like a separate self; my *thinking* brain said no way, don't you dare experiment on her! What if the blow to my brain had changed my pain-healing into something else, something savage I couldn't control? I didn't know how the power had come to me in the first place. Gift or curse, the compulsion was back and stronger.

Before I could touch her, Fiona blanched. She groped for her desk chair, but it rolled. Her knees gave and she fell against me. I caught her, eased her down and knelt beside her on the floor. Did I act without thinking then, or did I deliberately lay one palm on Fiona's forehead? It felt like coming home to a place I was born to be. The spikes of her pain melted in waves that rolled through me. To where? I had no idea. I didn't need to know. I sat back on my heels.

The lines around Fiona's mouth relaxed, her color returned. Graham slipped his hands under her arms and helped her up. She dusted her skirt, touched her hair. "How embarrassing, *fainting*, of all things!" I could see her going inside, checking for the migraine. "But ... my headache's gone!" She smiled into her husband's worried eyes. "You know, that takeaway *does* smell divine."

We feasted like people who had nothing to worry about except making their stomachs happy. Pain may trump all, but hunger runs it a close second.

Graham and I were collecting the debris from our meal when Fiona's phone sounded. She took the call beside the frangipani tree in her courtyard, slid the door closed so we heard her voice, but the words were muffled. I watched her through the glass. She stayed there for a minute after her conversation was over. She stared up at the sky, still as a sculpture, blue daylight bathing her face.

When she rejoined us, she looked sour. "Richard Morgan, Detective Inspector, etc., asked me to give you a message, Stevie."

"Yes!" I pumped my fist in the air. "He wants to question me again. This time I'll *make* him believe me."

Fiona quashed my hope. "No, actually, it appears you won't be needed to give a statement beyond what you've told him and neither will I. They've called off the investigation."

I gasped. "What? Why? That's not right. They can't do that!"

"They can and they have. The police are convinced Waleed drowned himself, but the cause of death will be declared an accidental fall. The family has influence and a reputation to protect. They don't want what they see as the scandal and dishonor of his suicide made public. It's intolerable for them to live with privately as it is."

"But I know it *wasn't* suicide! *Something else* happened to him. This isn't fair to Waleed!" I ran out of breath and realized I'd been shouting at Fiona. She didn't need that.

She flumped into her chair. "There's a threat implied— no, *more* than implied. The detective passed along a message from Waleed's family. They want *all* talk of Waleed's death silenced. If we, including you, keep stirring things up, they're afraid people will keep gossiping, spreading the suicide rumors. They'll need someone outside their circle to blame for driving him to it. It appears that would be me 'for exploiting Waleed's mental distress and depleted physical state, while selling his paintings at a significant profit' for myself."

Graham recited a string of colorful Aussie curses before he said anything I found intelligible. "They've got no bloody grounds for that! They couldn't win a judgment against you."

"Probably not, but they'd make our lives misery in the meantime and they know it. The legal fees alone! They'd slur my reputation in the art world, too, sabotage it with their lies. And, of course, they'd see Stevie got thrown out of the country. They want all the talk to end *right now, or else.*"

I was shocked wordless, tied in a knot at the injustice to Waleed and my powerlessness to make it right. Graham noticed and spoke to me kindly. "All we have to do is cooperate and be quiet. And why shouldn't we? What harm will that do?"

Fiona jumped up and kicked off her stilettos so hard one flew across the room. "Oh, God, I *loathe* being blackmailed!"

She pulled an old smock from a closet and wrapped it over her dress. It became clear she was intent on working out her anger cleaning the gallery. She set Graham to washing windows.

I tried to help, but Fiona shooed me away. "No, Stevie, you deserve some diversion." She thought a moment. "I would try shopping if I were you." She gave me directions to her favorite Darling Street boutiques.

Kristina Bak

Likely they both needed a break from my angsty presence. That suited my purposes. A plan had formed in my mind and, while I knew it was wrong to deceive Fiona and Graham, I didn't want them interfering. I promised to visit the boutiques, then go back to my hostel for an early night.

CHAPTER 15

Retail therapy was futile for me. I'd never been a fashionista; for years I'd shopped with Winter and bought what she did. I went to the boutiques so I could tell Fiona honestly I had. I bought a beige linen sundress I thought made me look older and selected an overpriced pink tee shirt, "Sydney" written in sequins across the chest, for my mom. I took my purchases to my hostel room and settled in for some online digging. Eventually I found the address I needed. I changed into the new dress and called a ride service.

The driver assured me he knew a way there around the worst traffic, at least until the next crunch came. I watched out the window and followed our slow progress on the GPS. We forged across a busy bridge over Iron Cove and the Parramatta River, into the leafy North Shore suburbs where the going was easier. My destination turned out to be a midcentury modern high-rise dominating a point that protruded into the harbor. The building cast a long, late afternoon shadow. It was twenty floors taller than its neighbors. I could almost hear my Mom going nuts over the "unique view property," obviously predating height controls in the wealthy residential district. I paid the driver and tackled my next challenge: how to get inside.

I'd pictured a neighborhood like the one around Lyrebird House, where I could explain myself to another human being at the door. Now I hoped for security screen time instead. I finger-brushed my hair over my scar to make a bland, respectable impression, but the building's security turned out to be as flawed as human nature. A dad leaving with a rowdy toddler in tow distractedly held the outer door for me. Inside, I buzzed the Tanoos penthouse and, to my surprise, the inner lobby door immediately clicked unlocked.

Apparently no one was monitoring the video feed, because the barefoot young woman who opened the penthouse door on the twenty-third floor looked equally surprised. Her eyes widened, then narrowed to slits. "Who are you?" Her voice was husky. She held a pungently smoking spliff in one hand and kept the other on the door. She was long-faced and square-shouldered, maybe early twenties, but haggard, with dark rings around her eyes.

My courage wavered. The door began to close. "Stop! Please. I'm a friend of Waleed's...*was* a friend."

"My brother's friend?"

"Your brother's, yes, perhaps the last to talk with him before..."

She looked me up and down. "Not press? Not police?"

"No, none of that. My name is Stevie. I have information for you, about Waleed."

She gave in with little grace and led me into a living room where gold drapes covering floor-to-ceiling windows diffused light over a plush white carpet. "Sit down." She was curt, apparently accustomed to giving orders.

We sat opposite each other on beige leather sofas with a white marble coffee table between us. Her face, without a trace of makeup, was like Waleed's if he'd never smiled in his entire life. She wore a jade green silk shift. Her only visible extravagance was a spectacular diamond ring on her left hand.

"You're Waleed's sister?"

"Olivia Tanoos, we've established that." She tucked her straight brown hair behind her ears with sharp gestures. "He was two years older but you wouldn't know it. I had to be the responsible one." Olivia stubbed out her smoke viciously in an onyx ashtray. I inhaled deeply before vent fans in the ceiling went on, cleansing the air, but the hit didn't relax me.

My short dress had ridden up and my thighs were sticking to the leather sofa that bizarrely matched the dress's color. I'd forgotten how linen wrinkled. What was right to say? "I'm sorry for your loss. I can only imagine how painful this must be for you and your parents."

Olivia's voice sounded flat, as though she had no energy left for emotion. "No you can't, you have no idea. Our parents were in London when the police rang them. Mum had to go to a clinic, in shock, Dad says." She lit a new cigarette and waved it toward a holograph photo block on a sideboard. A younger, conservative Waleed stood between his vividly good-looking parents. She spoke bitterly. "Waleed hurt Mum in his life, now he's nearly killed her by the way he chose to die."

"That's why I've come. I don't think he *chose* to die at all."

Olivia blew smoke, dragon-like, in a double stream from her nose. "Good, that's what we want everyone to believe. Believing it will make it true. People die in boating accidents. There's no disgrace in that."

"*Boating* accident? I was at the ferry dock, Olivia. I'd talked to him an hour before. He didn't go boating in the meantime."

She stumped out her cigarette half-smoked. "Don't be obtuse! A ferry's a boat, isn't it? Near enough. It's bloody well better than the alternative. Look, I think we're done talking." She stood.

The door buzzer sounded. Olivia answered tiredly without bothering to look at the screen. "Who is it?"

A man's voice growled through the wall speaker. "Who the fuck d'you think it is? Let me in."

The room had dimmed as we spoke. The abrupt subtropical evening caught me by surprise. Olivia touched a control and the drapes lifted like a theater curtain. I must have looked foolishly agog to her. "Have a look then, before you go."

I did all but press my nose against the glass. No theater I'd seen could equal the panorama—the Sydney Opera House's famous white shells and the Harbor Bridge, both illuminated; the city's towers and boats on the harbor spangled with lights, all doubled in the water; a crimson sunset dying to the west. Olivia ended the show, turning on room lamps. The windows reflected me, skinny and disheveled in my wrinkled dress, and the entrance of a man so strikingly handsome that I turned and stared openly at him. He stole a look at his reflection, then at me. "Who's this?"

"Never mind, she's leaving."

He ignored Olivia and came to shake my hand. "Laurence Tanoos."

Olivia stepped beside me. "Laurence is my cousin and fiancé."

"I'm Stevie, a friend of Waleed's."

"A Yank friend, eh? You from his squat?"

"No, staying in Balmain."

"Not one of those art wankers then. How'd you know him?"

Olivia put her arm firmly around my waist. "She's got a plane to catch. I'll see you down, Stevie."

In the elevator Olivia dropped her feigned affection, ready to have me gone. "Did you drive?"

I shook my head.

"No use calling a ride, you'd wait here hours. The ferries dock at McMahon's Point—you'll see it from the car park. No point avoiding ferries, is there?" Her voice turned harsh. "Look, what Waleed did is nothing to do with you. It's a family matter. We've got it under control. Stay out of it and leave us alone."

That was beginning to sound like a mantra. Olivia didn't linger at the lobby entrance any longer than she needed to be sure I left. I saw car lights not moving on the Harbor Bridge and one of the newer ferries approaching McMahon's Point. I ran to the dock to catch it and rode across the black water on the outside deck, my cardigan buttoned against the moist night wind, wiping my nose and my tears with its sleeve.

Kristina Bak

CHAPTER 16

Next morning, Fiona called sounding harassed. "So sorry Graham and I can't give you a proper Sydney tour. We have to deal with those clients I blew off yesterday. But, dear, a city bus goes straight to the botanical gardens from Balmain and you can walk down to the opera house from there."

I put on a lightness I didn't feel. "No problem, Fiona."

"This way, you won't have to go *near* the ferry. The busses are slow and overloaded, but they generally get where they're meant to go. We'll meet you later for dinner."

Fiona's idea was as good as any other. I had no new plan. Jet lag, grief, and neural pathways yet to reconnect made my brain like the Sydney airport, some areas inaccessible behind dirty translucent barriers. In one direction my dad waited, in the other Waleed begged for justice— between me and them was a maze I couldn't begin to negotiate. And Nate? *Forget Nate!* What was I even doing here, witless and paralyzed? My thoughts scrabbled like cockroaches in my head. Sightseeing alone, free from everyone else's static, would be better. At least, it couldn't make things worse.

I picked my sundress and sweater from the floor where I'd dropped them, dressed quickly, drank some flavorless but free hostel coffee, and set off for the bus stop. The bus arrived almost on schedule. Having scored the last seat at the front, I wasn't troubled by bumps that made the growing press of standees in the aisle grab for support. Chatter in Antipodean English, Mandarin, Spanish, Arabic and who-knows-what competed for auditory space as the bus filled. Near the Anzac Bridge I spotted the exit that led to the *Mary Murchie*. What if Graham hadn't asked the old sailor the right questions, hadn't communicated the urgency of my search? By the time we'd reached the end of the bridge I had a new plan, or part of one.

The bus traversed the city center, where people thronged the sidewalks and rich sun shot down architectural canyons. Beyond that, I got off at a park called The Domain and followed signs to the Royal Botanic Gardens.

There, at a bed of blooming roses, I buried my nose in blossoms, comforted by their perfume so much like the gardens at home, then traipsed on through an exotic succulent collection and into a bamboo forest. The city sounds and crowds ebbed. I stopped, alone on a path in a tunnel of greenery where bamboo stalks clicked, stirred by an imperceptible breeze. I took a deep breath, perhaps the first since I'd seen Waleed's corpse. My peace didn't last.

"Stevie! Oy, Stevie, hold on!"

I turned as Nikki bolted around a curve in the path, her emotional presence scarcely controlled in her body, as if her skin strained to contain her. She wore knee-length leggings, espadrilles, and a tie-dyed top that stretched over her melon breasts, more a reminder of her nakedness underneath than cover for it. Her face was pearlescent in the leaf-filtered light.

She bent over panting, hands on knees, then straightened and re-did the clip that was ineffectively holding her heavy hair. Her body radiated heat. She poured out her breathless explanation. "Fiona said you were coming here on the bus. When I caught it on Montague Street, I didn't see you for the crowd, then when we got off and I did, I had to get my bike from the bus rack and lock it up, because bikes are banned in the gardens. I need to talk with you about Waleed."

My energy drained away. I wanted to lie down in the bamboo shade and make her leave me alone, but that would be cruel—she was grieving, too. "To be honest, Nikki, I came here to put Waleed out my mind, but if you want to talk, I'll listen."

She impulsively gripped my shoulders. "No, no, I don't want you to listen to *me*; I want you to tell me what *you* saw, how he died. I can't stop picturing it every which way. I can't sleep for imagining. I have to know." Her grip on my shoulders tightened. Her eyelids were swollen, her eyes glazed with tears.

"Okay." I agreed out of decency and to make her let go. "Walk with me. I doubt it will help you sleep any better."

I was creeped out at having been followed, but here, far

from other ears, I could ask Nikki my own questions. We wandered on side-by-side, following the path through sun and shade, letting occasional runners and rambunctious children with their moms or nannies pass us. I told her about meeting Waleed at Lyrebird, then spotting him floating in the water. I edited as I spoke, saying nothing about his appointment at the MCA, or his latest paintings. He'd wanted Fiona to know first. Nor did I describe how Waleed looked dead. That wouldn't help Nikki. She sensed something missing.

"What'd you two talk about? Did he mention me?"

If she wanted to be the centerpiece of Waleed's attention, I disappointed her. "We talked about the the magpie paintings. We were practically strangers, so, no, he didn't mention anything personal. He was happy the show had gone well."

"Huh! Tried to sell you a painting, knowing him. He had a business sense. Probably got it from his dad. He hated when I said that." Nikki's voice broke. "Sorry I'm so weepy." She gulped and went on. "Youssef pushed Waleed to give up art and join the family business. Big developers, you know, projects on the harbor. He called Waleed a disgrace to the family name for hanging out with dregs. That was us. Youssef threatened to disinherit Waleed, started grooming Waleed's cousin to work with him."

"His cousin?"

"Laurence Tanoos. I wouldn't go near that scumbag, neither would Waleed. Lately, Waleed was reconciling with Dahlia, his mom."

"What about sisters or brothers?"

"Only Olivia. She consults to software companies in

India. She'll inherit the family business now that Waleed's … gone."

We came to a grove of trees. Something rustled overhead among their broad leaves; the air went musky and foul. I looked into branches teeming with shifting, pendulous fruit bats. Nikki pulled my arm. "Bat Alley, we call this part. Best not stand here looking up. They love the fig trees almost to death at night, then hang here in the daytime. The city's been discouraging them for generations, human generations, I mean, but it's hopeless."

We left the trees for wide lawn sloping to a harbor cove. "Waleed and me, we used to come here. He liked this place better than the beach." Nikki's composure broke in a choked sob. "Too many memories, I can't stay." She hugged me tightly, the way a child might, then ran back the way we'd come.

I was relieved to be free of her. I slipped off my sandals and went on downhill barefoot, the grass cool under my feet, tickling my toes, soothing. White-feathered ibis waded in a tiered ornamental fountain. Couples took photos and held hands, kissed, reclined embraced where tall flower clumps offered a little privacy. This was a good place for lovers. At the bottom of the slope, I leaned against the warm rock sea wall and, with an irrational stab of jealousy, pictured Waleed holding Nikki there. Small waves splashed against the stone. Alchemy of sun on water created another blue-green hue I couldn't name. No matter what horrors the harbor contained, I'd never seen water more beautiful. I put on my sandals again and followed the sea wall path. It led to my left along the cove, out of the gardens to the opera house.

From a distance the Sydney Opera House had looked as light as origami, so ubiquitous it was hard to see as anything more than a cultural icon, a background for the New Year's Eve fireworks. Close-up, the building revealed itself in solid parts, like stupendous seashells stark against the sky. I had to share it with *someone* besides the other gawping tourists. I called my mom. She was impressed, or tried to be, but her worry for me broke through.

"If you change your mind, sweetheart, you don't have to do this. You can let it go and come home."

Our call ending on that note spoiled the opera house for me. I was pressured from two sides now by people wanting me to give up my searches—the one for my father that had brought me here and the one for truth I'd stumbled into. Up the harbor, beyond the bridge, I saw the high-rise where I'd wormed my way into the Tanoos family's penthouse. Had I been out of order intruding into their grief? Had I misconstrued everything? I refused to believe that; I had to trust my intuition, but I was on shaky ground. I needed more evidence.

Expensive-looking outdoor cafes bordered the plaza between the opera house and Circular Quay, where the ferries docked. I resented the people who lunched there, laughing, chatting, sun glinting on their wine glasses. I had no one to eat with, even if I could afford these places. My stomach was empty, but I had more important things to do. I hurried past the ferry terminal, up George Street and into Sydney's glass and steel business core, to find the bus returning the way I'd come.

On my way, I thought about my conversation with Nikki. Waleed's death *could* have been the accident his family was presenting to save face. Some people might believe what *they* didn't—that he'd tripped on the dock, fallen off, knocked his head against something—more likely if he'd been drunk or drugged, a disoriented tourist, a child, or other *ifs* that weren't the case. Odds were against his simply being clumsy and my gut insisted it wasn't true.

If someone had wanted Waleed dead, followed him, and taken the opportunity, it must have been someone who knew him. I hadn't liked Laurence Tanoos, but until Nikki told me about him, he hadn't seemed a possible murderer. It should have been the other way around, Waleed bitter at Laurence supplanting him as his father's favorite. Waleed's mom encouraging a family rapprochement put Laurence's status in jeopardy. Marriage to Olivia wouldn't give him power and control if the eldest Tanoos child, and only son, returned to the fold. Had *Laurence* arranged his cousin's "suicide?" Impossible for me to prove.

My other quest might be impossible, too, but I'd barely begun. I wouldn't leave Australia without finding my father and I wouldn't give up on Waleed. I was becoming expert at ignoring impossible odds.

CHAPTER 17

I wedged myself into standing room on the bus this time and got off at the stop I'd spotted earlier. It was an easy walk from there to the the *Mary Murchie* dock.

The clangor in the workshop didn't let up at my entrance. My connection with Graham and with Marco de Torino Blandis gave me license to be there. The "old salt" overseer sat on his high stool. I caught his eye when a worker dragging a cable nudged him and tipped a nod in my direction. With the effort a younger man would take to climb down a cliff, he descended. Leaning on a cane, he signaled me to follow him into a room not much larger than a closet, partitioned off from the bustling workshop. Two chairs and a cluttered desk with an outdated laptop made it an office. It was close and hot inside with the door shut, but not so noisy.

I smelled the old man's briny sweat as he offered me his hand in greeting. It was a sailor's hand, hard and padded with muscle. "G'day, love." His smile disclosed perfect white teeth, contrasting so violently with his withered purplish lips and general deterioration they could only be false.

"I'm Stevie Wales. I've come to ask you about …"

"Aye, I remember you and the question. Call me Popeye,

as me mates do. 'Ave a seat." Of the various Aussie accents I'd encountered, his was the most nearly impenetrable. He lowered himself into the creaky desk chair, I took the metal folding one. He cleared his throat, hacked something into a crumpled gray handkerchief, wiped his mouth, and scratched under his scant beard. "Wales. He'd built a seaworthy craft."

"You knew my dad?" I wanted to jump out of my chair and hug the decrepit sailor. I gripped the edges of the metal seat and held very still to listen.

"Only the way we all knew one another in the North, in the pubs, telling tales and lies. He was a Yank who sailed over single-handed, so he stood out. A bit up hisself at times, but not a bad sort."

Could it be this easy? "What happened to him?"

"I hired onto a Malaysian freighter bound for Brazil, one last voyage before me body went crook. I don't recollect he was in Darwin next time I made landfall there. Later, I heard he'd been caught out in a bad typhoon."

I shook with impatience. "But now, where is he now?"

Popeye rubbed his chin. "She was an ugly storm. He didn't know conditions like the locals did."

No, no, no! "Are you saying he's *dead*? They told us they found wreckage."

"Yair, 'struth, but you hear strange tales about the shipwrecked, how they wash ashore. It's only I've not seen nor heard of him since."

"But if he washed ashore alive, where could he be?"

Popeye chuckled like bones rattling in his chest. "Anywhere. Up there it's more empty than not, specially now, what with the climate change, seas rising, storms getting bigger. The last typhoon took most of Darwin, again. I wish I could tell you better, but words wouldn't make it true. You want to know more, go find one of 'em who stayed on. If your dad's alive and doesn't mind being found, somebody's gonna tell you."

"Doesn't mind?"

"The North's a place people go to disappear, new names, new stories. You don't ask a bloke too many questions and don't answer too many yesself."

The distance from the workshop to Balmain felt longer on foot. No busses came, so I hiked uphill with Popeye's warning echoing in my mind, "a place people go to disappear." Why would my dad want to disappear and leave Mom and me behind? It hurt too much to consider. Going to Darwin was more urgent than ever, now that I'd spoken with someone who'd actually seen him there. I'd told myself a story—Popeye's recollections made it real.

When I reached the crest of the peninsula, I was footsore and hungry. Darling Street's smaller scale felt cozy after central Sydney's slick impersonality. Cafe tables crowded the sidewalks, made narrower by the parked baby strollers so excessively equipped the mothers might camp there for months. I lucked onto a table for two just vacated by a woman cradling a yappy baby-sized dog.

A guy slid into the other chair. "You have to order and pay inside. I'll hold the spot. Make mine a short black."

It was one of the de Torino Blandis twins. I made a guess. "Lucco?"

Today he wore a blue knit shirt with a tiny embroidered golfer on the pocket. "*Tony*, and not half the no-hoper my brother makes me out to be. A nice coincidence, isn't it, you and me here? Go in and order for us."

I didn't like being hijacked by Tony. I figured he was, in fact, exactly what his twin had labeled him. I obeyed, to buy space to think. As distasteful as his company was, he'd been a family friend of Waleed's and therefore a potential information source. Slanted information, for sure, since the two families had closed ranks around the "accident" narrative. Was the families' accord simple loyalty, or could it be a corrupt connection between Laurence Tanoos and the twins? From my position in the queue of coffee supplicants I saw Tony flirting with a server. He eyed her buttocks as she turned to bring a tray of empty cups inside.

Tony grinned when I reclaimed my seat, a friendliness at odds with his scarcely veiled threats at our first meeting. I wouldn't let him control the discussion this time.

"So, Tony, do you live in Balmain?"

"I like this place."

An answer without answering—I'd have to fight for control. The server brought our drinks and a sticky pastry for me. I ate it fast and messily, too hungry to try to preserve my dignity. I licked crumbs off my fingers and tried another conversational gambit. "It's odd that in a city of millions, I'd run into the same person two days in a row."

Tony touched the corner of his smug mouth to show me I had crumbs on my face. "Not so odd in Sydney. Every suburb's its own village. You see the same faces over and over. You get tired of them."

I was already tired of Tony. I wiped the crumbs with the

back of my hand. "And when they're gone?"

His grin wilted. "You're on about Waleed, aren't you? Yeah, I'm sorry he died, but the only thing we shared was we both hated working for our family businesses. He had a choice, I didn't. I envied him that, but I reckon I land up better than he did. His choice wasn't such a good one."

"Are you saying his choice to be an artist is what killed him?"

Tony stared up the street and licked his lips. Two girls held his interest, their cropped jackets and hip-slung skirts revealing a remarkable spread of naked skin.

"Something did, didn't it? It's done, nothing left but the funeral. Youssef and Dahlia are flying in tonight, so it'll be tomorrow, family, private and quiet."

"So Mrs. Tanoos is better?"

He looked askance at me. I wasn't supposed to know anything about Dahlia; he wasn't supposed to know I did. I'd be safer playing clueless with this thug. He didn't answer my question.

"Death happens, we have to get over it, move on. Have you seen the Blue Mountains? Can't miss them on your holiday. Take the Katoomba train tonight, get your mind off things. A mate of mine runs our hotel up there. Tony de Torino Blandis sends you, they give you a big discount, treat you like a royal. I'll let them know you're coming." Tony took out his phone, prepared to make me a princess.

"No thanks, Tony, I'm on my way to Darwin."

"Darwin? So, ah, good, good. See the crocs." He popped his phone back into his pocket, obviously relieved.

I let him leave first; I didn't want him watching *my* buns. Apparently his business with me was over as soon as he heard I was heading out of town. I stood to go and three women swooped for possession of my table, like greedy gulls. On the clogged street Nikki appeared, pedaling her bike among the cars, full on, holding her own amidst the motorized traffic. I waved, but she didn't see me.

———————

Graham and Fiona took me to dinner at a Nepalese place—six tables, turquoise walls with blown-up photos of the Himalayas, and, over the kitchen door, a shelf holding a Buddha, artificial flowers and incense sticks. The two reminisced about trekking in those mountains before kid and careers, while I devoured potato samosas and pumpkin curry. At meal's end, while we drank our tea, Fiona asked me about my day.

So much to tell, or not tell. "I did what you said, the opera house and the botanical gardens."

"Oh good! I'm so sorry we had to leave you on your own. My clients took lots of handholding. Every one of them was gobsmacked with how Waleed's magpie paintings looked in their homes—too powerful to hang over their dining tables or in their bedrooms, not background works you can ignore while you eat, or see last thing before you go to sleep. We found the right locations and adjusted their lighting. We only got to half. The rest are waiting for me tomorrow."

"It was fine. I wasn't on my own the whole time. You told Nikki I was going to the gardens?"

"Oh, too right. She rang me this morning, keen to talk with you face to face."

"She caught up with me. We walked together. I saw her

later, too, riding her bike up Darling Street."

"Their collective's in Leichhardt, past where Darling Street turns into Balmain Road. She was probably riding home."

Graham nodded. "True, she bikes everywhere. That's why she's got those well-developed thighs and calves." That earned him a frown from Fiona.

I rescued Graham with a question for him. "Is it common to meet Tony de Torino Blandis around there, too? I ran into him at a cafe this afternoon, or he ran into me. He said I should go to some resort in the Blue Mountains, that he'd arrange for me to get special treatment."

"Unusually kind for Tony! They're not mountains like that, you know." Graham pointed to one of the photos on the wall. "Or by your American standards either, not high elevation. The adventuresome part is hiking downward into the canyons. Every year bushwalkers get lost on animal paths, die from exposure or snakebite. Tony's family owns a fair share of the Blue Mountains resorts. They and the Tanoos family control some of the most valuable real estate in New South Wales. They're pressuring the government to let them build a mega-hotel on the harbor front. One of Waleed's conflicts with his father, in fact. He belongs … *belonged* to an alliance fighting the project."

Fiona wrinkled her nose. "Rotten of them, recruiting the developer's own son as a mascot. The irony is, their foreshore development will be moot soon, nothing more than a place to anchor a boat if the Antarctic ice shelves keep breaking off. For now, properties with harbor glimpses are so valuable people poison trees for the view. Other people's trees."

Kristina Bak

Nasty questions occurred to me. Had Waleed's mother been trying to lure him from that opposition with her peacemaking efforts? Had Waleed's father assigned her the task? I shook off my conspiracy qualms; I wanted to believe in the human heart's basic goodness. Fiona must have read distress on my face. She changed the subject, but what she said next sent doubt about human goodness shuddering through me:

"Here's something mind-boggling; Raven sent me a detail photo of a new painting today. It looks stunning! I didn't think he had it in him. He says he has a series. If the paintings are as good as that detail suggests, I'll include him in my final show." Fiona's eyes filled with tears. "It's too late to help Waleed any more, but he'd be happy I was helping his closest friend. It's the best thing I can do in his memory."

CHAPTER 18

Air bubbles streamed from my mouth in a soundless scream, salt water filled my lungs. Tough slippery kelp twisted around my neck, tighter and tighter, dragging me down. I raked at it with my nails as I sank. Waleed's pallid dead fingers, rotting, beckoned from the murk.

No! I fought up from beneath my pillow and lay searching the morning for the brink where dream and waking meet, painstakingly sorting one from the other. A warm rectangle of sun fell across my bed from the high window of my hostel room. Muted traffic sounds came from outside. Yesterday's clothes were where I'd dropped them, on the floor with the others spilling out of my open suitcase. Still feeling half-asleep, I showered, put on my sweater and skirt, threw my phone and sunglasses into my tote bag, and went out with a disorienting sense of having made a narrow escape.

On Darling Street, Balmain's population was enjoying Saturday brunch. The weather held glorious. All the sunny outside tables were full. I scrunched into a spot at a busy cafe counter and ordered espresso and a buttered scone. While I ate, I confirmed a Monday flight to Darwin. My heart stuttered with fear I'd fail, wrong about everything,

Kristina Bak

about my dad, about Waleed, but if I didn't try, I'd never know. Not knowing didn't suit me, neither did waiting. Salvation lay in action.

One thing I could do between now and Monday: prove to myself my suspicions about Raven's paintings—suspicions so outlandish I refused to mention them to Fiona—were wrong. If this was grief-crazed paranoia, no one else needed to know about it, to cut me slack for my warped thinking, feel sorry for my possibly misfiring brain. I *wanted* to be wrong about Raven. I wanted his help to get into Waleed's studio, to take my own photos of Waleed's last paintings to show Fiona as he'd intended. She'd see they weren't the paintings of a person on the verge of suicide. She would know what to do with that information, wouldn't she? This was her country, not mine; there was too much I didn't understand.

The espresso fortified my resolve. I marched inland on Darling Street, past the library, courthouse, police station, pubs and shops, following the route my GPS dictated, to the Rozelle Saturday Market. In a plaza filled with market stalls, festive with banners and food smells, I threaded through milling bargainers and competing shouts from vendors until I was sure I was going in circles. I stopped where a veteran in worn fatigues played "Waltzing Matilda" on an amplified violin, his hat optimistically upturned at his feet. I tossed in an Aussie coin for good luck and, right away, spotted Lala at her clothing booth. She had two rolling dress racks and a wavery full-length mirror under a striped sunshade.

The array on those racks was what set Lala's enterprise apart from others I'd seen in the market, where used-and-unfashionable was grandly renamed "vintage." Lala had deconstructed and remanufactured garments for drama and glamour with exquisite detail. The well-dressed women buying them didn't look like people who needed to shop for bargains. She couldn't be long for the outdoor market venue before somebody important picked up her line and the prices reflected its collectibility. I saw her notice me checking the tags.

She didn't return my attempt at a smile. "Stephanie, isn't it?" Her voice was lilting, her attitude all business.

"It's Stevie. Hi, love your work." I must have let my surprise show.

"Right, *Stevie*. What did you expect, cheap knock-offs?" Lala wore a drift of bronze-colored chiffon and a brocade jacket embroidered with crystal beads that danced and threw rainbows as she moved. Her lipstick was shocking orange.

"No, Lala, but I didn't come to shop."

Lala diverted her assistance to a customer eager to pay. She was no more friendly to her than to me, so I didn't take it personally when she turned back frowning. "Not shopping, but you're here?"

"I want to ask you about Waleed."

"Nikki says she talked to you yesterday in the gardens." It sounded like a dismissal.

If I was going to pry, I had to expect some rudeness in return. I held my temper. "We didn't talk long. Being there upset her. She said it was Waleed's favorite place, he liked it better than the beach."

"Well he would, wouldn't he? Waleed couldn't swim. He kept it secret from everybody but Nikki, when he thought they'd marry. He knew if he went to the beach with his mates, sooner or later they'd find out and they'd drag him into the surf as a prank. He was scared to death of water. In the end he was right. He should have stayed away from it, but that's hard to do in Sydney, water all around."

"You don't think he wanted to kill himself?"

Lala puffed through her neon lips. "How would I know? It's not like I saw him lately, is it? None of us did. He locked himself in his studio, wouldn't let us in, only went out for food and paint, more paint than food from what I could see. He was away with the pixies, not with us. God only knows what he was doing in there. His magpie show was such a winner, probably making more of the same."

She pulled a tissue from somewhere in her dress and dabbed her nose. "I miss the fucker. The only good thing about him being dead is we all owed him money for one thing or another. Not that he'd ever collect from us. He was like that, before, sharing everything."

"You haven't gone into his studio since he …?"

She looked appalled at the thought. "I couldn't, not yet. Raven might have, if he found the key." Talking about Waleed seemed to have softened Lala's attitude toward me. "Look, come shop next Saturday when this has sunk in a bit. I'll help you choose something. My creations would suit you."

"They're works of art, Lala. I'd love to. One more thing, do you think Raven would be home right now, so I could, you know, offer my condolences in person?"

CHAPTER 19

With Lala's directions, I took a bus out Balmain Road to Leichhardt, got off at a Peruvian restaurant on Norton Street, and worked my way through the busy shopping area. Some blocks on, I passed the cavernous entrance to a parking garage, then turned down a double row of undistinguished semi-detached houses built right up to the sidewalk with no gardens and no occupants in sight. I wondered uncomfortably what kind of people watched me from behind their barred windows and shifted my bag so the strap crossed my chest and under one arm for security. At the street's dead end, in the center of a graveled lot dotted with random piles of masonry, sat the crumbling brick warehouse.

I climbed several concrete steps and knocked on the locked steel entrance with no result except hurting my knuckles. I found a broken brick among some rubble and pounded harder and louder. Boots clanged down a metal stairway. Raven opened the door. He looked less masterful and like he hadn't shaved or changed clothes since the day Waleed died, his shirt limp and soiled. His hair hung lank around his face. He toweled midnight blue paint off his hands with a rag.

"Stevie! G'day, you looking for Nikki? She's surfing with

Col at Bondi. Lala's doing the market. It's only me here."

I put on my best ingenuous American grin. "Didn't Fiona call? Sorry to bother you when you're working, but she told me you had some awesome new paintings. I'm hoping you'll let me sneak a look." So far, it was true and easy to sound convincing. The crucial part came next. "My mom, in Seattle, wants to buy some Aussie art. I told her what Fiona said about yours."

Raven stiffened, like a dog scenting a rabbit. "Fiona's only seen a detail photo. Give me your mum's contact info, I'll show her more."

"No, Mom says if we're going to make a 'significant investment,' I need to see them."

Raven hesitated, but the temptation was irresistible. "Come in, then." He led me upstairs to a feebly lit landing with a caged freight elevator shaft and three more closed metal doors. "This isn't the best time." He seemed to be arguing with himself as much as talking to me. "If you come say Wednesday or Thursday …"

"Impossible, I'm flying out Monday."

His shoulders lifted with his breath, like a diver about to go off the high board, then he fished a key from his jeans pocket and unlocked the furthest door. We stepped into a high-ceilinged studio. Daylight streamed through mottled clerestory windows onto the paintings propped against three walls. That day in the gallery Waleed had spread his arms to demonstrate their size. The half-dozen canvasses were easily six by eight feet, blazing with color. He'd been jubilant with good reason; these were his masterpieces.

Did Raven really hope to get away with claiming these paintings as his own? Perhaps he could. They were enough unlike Waleed's magpie work that you'd need brushstroke analysis, or some other evidence, to prove they were his. Raven might acknowledge and defuse similarity, saying they'd inspired each other. Or maybe Raven was just deluded.

Waleed had left chaos around him as he worked. A filthy sink in one corner reeked of petroleum-based paint thinner. Piles of papers, tools and brushes, paint and solvent cans covered a wooden table. Lengths of framing wood and rolls of canvas were stacked haphazardly on the paint-splattered floor. In the midst of the mess, Waleed's paintings held me dumbstruck. I bit the insides of my cheeks not to cry.

Raven shifted his weight impatiently. "Your mum's a collector?"

I elaborated upon this hypothetical mother. "She'd like to be. She has a new house with lots of bare walls."

Raven bought my lie. "If she wants more than one piece, we can do a discount on the prices, direct purchase, cut out the gallery percentage."

"Cut out Fiona, you mean. Is that fair?"

"All's fair in the art world."

"The shipping costs…"

"Not so bad as you think."

"My mom would love these colors. It's gray where we live. Oils, aren't they? And that?" I pointed at a geometric design, like a coiled midnight blue feather, in the lower right corner of one of the canvases.

Raven spoke in a tight voice, aiming for the confidence and authority he'd exuded at the gallery by getting louder. "We sign with marks in the co-op. The feather is mine, a play on my name."

"And what was Waleed's?"

"… Waleed's?" Raven's eyes swerved. "A red spiral. He'd never say why. Waleed liked mystery."

"A red spiral, yeah, I remember now, on his magpie paintings." I squatted to examine a painting's corner. I touched the feather mark. My finger came away blue with wet paint.

"Hey!" Raven grabbed my elbow. I jerked free and wiped at more blue paint with my hand. A red spiral showed through the smear where the feather had been. "Bloody bitch!" He shoved me and I fell against a table leg. Empty paint cans clattered. Before I could get up he charged me, blue-stained fingers crooked toward my neck.

I shrieked at him. "Fucking liar! Don't touch me!" He flinched. I scuttled beneath the table and tipped it over between us, avalanching everything bouncing and crashing off its top.

Raven booted aside rolling cans and broken jars. I scrambled to my feet and snatched a gallon can heavy with paint. As he lunged at me, I swung the can by its handle with all my strength. I struck him hard in the chest. He yelped and toppled.

He raised his hands to fend me off from where he'd landed on the floor. For all his quick rage, Raven wasn't a fighter. He pressed his ribs gingerly, shot me a sidelong, open-mouthed look, crawled on hands and knees the few feet to the painting I'd smeared. He hunched there muttering, pushing paint with his fingers to conceal Waleed's mark.

I bounced on the balls of my feet. I didn't like how good I'd felt clobbering Raven in the chest, how much I wanted an excuse to hit him again. I was about *healing* pain, not inflicting it, wasn't I? But he'd betrayed his dead best friend, stolen credit for his genius. Didn't he deserve to hurt? Didn't he? I was Waleed's avenging angel. I relished Raven's fear and the weight of the weapon in my hand. "Why did you do it, Raven?"

"I didn't! I *didn't do it!*"

"You're so lying! The proof's right here."

Raven wiped his nose, rubbed his eyes, sank back onto his haunches. He spoke to the painting, plaintive, not looking at me. "So why did *he* do it? Why did he suck up to Fiona on his own? We're about collaboration, *one for all, all for one!* Why does he lock us out of his studio, out of his art? We'd be locked out of the building next."

"What, you're accusing Waleed?"

He swiveled around. His face turned up to me was smudged and streaked with blue. I took a threatening step toward him. Raven stared unfocussed, talking fast with shallow breaths. Spittle flew from his lips.

"Oh, too right, you didn't know, did you? Youssef Tanoos owns this place; the family can throw us out anytime. One show without the rest of us was bad, but Waleed says, 'Mate, *a rising tide lifts all boats.*'"

He got to his feet. "That morning, Nikki tells me he's gone off to the gallery. I go after him. We'll see Fiona together, so next time she shows us all or none. I get there too late, he's coming out. He's whistling, happy."

This was taking a turn I hadn't suspected, one that sent shivers over my skin.

"My head's exploding I'm so aggro. I hang back, I need to chill. When I catch up with him, alone on the ferry dock, he's all surprised smile and big hug, like this." Raven uncannily mimicked Waleed.

"He spouts about how well his magpies sold. I remind him he was lucky once, but he needs to stick with the rest of us, all together, like we always said. He says sorry, but no, he doesn't need us anymore. I argue with him until he opens his tablet and shows me a new painting. He's flat out quitting the co-op. I go berserk, slug him, maybe a couple times—I don't remember. Next thing, I've got the tablet and he's yelling and splashing around in the water."

I saw Waleed too vividly through Raven's eyes, flailing helplessly, drowning. I wanted to plug my ears, but I had to hear the rest. Raven was pacing; he'd gone hoarse.

"I feel better for having hit him. I reckon he'll find me when he gets out of the water. I take his tablet to the other side of the park and study every photo. I fuckin' envy him. He's right, he doesn't need us. Compared to him, except for Lala we look amateur. We'd drag him down."

Raven coughed to clear his throat, telling his story to himself, or to a jury, as though he'd forgotten I was there.

"The co-op's trashed, ruined without him. It hurts. I'm glad I dunked him, on principle. I could let him hit me for it, but Waleed's never hit anybody in his life. He'll be grateful I saved his tablet, anyhow. He'll dry off and we'll go have a beer, sort things out. I lay down on the grass and wait. He doesn't come. When I hear the ferry, I'm sure he's got on it and left me. No apologies then, no goodbyes, his decision, *everything's* finished. I come home, pack my kit to head south for Melbourne."

While I strolled in the sunshine, oblivious, titillated, daydreaming of him, Waleed had been dying in the water, or already dead. I had the means to murder Raven; I *wanted* to do it. I took a another step toward him and he seemed suddenly aware of me again. I couldn't do it. I woke from my mad, violent fantasy. "His paintings, how could you?"

Raven clenched his fists. "It's not wrong! I sell the paintings as mine, share the money with Col and Lala and Nikki, fuck the Tanoos family. We put the money into our art—a memorial to Waleed, in a way. He'd want that. I can't undo what's done."

I laughed without a trace of humor. "That's a scam, Raven. *You'll* get the glory. How will you convince the others to go along with your lie? They'll know you didn't paint these. You haven't told them how he died, have you?"

I'd crossed a tipping point, like the cold sweat moment on a roller coaster when you've dropped over the top. Raven's eyes went stony. He'd told me too much. He ignored my questions. He went from one painting to the next, stroking them like sentient things, mumbling to himself, or to them. I retreated backwards toward the door. In the shambles around the upended table, I saw the thin edge of a folded tablet. Waleed's? I bent to set down my weaponized paint can and surreptitiously slipped the tablet from under the mess into my bag.

Raven wheeled, sneering at me. "You can't prove anything."

"I won't keep quiet!"

"You don't belong here. No one will believe you."

"How do you know? It's not too late to confess, for

Waleed's sake. It truly was an accident. Wasn't it? A stupid, stupid accident? You didn't know he couldn't swim, did you?"

Raven caught his blotched reflection in a cracked mirror over the sink. He went closer and goggled at himself. "God, I look like a monster!" His face was a blue mask, the mask of tragedy with the turned-down mouth. He saw as well as I did the story he was weaving could have no happy ending.

I'd woven a story about Waleed, too, from the moment we met. I'd read his words, his eyes, his smiles, to mean what I'd wanted: mutual desire, fated, written in the stars, promising great things for us together. What *had* he meant? He'd promised great things to his four friends, too. Given time, would he have betrayed me as he'd betrayed them? I'd never know. "You're not a monster, Raven."

His voice sank to a murmur. "All the time I hear him calling me from the water. I plug my ears, he's louder. I haven't slept since he died. I loved him, my best mate. I need this to end."

I was drawn, reluctantly but irresistibly, to the pain I sensed in him, as I'd been to the pinto's. His body was rigid and visibly trembling, fighting emotions that threatened to tear him to pieces. The horse had taught me caution. I went to Raven in soft steps, not to alarm him, touched his back with my fingertips, then, braver, with my palm. He didn't resist.

I spoke to his face in the mirror. "Come with me. We'll tell Fiona Waleed did the paintings, the rest, too."

Raven appeared to consider his options, poor as they were. His lips moved in silent inner dialogue. His muscles relaxed, he sighed. I took my hand away. He ran hot water and scrubbed his face with soap until he looked almost normal. He inspected his reflection, eerily placid. "Right then, that'll do."

I hardly dared believe it, but I'd won. I'd eased his pain so he could think clearly and see the truth of his predicament. Together, we took a last look around the studio, then he let me out the door ahead of him and didn't lock it this time. Coming up, I hadn't cared how steep the stairs were. With Raven practically treading on my heels going down now, I envisioned another accident for him to explain. I shook off my misgivings. I'd persuaded Raven to do the right thing.

The instant we stepped outdoors, he shoved me. I windmilled for balance as I pitched down the concrete steps. The door crashed closed. I heard him running back up the metal stairs. I picked myself off the ground, a bite through my lip and gravel in my knees. Livid at being duped, I hammered the locked door.

"Raven, come back, I'm not leaving without you!" I'd tasted victory and it was good; I refused to fail. This time I'd stay well out of his reach.

I circled the warehouse. The only windows on the front were the clerestories, high and closed. The side walls were impregnable brick. At the back I found another locked door off a loading dock, beside it, the antiquated freight elevator. I fought open the elevator's rusted metal grille. Whether the machinery was functional, or safe, I risked it. The manual control lever was stiff. I put my whole weight into it and the elevator shuddered and creaked up. So *Ha!* Raven couldn't elude me.

I rode triumphantly to the second floor. The grille gating the landing there wouldn't budge. I could see the studio door, but I couldn't get to it. Raven had the last laugh, if you could call it that. I rattled the grille. "Raven! I'm here, come talk to me!"

I heard a racket. What was Raven doing throwing things around? Could he hear my shouts through the thick concrete walls? I prayed he wouldn't damage Waleed's paintings.

"Raven, I swear! I'll help you!"

I smelled smoke. It seeped onto the landing, thickened, then I smelled paint thinner. "No! Raven!" Something exploded in the studio. A human-shaped flame blundered out through the door. In frenzied disbelief, I saw Raven as the rising phoenix, though his fiery figure flew *down* the stairwell. Flames raged across the landing toward me, smoke seared my lungs. I wrenched the control lever. The mechanism stalled, then let go and gravity took over, like a sadistic carnival ride. This could be bad. I flexed my knees when the elevator hit the loading dock. The impact jolted me off my feet.

I scrambled out and lay coughing my throat raw. By the time I could breathe and stand, sirens blared. I staggered to the front of the warehouse supporting myself against the brick walls. A fire truck and aid car hurtled in from the street. I ducked as the clerestory windows shattered, shooting down hot glass.

I wasn't meant to see the blackened figure the firefighters salvaged. I retched at the smell—burnt, cooked. If Raven survived, it would be in this charred form shaped like him. My palms began to pulse. Did he feel pain? Did his spirit linger, bewildered? Something, or someone, had brought *me* back from death's border once. How terrible it would be for what was left of Raven to return! *Raven, go!* My abraded throat made me mute. Someone wrapped a silver blanket around my shoulders, bundled me into the aid car and covered my mouth and nose with an oxygen mask. A needle prick was the last I knew of that scene.

Kristina Bak

CHAPTER 20

The banner across the Lyrebird House entrance read "*Vale Waleed Tanoos*," farewell. Above the rooftops, lavender clouds soared in rococo arabesques, outlined in gold and pierced by rays like spotlights from the setting sun. The Sydney evening was glorious enough to break the heart of anyone who didn't live there and some who did, if they weren't already heartbroken. Five days since Waleed had died and the gallery filled with friends paying homage to his memory with food and drink and stories. We'd all been excluded from the family's private funeral rites the morning before.

Fiona had stripped the three rooms to bare white walls. Waleed's nearly life-size hologram portrait floated above a table decorated with candles and orchids, on the exact spot where he'd stood smiling, inviting me to lunch. Someone, Nikki perhaps, had laid a well-used paintbrush there in tribute. Lala added an orange scarf and a silver ear cuff, Col a bottle of beer. Seeing the lifelike three-dimensional image—Waleed among us, yet irretrievably gone—left me nauseous.

I stayed out of the way. The new flying-glass splinter

cuts on my face were mercifully minor, scabbed over, but visible, sure to stir up questions. Raven's death hadn't been announced. Authorities were trying to locate his family on the remote outback sheep station he'd alluded to, but never named. I'd been forbidden by the police to say anything about him, or about being at the fire scene, to anyone else but Fiona. Fiona, of course, had told Graham. Nikki and the others knew nothing about my role. They'd been locked out of the warehouse and shocked into discretion by investigators. Inevitably, rumors had festered in the day since the fire and they flew around the gallery now, too. No one could miss Raven's absence tonight. It was only a matter of time before the news broke.

I was astonished when Waleed's parents and Olivia arrived. The party faltered; the three stood at its edge until Fiona hurried to draw them in. I recognized the couple from the photo I'd seen of their younger selves, though they looked diminished by years and by sorrow. The truth, that Waleed hadn't killed himself, had certainly been leaked to them through their powerful connections. Perhaps, relieved of their toxic shame and guilt, they'd come to make amends with Fiona, or to feel closer to their lost son.

Everyone went quiet when Graham dimmed the lights and illuminated a large projection screen against a wall of the middle room. Word of Waleed's lost paintings *had* gone around; now they sprang to phenomenal life. *Oohs* and *ahhs* rippled through the gallery at each image, one morphing slowly into the next. When we'd seen all six, a final photo appeared, Waleed with one arm around Nikki, the other around Raven, laughing together with Col and Lala, the five of them buoyant with love and hope and ambition—all that Raven hadn't been able to live with losing. It was the only other image besides his paintings Waleed had saved on his tablet. Out of the hush came Col's applause; Nikki picked it up and then Lala. When Waleed's parents joined in, so did everyone else. The applause was tearful and long, farewelling Waleed and, as only a few of us knew, Raven.

Although I'd failed Raven, my instinct to steal the tablet from the studio had been right. My bag slung across my chest had survived and, in it, Waleed's tablet with the only complete record of his brilliance. He'd been careless in documenting his work, sure of his studio's security. Eager to get to the MCA, euphoric at the prospect of art world fame, he'd put off saving the new photos anywhere else. Two had died for those paintings, one by water, one by fire—I hadn't been able to save *them*. My chest tightened, holding in a wail.

Was I cursed that men disappeared or suffered ghastly deaths around me? Who would be next? Would I travel through life trailing male corpses? *Don't lose it in front of all these people!* I escaped outside and sat hyperventilating on the sandstone steps warm from the day's sun. Being alone calmed me. The night was anything but quiet with light and voices pouring out through the open windows. I felt my foreignness. Aussies I'd met showed emotions more overtly than I was used to. I envied them that. My new cuts expressed my anguish better than I could, my history written on my face. How would I change if I stayed in Sydney for a month, or a year?

Useless musing. This was a stopover on my search for my dad, somewhere two-and-a-half thousand miles to the north; I was overdue to leave this city where death weighed on my heart and my conscience. Everyone, including the police, assured me I was an innocent witness to the tragedies, but I kept falling down the rabbit hole of what I might have done to stop them.

After the medics released me, I'd spent hours in a dingy, over air-conditioned room at the Balmain police station being debriefed by Detective Inspector Richard Morgan. Now I was dismayed to see him follow me outside. I hadn't noticed him among the mourners. Perhaps as camouflage among artists, he wore a black shirt and slacks that fit better than what I'd seen him in before. Without his suit and tie and with a drink in his hand, the detective looked younger and less uncomfortable. He leaned on the parapet around the porch, evading the light from inside, so his expression as he spoke was hard for me to read. "This wouldn't have happened without you."

My voice was croaky from yesterday's smoke. It hurt to talk, but Morgan provoked me into answering. "You think I need to hear that? I know Waleed wouldn't have died if I'd kept him longer at the gallery. Raven would be alive if I hadn't confronted him. I can't feel any worse about it."

"That's not what I meant. Who knows what might have happened *if*, because it didn't. I meant, you saved the photos of Waleed's burnt paintings and you found answers his family needed. Raven's own demons created *his* fate. Don't credit yourself."

I didn't answer. I wanted him gone, but he stayed.

"I came out here to thank you."

"For what?"

He ran a hand through his unruly hair. Could the tough man be nervous? "I was called off the investigation into Waleed's drowning. You knew that. But there was conspiracy talk my superiors wanted to end. The Tanoos family's in high-stakes development and that's never been clean here, or anywhere else—fortunes made and stolen, villainous pols and bureaucrats, backstabbing, mudslinging—comical if it wasn't so ugly. Meanwhile, my so-called career was in a pretty squalid low. I don't deny it. I'd made some mistakes, annoyed some important gents. Seriously annoyed, dangerously important. At best I was about to be sent home to Darwin with my tail between my legs."

"You're from Darwin?" I didn't care about the detective's tale of woe, but *Darwin* snared my attention.

"Far from and long ago, but a retreat to my unsavory origins to save my skin was imminent, until you, my dear girl, catapulted me into a promotion. You solved the mystery and, I confess, I claimed the credit. For now, I'm the golden boy." He finished his drink and crushed the paper cup. "So I have a proposition for you, to prove to myself I'm not a bad bloke, show up as an honorable man, launder my karma, as it were."

"Why would I want to help you do that?"

"Because, you want to find your father." Richard Morgan turned toward me and smirked in a way I despised. In the course of his investigation, someone had told him why I was in Australia.

I admitted it. "I'm flying to Darwin tomorrow afternoon."

"Right. I'm going with you. The North's not a good place for a young Yank sheila to be waltzing around. You'd be lied to at best. The worst that could happen? It won't with me there."

I rose abruptly. "Fuck off! I don't *want* you with me. I can take care of myself."

He grasped my wrist and held it, not so it hurt, but enough to stop me from storming away. He kept his voice level. "Without me you're going nowhere. I can have you declared a person of interest in Raven's death. You can be stuck in Sydney while the wheels of justice grind, etcetera. Believe me, you've got Buckley's chance of finding your dad without my help and I can't in good conscience let you prance off Back of Beyond alone. Besides, I have holiday time due me. I need a rest from so-called civilization. Do we have a deal?"

He released my wrist and offered a handshake. My only choice was to accept his company. Though being coerced into it irked me, having my own personal detective might be the only good thing to come from my time in Sydney.

Part Three

The Deep North

CHAPTER 21

I'd refused Morgan's offered ride to the airport, an error in judgment that left me running through the terminal at last call for the non-stop to Darwin, my backpack jouncing, my carry-on swerving on its rollers. I was the last to board. The detective had apparently used his police resources to commandeer the seat next to mine in the row of three. He stood and stepped over the knees of the person sitting in the aisle seat. "I don't need the window, I've seen it too often. You sit there."

I planted myself standing in the aisle. "I don't take orders from you."

He seized my carry-on without asking and stuffed it into an overhead bin. "It'll go easier if you can sort an invitation from an order."

The flight attendant defused our confrontation, urging me into the seat by the window.

I took some satisfaction at takeoff seeing the brave detective was a white-knuckle flyer. He unclenched his hands and opened his eyes as we leveled off. I pretended not to notice. He'd changed his look to khaki pants and safari shirt, costumed for the occasion, as usual. Who was I to judge his appearance? Had I looked in the mirror before I left the hostel? I'd dressed in the first clean things I'd pulled from my suitcase before I zipped it closed in my hurry to go: khaki shorts and jacket. Great, Richard Morgan and I would be a matched pair.

Fiona had implored me to stay longer, until I healed completely, and Graham threw his weight behind her, promising three good meals a day to fatten me. Morgan finally persuaded them I'd be safe. I'd left them with hugs and tears. Too many tears had fallen since I'd arrived in Sydney.

The flight attendant was staring at me, her hand poised over a drinks cart. The detective answered the question I hadn't heard. "Give the girl a lemonade."

I had to stop doing that, drifting in my thoughts. I thanked the woman for the can she plunked onto my tray, to prove I wasn't the basket case her solicitous look implied. Morgan opened it for me, adding another command.

"Drink that and have another. Rule number one, stay hydrated in the tropics, or you'll be no good to yourself or anybody else."

I was tempted to empty the lemonade in his crotch, but I *was* thirsty. "Now you're laying out rules for me? I'm not a helpless child."

"Stevie … oh, may I call you Stevie?"

"*My* rules, no sarcasm, no patronizing me, no bossing me around."

"Right, Stevie, this is what you have to know. There are lots of ways to die up North and I plan to bring you through our search alive. You're not to be some fuck-wit ignorant backpacker in for thrills."

The backpacker in the aisle seat studying the Darwin site on his screen harrumphed at that. *Our* search, Richard Morgan had said. Until now it had been mine. I was losing what little control of the situation I'd had.

There was no stopping him. "Forget what you thought you knew about Darwin."

He gave me more credit than I deserved. In this information-glutted era, I'd been counting on doing exactly what our eavesdropping seat mate was doing when the time came. What did I need to know that I couldn't learn online? He went on:

"Most of the old city, within a kilometer of the coastline, was razed two seasons ago by another killer typhoon. Happens with fair regularity now. Speculators and construction firms come up and do their shoddy rebuilding, then they go home to Bahrain or wherever, until another typhoon. I hear this time the good people of Darwin have run out of optimism and money, lots of them leaving their coastal property to the sea, those who can afford it going south, too many left behind with nothing to lose. Publicly, powers that be put on a happy face to keep visitors flowing in from overseas. So, the point I'm making? There will be times when I need to know you'll trust me and do what I say, not stop to argue or go the other way and make me rescue you from some lawless yobbo."

I gave him a scornful, lip-curled look. "Stop trying to scare me!"

"I wouldn't waste my time."

The pilot came on the intercom announcing an updated "footy" score to expletives among the passengers. I watched the endless red land unfurl. Richard Morgan ordered another lemonade for me and beer for himself. I wouldn't tell him I was grateful for the window. His allegiance to my purpose depended on his gratitude to me; any I admitted to him would only dilute what bargaining strength I had. I knew him, as little as I did, as a Sydney police officer defined and circumscribed by his profession. Who knew who he would be on his home turf? If he reverted to type, what type would that be? What could be less conducive to trust than a man saying "trust me?"

———

The Darwin airport was like a stage set—enticing scrims advertised beaches and jungle, but no more structure supported them than was necessary to get us travelers on and off our planes. We passed through into the tropical night, where hot, dank air closed around us. A few SUVs, several resort vans and taxis waited. Our Malay taxi driver just nodded to confirm the address the detective gave him. I had a sense the North was a no-frills place. I liked that. I wouldn't stoop to ask the detective where we were going. Streetlights were obviously one of the frills not considered essential to rebuilding the city; along our route only lights from houses punctuated the darkness. The house where we were dropped had a deep verandah walled with green shadecloth glowing from lights inside.

"Bloody hell, me long lost!" A man in shorts and an open shirt barreled out belly first. He grabbed Morgan. The two thumped each other the way men sometimes do, overcome by emotion, when they mean to say hello. I followed them through a flap in the shadecloth. The meaty

Kristina Bak

smell of something sizzling on a barbecue mingled with smoke from citronella mosquito candles. Two blue heelers, who hadn't made the effort to bark, lolled on the concrete floor. A woman and two other men, all in tank tops, shorts and flip-flops, lounged in mesh lawn chairs. These men looked disinclined to stir, but the woman joined the action and saved Morgan and our host from having to put words to their feelings. She reached up, pulled down the detective's head and gave him a smacking kiss.

"Dickie boy, you're losing your hair since we last met."

"Grateful to you for pointing that out, Mryna. You've gone a bit to lard yourself."

"Not so much as your worthless brother here. Who's the sheila you've brought?"

I'd hidden behind the affectionate patting and pinching that went with Myrna and Morgan's conversation. Now he pulled me forward by one arm. I had the disconcerting feeling she'd have accepted any explanation, from my being his newly-discovered daughter, to a piece of cradle-robbing on his part.

"This is Stevie, she's a Yank, but be nice to her. She's come looking for her dad and I'm helping her out, repaying a debt, so to speak."

They studied me, each in their own way, the men starting with my legs, Myrna with my damaged face. Her mouth pursed in distaste or sympathy, or from forty-plus years in the tropical sun. The examination lasted longer than courtesy would dictate in my part of the world before Myrna broke it off. "Welcome, Stevie. You've come in time for tea."

The meal was nothing I would call "tea." Greasy, steaming

sausages, potato chips from a package, and beer, lots of beer. Morgan unfolded two more lawn chairs and prevailed upon his sister-in-law to find me something non-alcoholic. After consideration, Myrna brought tonic water and lime "without the gin." This was food I would never get at home. I gobbled the sausages and chips. Morgan's brother dragged a chair beside mine and balanced his plate on his hairy thighs.

"Name's Jack. Over there's Max and Bradley."

I half-smiled at the two other men who responded with minimal lifts of their chins. Jack looked like a more dissipated variation on his brother's theme. He carried disappointment in his eyes as obvious as the beer belly that protruded from his otherwise lean frame, his bare scalp sunburned red. He spoke quietly, as though to save himself the effort more volume would require, or as if he usually left the talking to his wife.

"Dad done a runner then?"

"He's here somewhere, or he *was* here, thirteen years ago. He built a boat and sailed across the Pacific."

"Well, good on him!"

"He named it the *Stevie Colleen*, for me. Pieces of it washed ashore and they told us he was dead, but I know he's not. I've come to find him."

Jack attended to his beer and sausages. It wasn't a denial, or an affirmation, of what I'd said. He talked with his mouth full. "Ah, it's a funny old world. Some come here fortune hunting, some come for freedom, or love. Everybody finds something, not necessarily what they expected. Our old man lit here from the Vietnam war. He went into the uranium mine and when I finished school I followed him, pretty much by accident, never meant to stay, either. Then it got too late to leave and start over. Now the mine's closed, I'm out of work, on the dole, not a bad life day by day, but not really the thing for a man, and Myrna's sick of me whinging. We hope they'll reopen the mine—anybody, the Chinese or the Germans, or the Yanks—before I drink myself to death."

In the satiated silence, with the hissing barbecue turned off, I heard waves washing against a shore. "You're right on the ocean?"

"Oh, aye, used to be valuable property, can't be sold anymore. Lost our house in the last typhoon. This one's meant to be temporary, but that means diddly. Most of Darwin these days could be called that. Meantime, we've got first-rate beach access."

The sausages eaten, the men drank, sunk into their chairs like permanent fixtures in the floor. Only Myrna moved with purpose, collecting plates and bottles from where the men had left them. "Oy, Dickie, you dossing with us?"

"Since you invite me so graciously, pet, but Stevie needs somewhere posh. Gloria at her old place?"

"Hanging on. She gets backpackers now. The eco-adventure bush resorts get the deluxe clientele, what's left of it. She runs a tight ship. I'll call her, let her know you're coming." Myrna turned to me, all hint of joking gone. "You'll be safe at Palm Lodge with Gloria."

Myrna didn't seem easily daunted. I hadn't doubted my safety until then, despite Richard Morgan's warnings. He borrowed Myrna's car, an old Honda with broken-down seats and the smell of dogs, to drive me to Palm Lodge. All I could see by the headlights when we got there was a door in a white plastered wall overhung by trees.

The landlady, stocky, middle-aged, hair in an unraveling blondish topknot, greeted us in a vestibule with ill-lit hallways to the left and right. "Come home to us, Dickie? No more women left in the Big Smoke?"

"Good to see you, too, Gloria."

"Your ex came 'round last week; Patty's looking for a job. I had to tell her no."

"Yeah, too right. How's your Bobby?"

"Dead two years."

"Shit, sorry."

"I'd like to be able to say the same."

The detective's moment of silence seemed sufficient with respect to the late Bobby. "So, Gloria, this is Stevie. She needs looking after for a night or two, never been here before."

Gloria drew me away from Morgan. "No worries, Stevie, you'll be right. Got to watch out for the local boys. This one used to be an awful larrikin, him and his brother, in their day."

Morgan accorded me a sketchy salute. "I'm off then, leaving you in good hands. See you in the morning."

I didn't explain myself. Whatever Myrna knew, Gloria would probably know soon, if not already, and she had plenty to say on the way to my room upstairs. Our footsteps echoed in the hallways. The building was solid and spacious, with arched doorways and marble floors, but empty.

"I've run this place for thirty years. It's all mine now. Isn't it wonderful to be on your own? Nothing like it. Men get clingy at this age, they want their mums. We women thrive on being free. Here's yours, shower two doors down. I've got a tour coming in Wednesday, but tonight it'll be

152   *Kristina Bak*

quiet. Lock both doors when you sleep. We're walled, but no point being careless. Breakfast room is past the office, the way we came."

———————

Tiny lizards clung upside-down on my room's high white ceiling. White bedspreads covered three narrow beds. I opened my balcony door to the warm night smelling of eucalyptus, chlorine and decaying vegetation. Rampant vines climbed the walls from a garden lit by underwater lights in a swimming pool. Insects shrilled. Leaves rattled, alive with creatures invisible among them. A kitten-sized marsupial skittered across the balcony railing on dainty pink toes.

I called Mom. The phone signal was weak, the screen image pixelated, and the tropical night cacophony deafening. I stayed on the balcony, glad Mom couldn't see or hear me well. I hadn't told her about Waleed or the fire, only that a Sydney detective was helping me out of friendship with Graham and Fiona—a fib, not a lie. I marveled that she wasn't checking up on me, that she trusted and believed me, or had she given up on that and simply prayed for my survival? I hoped she was praying hard, because I wasn't sure what I'd gotten myself into here in Darwin.

CHAPTER 22

I was even less sure in the morning when Morgan came to fetch me. I'd slept, but if *he* had it didn't show. He wasn't a hairy man; the stubble on his cheeks didn't hide the gray tinge of his skin. He hadn't changed clothes, except to add a shapeless broad-brimmed hat. He smelled like seaweed. Had he gone into the surf fully dressed in place of a shower?

He caught my look. "Taking on protective coloration, got to blend in with the local lads if we're going about asking questions. A bit out of practice with the beer." He narrowed his eyes at the bright sun in the Palm Lodge driveway. "Had brekkie?"

"Gloria saw to that. Where're we going?"

"To the pub."

"More beer? It's 9 a.m.!" I balked at the open car door. He barely looked fit to drive as it was.

"You want to find old sailors, you go to the pub. I'm not that happy about it right now either. Get in the car."

Darwin's city center wasn't much to see. Whatever had been there before the last typhoon was gone, torn to toothpicks. The replacement buildings' impermanence was obvious, their shabby construction not committing them to the long term. Low-rise cafes and shops and pubs clustered together, uniformly uninviting.

Morgan made his choice without hesitation—a pub reeking of last night's beer and disinfectant, sparsely furnished with plastic-laminate topped tables and stiff chairs, with no pretense to any purpose other than efficient alcohol consumption. "This place has been here forever, not the same building, but the same blokes propping up the bar." He bought me a glass of mango juice, plonked me at a small table with orders to stay, and joined the men at the bar lifting pints for breakfast.

A few women occupied themselves with the gambling screens that were blinking and making merry musical sounds in an alcove at the back. Another plopped into a chair beside me and, without introduction, commenced a tête-à-tête in a raspy smoker's voice.

"Mango juice, good girl. I don't normally drink so early myself, but I'll tell you what, I'm leaving Darwin and flying scares me half dead, so a beer before takeoff ..." She looked a hard-used fifty, or a decade more, her face eroded and creased. She wore globbed mascara and mauve lipstick, charcoal eye shadow daubed on her eyelids. Her hair was dyed flat black, desiccated, light reddish roots growing out. She stank of cigarettes and hairspray. She set a travel case on the table, opened it to show me the gin bottle nested inside, and winked. "Emergency stock for in the air."

Shut up, shut up! Morgan was saying something about my father to the men at the bar. I wanted to hear what they answered, but I'd been raised to be polite and the woman droned on.

"I come out from Ireland to work on a cattle station as a young girl, thought I'd be living on a dairy farm. Ha! I was milk-white skin and hair red as the devil. They told me river mud was good for the sunburn and I should go lie in it, so I did, up to my neck, and saw those blokes up on the bank laughing at me. It was a crocodile place. The only reason the crocs didn't get me was they couldn't believe their eyes."

She barely paused for breath. "Now, where I live here in town, there's a family of goannas, the biggest one stands a meter and a half, near five and a half feet, on his hind legs. They beg until you feed 'em. You know goannas?"

I gave up on hearing the men's bar talk. I hoped the sooner I let this woman tell me her story, the sooner she'd leave me alone. "Goannas? No, what are they?"

"The big lizards, love, like Komodo Dragons. I get home the other night and they're waiting for me, sticking out their blue tongues, so I run around and come in the back. Then they leave a couple on the front verandah and the others follow me and they keep me trapped for an hour banging on both doors. But I'm leaving Darwin for good today, if I can work up my nerve to get on that plane." She levered herself out of her chair, empty glass in one hand, travel case in the other. "Pardon me, need another beer."

A bunch of backpacker boys claimed the next table. They were loud in Swedish, German, and Japanese with some concession to English, maybe the only language they had in common and the only one I could understand. "Trekked to Jim Jim Falls yesterday ... red boulders the size of cars ... rainbow serpent painting in this cave we had to crawl into on our backs ... off the cliff into the rock pool ... crocs at Sandy Billabong ... snakes in the trees ... taking off for Thailand tomorrow."

Kristina Bak

Morgan pushed away from the bar and took the chair between the backpackers and me. "Wankers, but there'd be no economy here without the tourists."

"What did the men say about my father? Do they know him?"

"Maybe."

"Maybe? Either they do or they don't!"

"We have to go to Jabiru, the old mining town. Easier said than done. They say the South Alligator bridge washed out in the last wet."

"The *wet*?"

"Two seasons up here. Now is the dry, what outsiders think of as autumn and winter. The wet is everything else, monsoons. I'll get Jack to drive us. He's bloody desperate for something to do."

"Someone told you my father's there?"

"Not so clear as that. The old bloke at the end of the bar says a mate of his up Jabiru way might've heard something. Before you get too enthused about it, you need to know the motto here in the Top End: *Why let the truth get in the way of a good story?*"

CHAPTER 23

We returned Myrna's dog-smelling car and Morgan rousted Jack out of bed. It took a pot of coffee before he allowed himself to be cajoled into driving us to Jabiru. He plainly savored making his citified brother beg for his help, until Myrna cut off the debate.

"Quit muckin' around, Jacko. What else are you gonna do today, you lazy bludger? Do me good to get you out of the house."

Jack tried to save face. "I'll take my gear, haven't been fishing up there for yonks."

Myrna's laugh sounded tart. "Don't bring any home. They say the barramundi glow in the dark these days. Stevie, love, take this hat." It was another floppy broad-brim like Morgan's. "Don't go out bare-headed, or you'll look like me by the time you're thirty."

I pretended I didn't know what she meant. She must have been delicately Anglo-pretty once. She looked none the better for the night before, either. "Sure, thanks, I'll wear it."

Myrna filled water jugs, packed a cooler, and fussed over me. "Make them get you sunblock, too, with mozzie repellant, and wear a proper shirt with sleeves."

Jack, stoked by caffeine, threw tools and cables and who-knows-what into his Landcruiser. The Landcruiser looked older than me—a no-particular-color workhorse, high on its axles, extra tires and gas cans mounted on the sides, a winch, a snorkel, spotlight, and gun rack—unnerving to me in the hazards it implied.

Myrna's warnings didn't add to my peace of mind. "The boys'll watch out for you, but you take care, too. There's always something waiting to bite you or eat you in the bush."

Jack didn't help. "Don't let the wife spook you, Stevie. She's spent half her life out there and look at her, she's fine." He patted her butt and kissed her goodbye. "Give us the tucker bag, Myrnie. We're off."

Jack took the road out of Darwin with bone-jarring speed, Aussie country rock blaring. His brother napped beside him. I was jounced around on the bench seat in back. Each time we met a vehicle like ours Jack raised one finger off the steering wheel in answer to the same laconic wave from the oncoming driver, but we didn't meet many. Jack had no wave for a passing shiny, air-conditioned van with a resort logo and darkened glass.

The road, irregularly paved and patched, ran through miles of spindly eucalyptus trees dotting sandy earth, the flat, sere landscape unchanging, the sun higher until shadows shrank and heat mirages lay cruel illusions of water over the road. I saw my first kangaroos, swollen roadkill on the pavement's verge.

Like a benediction, thicker, greener vegetation announced our arrival at a river where a bridge had once crossed. The river was no more than six or seven car lengths wide and the lack of a bridge didn't discourage Jack. He yelled over the music. "We can ford it. Look at the tracks here, others have today. It's the South Alligator, Stevie. Jabiru's on the other side."

"Are there alligators?"

"Crocodiles, Salties. Keep your eyes open, could see some. Hang on!"

I didn't have time to be scared before Jack took the river. The Landcruiser plunged in over loose rocks, bucked through midstream where water flowed halfway up the doors, climbed a sandbar. *Clunk.* Dead stop. The men swore. I wasn't worried. We were near the shore, the water a foot or two deep.

Jack cut the engine. "Could be worse, we're bogged, but we can dig free."

The men splashed out with shovel and pry bar. They dug and pried and cursed, three elements necessary to get the job done. It was stifling waiting inside. The windows were open, but the air was muggy and dead still. I fanned myself with my hat but it didn't help. I took off my shoes, opened my door on the downstream side, and dipped my toes in the water, blessedly cool. I slid out barefoot and let the water swirl around my knees. I waded a few steps into the river. It was silty; I couldn't see the bottom, but I found footing with my toes. Cautiously, I looked around for crocodiles. For the first time, with a frisson of excitement, I knew myself an adventurer, fully in this place. No one had told me *not* to get out of the car, but I stayed close. A log that had washed up into an eddy near the riverbank began to glide *upstream* in my direction. I blinked—an optical illusion, the heat blurring my eyesight.

Jack bellowed behind me. "Holy Christ! Get in! Move, move!"

His alarm terrified me before I recognized the danger. I turned and floundered against the current back to the Landcruiser. Richard Morgan tore open the door on the other side, dived through, jerked me in by one arm, and slammed my door shut so violently it hit my heels. Jack scrambled into the driver's seat.

The crocodile's scaled snout and pale underside surged out of the water like a prehistoric nightmare, jaws agape with gigantic cone-shaped teeth big enough to bite off my head. The Landcruiser shook as the creature crashed against it. Water splashed through the window. I screamed and threw myself into my rescuer's arms.

When the crocodile sank back into the turbid river, I sat up straight, rubbing my shoulder, too shocked to cry. "It tried to *eat* me!" Like cellular memory, DNA from ancestors with only their brains to protect them, now I understood *I could be food*. If I'd relied on *my* brain, I already would be.

Morgan, red faced and breathing hard, looked ready to take my head off himself. "Stupid girl! That's it, I don't owe you anything anymore. I should take you back to Darwin and leave you."

"No, *please!*" I gripped both his hands. Out here he seemed bigger, rugged and resourceful. I needed him on my side. "Thank you! *Thank you* for saving my life."

"Would've looked bad in Sydney if I hadn't."

Was that a joke? Jack snickered.

The detective didn't smile. He brusquely freed his hands from mine. "One more chance. From here on, you're piling up debt to me."

He took a rifle from the gun rack and stood guard while Jack finished digging out the Landcruiser. They stowed the tools and got in briskly, both as wet from sweat as from the water. On the other side, both men chugged beers from the cooler, ignoring my mortification. I needed to pee, but I would hold it for a stop well away from the riverbank.

———

The highway east of the river was worse than what we'd driven on so far. Jack dodged potholes without slowing. We met no one and the signs were unreadable, peppered by bullet holes. Jack killed the music as we drove into Jabiru. If Darwin was devastated, this place appeared eerily abandoned—low, widely spaced buildings boarded up, gardens gone to jungle, streets empty but for a few cars at the curbs, and unceasing cicada shrill. Jack parked at a shop that looked as neglected as the rest, except the door was open and the sidewalk out front was swept clean.

We entered through a hanging flyscreen. A shape materialized ghostlike from the dimness inside, a skeletal man in a white turban, his white shirt and pants so loose I could believe there was no body in them. He put his palms together and bowed.

Jack didn't bother with niceties. "Bahadur Singh, mate! How's it hangin'? Kath around?"

Without speaking, the turbaned man vanished through a curtain leaving us alone. As my eyes adjusted, I saw we were in a cramped grocery, its sparse stock meticulously arranged. The curtain heaved aside. A woman with dark eyes, a broad forehead, and smooth skin the color of burnished chestnuts joined us. She had no eyebrows or lashes and she wore a patterned headscarf artfully wrapped and knotted.

"What the hell, Kath?"

"Oy, Jacko, it's finally got me. Knew it would. Brought me some customers? Business is slow, but at least we got no competition now."

"Old Fong?"

"Carked it in the middle of the wet. We don't say his name no more."

"Sorry, yeah." Jack nodded my way. "This is Dickie's friend Stevie here."

Kath looked me over, clearly didn't approve. "Dickie! You do that damage to her? Thought you'd got past it. Besides, she's too young for you. Girl, you can find better."

"Um, actually, he saved me from a crocodile. He's helping me …"

Jack broke in. "Not what you think, Kath. We're looking for Bluey Rourke. You know where he's got to?"

Kath turned her fierce attention to rearranging cans of tomatoes and beans on a shelf. "What you need that piece of shite for?"

"We won't cause him any aggro, want to ask about a bloke."

Bahadur Singh had slipped back into the store and stood behind the counter. He bobbed his head barely perceptibly. Kath apparently agreed. "You'll find him in the mine boss's old place, around in the garden, but he generally won't see anybody. If you want him to talk you buy some chocolate. Chocolate's gone dear these days, supply and demand, but I've got a cache. Nobody around here can afford it."

Bahadur took two bars from a high shelf. I was about to pay for them, but Kath snorted at the sight of my phone. "Cash only up here, darlin'." Jack paid with coins and bills from his wallet. "Thanks, Kath. We'll see you."

"Better be soon, then. Tell Bluey Honey says his dole payment come. She'll bring the seeds he ordered on her next delivery."

Richard Morgan had been skulking in the background. He spoke for the first time. "Honey around?"

"Sometimes, but not to you." Kath disappeared through the curtain leaving Bahadur Singh to see us out.

As we drove through, the brothers feigned great interest in the town. I wouldn't let them off that easy. "Come on, Mr. Good Guy Detective, I'm catching that you've got a reputation you wouldn't want celebrated around Sydney."

Richard snorted. "Sarcasm's contagious up here. Don't credit the locals, always wanting to cut down the tall poppy."

Jack remained conspicuously speechless.

I relented. "Okay, 'Dickie,' but what about this place? What's happened to Jabiru?"

"The Ranger Mine happened to it. Uranium built it, uranium destroyed it, or climate change and Mother Nature did. A half century of mining uranium from an open pit bigger than the town, radiation leaks detected, reported, covered up. The company promised it was 'safe forever, fool-proof technology, government certified.' Then a typhoon to beat all typhoons walloped the tailings dams. No sooner the company got that cleaned up, or said they did, a bigger one blew them to hell, poured radioactive waste water out into Kakadu, into World Heritage listed wetlands. No one knows for sure how much."

Jack picked up the thread. "The company closed up shop and left. No amount of money can fix what they've done, no insurance company, no legal action. The Gundjeihmi Aboriginal Corporation, the Mirarr people, got a settlement from the courts, for what that was worth with half their homeland poisoned. Most of the traditional owners, especially the ones with kids, moved farther northeast into Arnhem Land."

My horror grew with their story. "Wait! You're saying this whole town is radioactive?" I sat forward and punched Richard Morgan's shoulder. "You've brought me to a place it isn't safe to live, where we'll get radiation poisoning? Where ..."

He kept looking straight ahead. "It won't kill us."

"It looks like it's killing your friend Kath."

He shifted in his seat, but wouldn't turn to look at me. "Too right, and likely Bahadur Singh. Kath's lived her life here, born in Kakadu under a paperbark tree out in the bush. Bahadur was a physics professor in Surabaya. He met Kath when he came ten years ago with nowhere else to go after his family was killed in a plane crash. He was working a security shift at the mine when the second typhoon hit, him and Jack."

I stared at the back of Jack's head while the implications of that set in.

"Here we are." Jack turned off the street onto a curving drive between two rows of tall palm trees. It led to a wide house with spreading verandahs, overgrown with red-blooming bougainvillea like the briars enwrapping Sleeping Beauty's castle.

A flock of pink and gray galahs lifted off, screeching, then repossessed the unmown lawn. A raggedy man in a hat that shaded his face stepped into the driveway, a rifle in his hands. Jack stopped and shouted out the window, waving. "G'day, ya old bastard! Don't shoot, it's Jack."

The man glowered into the sun. "Jack bloody Morgan?"

"Two Morgans, I got Dickie here, too, and a sheila."

"A sheila, heh. Why'n't you say so? Come through then but mind the chook."

CHAPTER 24

The old man's "chook" was a white cockatoo that followed him like a puppy, ruffling its wings, its sulphur-yellow crest feathers bobbing. When we piled out of the Land-cruiser the bird cowered and turned one ruby-red eye on the men doing that pounding, punching thing all around.

"I would'na shot you, haven't shot a man in years. I try for the guard drones round the mine pit, but the bloody things are too high up." The old man shifted his rifle to his left hand and shook hands with me with his other. It was hard and calloused. "I'm Bluey Rourke, love. Who're you and why're you with these disreputables?"

Jack tipped up his hat brim. "Fair go, Bluey. Stevie's had an earful of our shortcomings. Tell her we're good blokes."

"Better'n some, I give you that."

"Thanks, mate. We, ah, looked in at Kath and Bahadur's."

Bluey's cockatoo climbed onto his boot. He toed it gently off. "Yair, well…tea or beer, gents? And lady?"

A footpath led behind the big house, into a fruit grove—banana, mango, avocado, citrus. In contrast to his personal shabbiness, Bluey maintained an orderly Eden around a latticed gazebo covered in orchids and fragrant flowering jasmine. Bamboo made rustling walls around it.

I sighed with relief in the shade, out of the relentless northern sun. "This is so beautiful, like something from a fairy tale!"

"Ta, love. It's home. I've been at it some years. When I retired from the sea, I came to live out my dotage with my daughter and the grandbabies. Thought I'd take up golf. Nice town then, clean, friendly folks, public swimming pool. We still have the pool during the wet."

Richard Morgan guffawed at that. "Everything's a pool up here during the wet."

"True, but even so … Anyhow, when the mine went bad my daughter and son-in-law moved the littlies to Brisbane. I can't abide the city. I like it here and what harm can it do me? I'm old, my good looks lost."

Bluey raised his hat, watching for my reaction. The left side of his face looked scraped to the bone, one nostril and part of his upper lip missing so that his mouth formed a perpetual sneer, teeth yellowed like the crocodile's. I was worse for wear as well, but my shock must have shown. He turned the other cheek. "Stay to my right, love, and admire

Kristina Bak

this noble profile." He was joking, but there was truth in it. He had been a handsome man. "The sun of the Antipodes taxed my Irish skin, as it does. The surgeon saved my life and half my face. Now, what can I give you?"

He couldn't have missed the shopping bag Jack carried. He had his eyes on it as he asked the question.

Jack set the bag on an ornate wrought iron table rusting under an arbor. "Don't trouble yourself, mate. We did a BYOB and threw in prezzies for you, too."

Jack unpacked bottles of beer and the chocolate bars. Bluey pounced on the chocolate. Jack opened a beer and passed it to me, tepid, but a safer choice than radioactive tea. Bluey ducked into his gazebo. We made ourselves comfortable beneath the arbor on antique wooden chairs meant for a formal dining room.

When Bluey rejoined us, sporting chocolate smears around his mouth, Richard Morgan tipped his beer bottle to him. "Nice digs. Last I was here you were camped in the old Crocodile Lodge."

Bluey thrust his tongue into the gap on his mutilated side, licking off the last of the chocolate. "The lodge was too empty, the rooms haunted-like when the others took off, and inside sprouted mold without the air-con. I went right to the top, the boss's house—too indoorsy. I brought some furniture out here and left the house for the termites. You'd have to take a machete to the bougainvillea thorns to get in there now. Those years on ships made me what I am. I like my quarters trim and I like the wind and the stars. If I get bored I go on a pig hunt, or buffalo. Plenty of feral game around tearing up the land. Mostly I fish."

Jack perked up at that. "Barramundi good?"

"You wouldn't credit it—thirty, forty kilos, some of them, since the tourists and commercial fishers went. You want to throw in a line? Something to take home to Myrna?"

I could see the effort it took Jack to say no. "Myrnie wouldn't let me in the door with one nowadays."

"So you didn't come Jabiru way to hunt or fish, which brings me to the fact, aware as I am of my own charms, since you rock up bearing gifts, you need something from me."

Richard Morgan passed him a beer. "A yarn, Bluey, about a bloke you may have chanced on when you were cluttering up the pubs in Darwin. A Yank who sailed over on his own in a boat called the *Stevie Colleen.*"

"Heh, I knew the name rung a bell." Bluey studied me now. I tried to meet his eyes without looking at the disaster he wore for a face. "A young bloke, wasn't he? Full of himself like they are before the sea smacks them down some. Not a bad one, good for a drink and a chinwag. Never talked about where he come from, nor bragged about what he'd done, only grand things he fixed to do."

What he said hurt me. I didn't want to show the emptiness I felt, but I had to ask. "He never talked about his daughter?"

Bluey looked at me with eyes full of pity I didn't want. "Not in so many words, love, but he was exceedingly proud of that vessel he'd built, and what a sailor names his yacht tells you where his heart is. I can't bring to mind his name, you see, but I recall the *Stevie.*"

"Sam. His name is Sam."

"Aye, Sam, and he was bound to sail her around the world."

"And home?"

"That would be implied, love, but the details are lost to me in time."

"What happened to him? Where is he now?" So close to the answer I didn't dare hear it. "Wait, no, not yet." If I were to lose the faith that smoldered in me, this would be the moment. I wanted to prepare for its being gone.

Bluey swigged his beer. Bright green parrots with red wings landed in a tree above the gazebo and began noisily ripping at its fruit. Richard Morgan shifted his feet. "Stevie …"

"Okay, please, I want to know everything about my father."

Bluey wiped his mouth where the beer dribbled out. "Not *everything* about him, what I heard. He set sail across the Arafura Sea, round Cape York, and south to Cairns to beat typhoon season. He weren't stupid, but cocky with strength and success, and didn't know these seas the way he needed to. He'd only seen 'em quiet. A storm blew up fast and caught him before he reached the Torres Straits."

"I know the part about the storm. We got the report and I dreamed it."

Bluey nodded. He didn't seem to find my dreaming strange. "This next I can't swear to. The bush telegraph had it a Ylongu woman pulled him from the surf, near dead. I never heard another word about him."

I veered from hope to despair and back. "So he could be somewhere around here!"

"Not impossible he could be." Bluey turned from my elation. "You boys might find old Gerry around the Border Store. Tell him I put you on to him. He's kept good track of his people since they lost their battle against the mine. He watches that border close now, knows where everybody is when nobody else does."

Bluey escorted us back to the Landcruiser, his chook hustling at his heels. "Thorium-230 in the tailings has a half-life of 80,000 years. It'll outlast me, but I'll give it a good go. Sure you wouldn't like to take some fruit from my garden, Jack?"

"Kind of you, mate, but my companions here are squeamish about the radiation. Can't imagine why. Next time I'll bugger off alone. We two can go fishing."

CHAPTER 25

Jack backtracked out of Jabiru and headed northeast without consulting us passengers. Leaving town we passed a wall laden with graffiti: *We are Not a US Colony!* the US replaced by *Chinese, Canadian, Mexican, Korean,* each crossed out with *White Australian* the current reigning favorite to hate. The sun was angling low. Jack glanced at me in his rearview mirror. "You right, Stevie?"

I'd exhausted the last of my adrenaline at Bluey's. I would have fallen over if not for the seat belt, but I didn't want the two Morgans to see my weakness. "Of course."

"There's camp sites and rooms at the Border Store. The wife threw in her swag for you to sleep in."

"What's the Border Store?"

"Last stop between Kakadu and Arnhem Land. If Bluey's right Gerry'll turn up. He can grant us permission to cross in if we need to."

"Why do we need his permission?"

"He's one of the elders. Arnhem Land belongs to his people. They're watchful over who they let in. In fact, Dickie …"

Richard Morgan passed an open beer to his brother. "Put that in your gob and shut it. We were batshit young then. It got settled and we ended right."

I nodded off.

Jack startled me awake."Brumbies!" He braked hard to let a herd of horses, manes flying, gallop across the road, grays with one or two darker among them. "Feral, like the pigs and buffalo. History on the hoof, Stevie. They say grays predominate because Paddy Cahill liked that color. He's a local legend, brought their ancestors in more than a century ago. They're fattening on the grass now before it dries up."

I watched until they disappeared in the red dust behind us.

When we got to the Border Store, eucalyptus trees cast long shadows across its empty parking lot. It looked like detritus from Darwin had blown here in the typhoons and been mistaken for buildings. Miscellaneous signs on the ramshackle structures announced Motel, Cafe, Tour Booking, Food and Bait, Souvenirs and Fuel. The place seemed deserted until someone called from a platform built atop a sizable steel water tank over the central store. "Cooee! Help yourself to beer from the cooler and come up."

Richard Morgan kept his voice low. "Is that Quint? That shit-for-brains? Thought he left for Perth with the last tour bus out."

Jack spoke quietly, too. "I know, you wouldn't credit it, but he couldn't part with Gav and Gav wouldn't go. We don't talk about it. They own the place now."

A shaky aluminum ladder led to the building's flat roof and to rungs nailed on timbers bracing the steel tank. I climbed behind the men. It wasn't easy with the can of soda I'd chosen over beer in one hand. "Richard, why are we doing this?"

"To watch the sunset. It's like a Top End religion, the only religion for most of us whitefellas. And will you kindly not call me Richard? It's *Dickie* in front of this lot."

"This lot" was motley. Of the three guys on the platform at the top of our climb, Gav was the one with astonishing movie-star good looks, from his rippling blond hair and sumptuous lips, to his tanned beefy legs in fraying khaki shorts and well-worn ankle-high boots. I recognized Quint because he was watching me watch his Adonis. Quint was mid-height, mid-thirties, decent-looking.

You couldn't say the same for the third person. He was closer to my age, short, with sunbaked acne scars and thick wire-rimmed glasses. His eyes blinked too much. I caught the name Mickey attached to him in the greetings, but there were no formal introductions or male bonding displays. We all turned our faces to the setting sun's performance. The sky was generous with its spectacle, lending itself to each of us, so we were lit like a frieze of six red-gold gods.

Once the sun dove beneath the horizon, we degenerated from ethereal beings to smelly, fleshy creatures mosquitoes drilled for blood. By what little light remained Gav noticed me slapping at them. He'd looked the archetypal Aussie hero, so his upper-class English accent surprised me. "We need to get you inside ... *Stevie*, did you say? This season the mozzies aren't so bad, but they can be damned uncomfortable, not to mention mutating malaria and Dengue Fever. Long sleeves, long trousers, that's the ticket. Down you go, feel carefully for your footing, watch that third rung."

He kept up his advice and instruction while I retrieved my repellant and more protective clothes from the Land Cruiser, then left me at the store's restroom to change. I expected him to be waiting when I emerged, smelling of soap and mosquito repellant. Instead it was Quint.

"Gav's gone to the cafe, to cook dinner. You have to forgive him if he bosses you a bit. He hasn't had a tour to guide in months. Everybody's scared of the radiation around the mine. Gav loves taking care of people—like a herding dog, he needs to work or he goes bonkers. But don't mention dogs, please. His Kelpie, Matilda, got taken by a croc in the wet this year and he's mourning."

CHAPTER 26

*I*n a bleakly lit corner of the cafe, our company made a lonesome cluster. Around us were chairs and tables where fifty people could be fed, all empty.

Quint served more beer. "When the last typhoon struck, Gav and I were in the bush, guiding Swiss archeologists to see rock art. We camped in a cave while the storm passed. We knew it was bad, but we didn't know what happened at the mine. Reg offered us the business, mates' rates, the minute we came back through, said he was going home to Queensland, happy to give two young blokes a foothold here where he'd enjoyed good times. We bought this place for practically nothing, but nothing was what we had and we were swindled. Reg guaranteed we closed the deal before we heard the mine report. We didn't foresee tourism was doomed."

Mickey strutted from the kitchen wearing a once-white chef's apron tied under his armpits, his legs so short only his boots showed beneath the hem. Without his hat, his head looked too big for his straggly hair. He dropped a handful of forks on the table in our general area. "Quit'cher whinging, Quint. It's a good life." His voice was nasal and annoying.

The men swilled beer and wove rambling tales about fishing and hunting and the almost nonexistent tourist trade. I hadn't dared eat anything in Jabiru, but with my stomach about to cave in, radiation wasn't so high on my worry list. By the time Gav made his entrance bearing a tray piled with roast pork in one hand and a heaping bowl of mashed sweet potatoes in the other, I was far more concerned that he didn't drop them.

Mickey schlepped mango slices, a loaf of biscuit-like damper, and a carton of palm oil butter and took his seat across the table from me. He snuffled wetly, mopped his pocked face with his apron, forked himself a slice of pork. "Killed this one myself two days ago. Place's overrun with pigs, shoot one, ten more spring up. They root out the native plants. Nothing discourages the vermin, but they're good to eat."

It strained my imagination to picture Mickey stalking prey, even feral pigs. I figured he was exaggerating to impress me. Did he see me as a match for him with the scar and cuts disfiguring my face? The pig was stringy, but with salt and crusty damper it went down. The men shoveled it in. Dessert was beer, of course. The men's belches filled gaps of satisfied contemplation over their empty plates. I ate the last mango slice and licked my fingers.

Partly to avoid Mickey's palpable fascination, I turned on my phone to retrieve my messages. Nothing. "No reception here?" My question was general. Gav answered.

"Nothing official. We pirate off different satellites when we need to. You want Quint for that."

"Why Quint?"

"Electronics genius. He was with ASIO, Australian Intelligence, before he saw the light and came here."

More, like, saw *Gav*, but whatever. I kept that thought to myself.

"Also, he'd done some whistle-blowing in Canberra and needed to leave." Gav called down the table to Quint. "Oy! Here's a damsel in digital distress."

———————

Quint's setup looked crude, mismatched screens on a desk in an unused motel room. That wasn't much of a distinction; the motel consisted of ten rooms, all of which appeared to be unused. The complicated part, Quint told me, was tracking the passing satellite signals and using them while they were in range without being detected. "I download movies. We don't care much about news from the outside."

"What movies do you like?"

"What movies? Uh, nature shows."

"What, you're half-drowned in nature!"

"I mean, human nature. You know."

I read Quint's discomfort in the color rising up his neck. It was sweetly old-fashioned to see a man still embarrassed about watching online porn.

He went all business. "I need your user name, your passwords. We're coming to a portal now."

Primitive! When was I last out of signal range? I didn't like giving up my data. "I'll put those in myself."

"No, I'm the only one who knows the encryption code. I invented it. I can pull in your messages, but you can't send anything out. This has to be quick. I, ah…can't afford to be traced."

"ASIO?"

"I left somewhat under a cloud. I don't fancy prison."

"And you're telling me because?"

"You're a Yank, you're with Jack and Dickie. I figure you've got a thing or two to hide yourself. Besides my name—"

"Isn't Quint. I get it. Anyone comes too close, you do a disappearing act."

"Boundless bush hereabouts."

I gave him what he needed and my messages downloaded in seconds, not that there were many. Quint shut down his connection and transferred them to my phone, chuckling at his own skill. "Playing hide and seek with them."

"Like Peter Pan."

"Too right. I'll never grow up, absolutely refuse to."

"Thanks for this."

"No worries."

Back in the cafe Mickey was washing dishes, Gav and Jack one-upping each others' exploits, Richard Morgan listening with his eyes closed. Quint left an empty chair between himself and Gav. Why? It wasn't as if we didn't know, or as if anyone cared. Or did they in this remote place? I had to admit I knew close to nothing of how people around here saw things. I sat on the cool tile floor against the far wall and started scrolling through my downloads.

One from my mom was first. In the garden on a sunny afternoon, a breeze ruffled her hair and her lilies. "Hi, sweetie, we're so relieved you're not alone there. We worry. We think about you all the time."

The second message was a surprise. Olivia, Waleed's sister, somber, but polite. "Stevie, my parents are grateful to you." Her voice quavered, but she went on formally, reading from a script: "Although Waleed's latest paintings were destroyed in the studio fire, the surviving photographic images are excellent quality and will have reproduction value. My mother, especially, wants you to have the one I've attached. Rights to it will be transferred to your name in perpetuity. We ask your permission to include it in a documentary about Waleed and his work to be produced in the coming year."

I had no idea what Olivia's's message meant in monetary terms. Seeing the painting here was like a visitation from another planet, alien and unexpected, like rules of reality had been undone and Waleed could return, too.

I didn't realize I was crying until Richard Morgan came and squatted beside me. "You right?" He scowled when I told him what Olivia had said. "I didn't fool them, then, did I? They knew it was you broke the case. Good they didn't let on to my chief. Look, put that phone away and get some rest."

I'd have resented him telling me what to do if I hadn't been dead on my feet. The motel room Gav assigned me had a cracked window, a dribble of lukewarm water from the shower head, and a distorting mirror. At least the window was screened to keep out the bugs in the heat of the night. I flopped across the bed's bare, mold-smelling mattress, fully dressed.

CHAPTER 27

Footsteps passing my room dragged me from sleep. I smelled my own fear. How well did I know these men? The only one I'd met before yesterday was the detective and nothing I'd learned about him since we'd been in the North was reassuring, except the fact he'd saved my life. What, exactly, did he think I owed him for that? He had his promotion, what more did he want from me? What *did* men want from young women? Ridiculous, I was winding myself up. *Relax, breathe.*

"Stevie…" It was Jack, speaking low to not wake the others.

"Go away!"

"Get up, there's someone wants to meet you."

"No!"

"Gerry's here, Stevie."

I sat up and rubbed my face. The pork lay like lead in my stomach. I groped the wall for a light switch. One light went on outside. I opened the door, blocking the way in with my body. What had I expected of an Aboriginal elder, that he would be naked and painted and carry a spear? Gerry rocked on his heels from my nearness, then regained his poise. Other than his darker skin and eyes deep set below his broad forehead, he looked like what I'd seen of the standard Northern Territory bloke—weighty around the middle, wearing khaki shorts, a tee shirt, and the same beat-up leather ankle boots they all wore. Jack stood beside him. They were alone. This confused me. "Where's Richard, uh, Dickie?"

Gerry peered around me into my room. "Not in there?"

"Why would he be?"

Jack gave me a look I couldn't interpret, then spoke with more formality than usual. "Gerry, this is the young lady I told you about."

"Welcome to my country. Come and talk with me." Gerry's voice resonated with authority it didn't occur to me to defy. "Switch off that light first."

I flicked off the light and went outside. Jack drew back and left me with Gerry. The border buildings were unlit, but the Milky Way swept over in unfamiliar opulence, so brilliant the stars danced and we were silver-highlighted shadows, more voice than substance.

"Why have you come to my place, Stevie?"

"To find my father, Sam Wales. Do you know him?"

"What will you do if you find him?" No one had ever asked me that, but the answer was obvious.

"I'll take him home. We'll go home together."

"What if he's already home?"

"No, he hasn't been for years, he's been lost nearly my whole life."

Gerry's silence stretched uncomfortably for me. My words whirled in my mind and came down in a different shape. Gerry let me work it out on my own. "You mean, *home here.* I don't care, I need to see him, talk to him, touch him, look into his eyes, hear his voice." I'd never said it this way, but it was true. "My lifeline's broken, I'm out of balance until I find him."

"You think he wants to see you?"

That question hurt. "I can't believe he's forgotten me."

Gerry paused so long, I thought he wouldn't answer. He studied the stars, then spoke gently to me. "Maybe he wants you to find him, maybe not. It's his story, but it's yours, too, so he can't choose how it ends, if it ends. Nobody can control that belonging, father to child. You go out there, you look around, you may not like what you find."

"But I'll *know. Please*, is he here?"

"I have an idea where you might look. I'd be wrong not to give you a hand." His voice sharpened, commanding again. "Croc Man can take you upriver tomorrow. These yobbos aren't going." Gerry bunched his lips toward Jack.

Jack protested. "Oy, Gerry, that's not right. We need to take care of her."

"You saying this young lady won't be right with my nephew? He'll treat her like one of our own. She'll be safer than with your bloody brother." He turned to me. "No worries."

CHAPTER 28

I went back to bed and lay trying to sleep until the stars waned. The first birdcalls came. A kookaburra's manic laugh sounded, answered by another from deeper in the trees, where I would be going, where my father might be. The sun came up as I stripped off yesterday's stinking clothes. A mosquito bite added a red lump over my cheekbone, but the glass cuts were healing and I looked no bonier than usual. I showered and rubbed insect repellant onto my arms and legs, its acrid citronella smell my cologne.

Gerry had been circumspect, careful not to encourage me too much, but he hadn't fooled me. My father was alive and I was certain Gerry knew where he was. Richard Morgan rose some notches in my esteem; whatever his character flaws, he knew who to ask to find answers and he kept his word. Why had I imagined he'd want to mess with skinny, scarred me?

In the cafe, the men tucked into plates of damper and fried pork like a pack of dingoes gorging on kill. I'd hoped the person Gerry called Croc Man would have arrived, but it was last night's crew, minus Jack. I joined them and served myself. Mickey smiled, too eagerly. I avoided his eyes. Quint sat back and watched us as Gav made sure I ate. Gav looked older in the morning light, his skin coarse, lines framing his beautiful mouth, his eyelids drooping at the corners. Richard Morgan was unshaven and red-eyed. He swabbed his plate with a bite of damper and finally spoke to me.

"You'll be in good hands, the best for where you need to go. Mickey knows every sand bar and tributary between the escarpment and the gulf."

Mickey? That had to be a slip of his hung-over tongue. I corrected him. "Gerry said his nephew Croc Man was going to take me upriver."

"That would be right, Croc Man."

Mickey grinned, food bits stuck in his uneven teeth. "That's me."

My shock had to show. They were joking. In a second, everyone would have a giggle at my expense. I turned to Gav, who looked the brave bush guide part, but no. "Mickey killed a saltie with a spear and a knife when he was thirteen. It was a monster, had boots and a watch in its belly."

Mickey blinked modestly behind his smeared lenses. "I don't *like* to kill them. They know me. I talk to them."

No one was laughing. I'd be alone on a saltwater crocodile infested river with this near-sighted, lascivious boy who *talks* to them?

"I don't communicate so well with the snakes, but we sort it, leave each other in peace."

Okay, good, and snakes!

Mickey passed me a mug of coffee. "We'll leave right after breakfast. Bring your swag for camping."

The detective tried to reassure me. Whether I liked him or not, he was my last link to anything familiar and remotely safe. "Jacko's gone home to Myrna, but I'll hang around here, do some fishing, hunt pigs and water buffalo, a real holiday." He didn't look particularly thrilled at the prospect.

He brightened a few minutes later when a dusty four-wheel drive with an Australia Post logo on its side rattled to a stop outside the cafe. Everyone went to meet it. The woman who climbed from the driver's seat had to be Honey. From her untamed corkscrew curls to her toes in rubber flip-flops, she was honey-colored, dark golden brown, even her ardent eyes that caught on me and Richard Morgan, then skipped to Gav. If Gav were Adonis, Honey would be his Aphrodite, if either interested the other in that way. Honey began unloading her truck. "I brought your flour and tea, love."

Gav went to help her. The detective disappeared. He showed up twenty minutes later, when the supplies and mail had been stacked inside on a cafe table and Gav was pouring coffee for Honey. Morgan had washed and changed his shirt. His hatless hair was wet, slicked back, his cheeks smoothly shaved and pink. Was he blushing?

"G'day Honey."

"G'day Dickie. What's up, besides the usual?" She tipped her head toward me.

"Ah, this's Stevie. Brought her from Sydney to look for her dad."

Honey looked at me directly for the first time. "Your dad's up here, love?"

"I'm pretty sure Gerry thinks he is."

"Your dad a Yank, too?" Her question sounded like more than simple curiosity.

Mickey cleared his throat. "I'm taking her upriver today. Gerry won't let Dickie go in."

"I see." Honey scrutinized me with a look I read as concern. "Well, good on'ya." She rummaged through the pile on the table and retrieved a bulky padded envelope. She passed it to Mickey. "Can you deliver this for me, if you happen by that camp?"

Mickey took the envelope without checking the name. He frowned over it. "Get your things, Stevie, and meet me in the store."

So I was to take orders from Mickey now. I didn't like it, but I didn't like a lot I'd had to do in Australia and I hadn't planned this to be a pleasure trip. If I missed the subtleties of what was going on around me, what difference did it make as long as I was getting closer to my dad? It didn't take much to know there was a backstory for Honey and Richard Morgan. While I packed, I saw them pass my motel room in tense negotiation.

Quint drove Mickey and me to the river in a van meant for tour groups that weren't coming anymore. Too large for the three of us. The aluminum dinghy waiting on the riverbank, in contrast, looked far too small for two, scarcely longer than Mickey's legendary crocodile, but then, the river wasn't wide, either. Mickey stowed our gear among other boxes and bags. I lifted my phone to take a photo. Mickey plucked it from my hands. "Too easy to lose where we're going."

I felt like he'd taken a part of me. He tossed my phone to Quint who caught it neatly, one-handed. Quint cut off my protest. "It'll be safer here. I'll be sure you get it back." What was going on? I knew it wasn't a question of safety. My uneasiness without my phone added to my resentment toward Mickey.

He and Quint slid the boat into the water and held it steady. As a child I'd been obsessed by boats, watching fruitlessly for my dad's sails coming into Eagle Harbor, but aside from trial runs on the *Stevie* into the San Juans—which I wasn't sure I remembered, or recreated from my mom's photos—until Sydney, I'd avoided going onto the water in anything smaller than a Puget Sound ferry. To me, boats had come to mean loss, peril, sadness. I stepped in hesitantly and sat where Mickey told me, at the front. He took his place at the stern and started the outboard motor. Quint pushed us off and we were launched.

One hand on the tiller, Mickey aimed us up the middle of the river. I faced forward in the narrow prow. The river flowed smooth, opaque brown, fringed by white-trunked eucalyptus and dense green trees growing down to the water. A stone escarpment jutted in the distance, its jagged horizontal strata so red in the early morning sun they looked like the land's torn flesh against the sky's unmarked blue. We rode low in the water. The motor putted against the current.

"Oy, Stevie, take a look over there to your right." Mickey's tone made it clear he expected to be obeyed as captain of our craft. "Keep your hands and elbows inside the boat."

On a sandbank, a twelve-foot crocodile reposed, tail toward us, the sun throwing its heavy scales into relief. On the other bank, some yards to my left, two more watched us pass. I tucked my elbows close to my sides and drew in my feet from the boat's hull, too thin between the water and me. Like a monster movie sequence, enormous crocodile teeth biting through it, dragging me under, played and replayed in my mind. The Morgans weren't here to save me and I had no faith in Mickey. I breathed into my belly to control my fear. "So, uh, *Croc Man*, how far do we have to go?"

"Not so far as you might think."

"How do you know what I think?"

Mickey went quiet.

What *did* I think? That this was a taxi? I hadn't paid anybody anything, not for food or lodging or information, since I left Sydney. I'd been riding on Richard Morgan's indebtedness, but I'd used that up. So what was the deal? What did these people want from me? Everyone wanted something, didn't they? Was that why I'd instantly loved Waleed? He'd seemed different, guileless. I shivered despite the day's building heat.

"Sorry, Mickey. That was rude."

"No worries. Lots of people get scared out here. Sometimes it makes them crazy."

I turned aft, to face him. "You don't get scared?"

"I was born here, it's my home. I love it. The only thing that scares me is the poison and it's too late for me on that."

"The poison?"

Mickey steered and scanned the river ahead, not meeting my eyes as he spoke. "My dad came over from Scotland for a job in the uranium mine when he was sixteen. He met my mum, Gerry's youngest sister, staying in Darwin for school. Dad had already been exposed to too much radiation when they got together, but he didn't know it. The cancer killed him when I was a baby. Mum's people took us in." He told his story with no trace of self-pity. "They say the poison is why I never grew tall like my eastern cousins and my hair falls out. Since the last bad spill, my family's gone away, but some of us won't leave this place. Look around, how could we?"

No crocodiles in sight now, only white herons like Japanese brush paintings against dense greenery. Mickey opened a covered creel at his feet and produced a fish. "Watch this." He stood, raised the fish in one hand. A huge gray and white bird plummeted from a treetop. It swooped over us, its wingspan wider than our boat, seized the fish in talons that looked big enough to take Mickey, too, and flew off with a loud triumphant *ank-ank*.

Mickey gave it a name I couldn't have repeated, then interpreted for me. "Sea eagle, one of my best mates on this stretch. She expects a gift when I come." He sat to steer again.

"The radiation doesn't hurt the animals?"

"We'll know in more generations, but be careful what you eat here, not too much fish. I've brought bottled water for you and we won't stay long ... in case."

"But my dad!" How could he live here?

"We're going to call on a bloke who could be him, or not. He doesn't have the name you said, but names are easy things to change, when there's a reason."

My heart sank. Of course it couldn't be him. "Why would my father change his name?"

"Why does anybody? To hide from their past, their present, their future, who knows? This bloke's a Yank. Odds on, Immigration don't know he's here. He'd be deported for sure if they caught him."

Kookaburra laughter resounded over the river, diabolical, ridiculing my self-importance. I was a ripple passing through the tragedies and dreaming of the people who belonged in this place. My grieving Waleed, my longing for my father, were trivial in comparison. Still, they were *my* grief and longing and they consumed me.

Heat shimmered on the water. Everything stayed much the same, suspended, to my eye, though I suspected not to Mickey's. We'd gone on this way for hours when Mickey angled in toward the shore. "Keep your head down."

Of course, I looked up. We were on a collision course with the trees. I grabbed my hat as branches clawed at it. We entered a tributary, unnoticeable to anyone on the river unless they knew it was there.

Mickey maneuvered the boat further into the overhanging trees' thin shade. He bumped against land, cut the motor, and let midday quiet flood the space. "We'll take a break here for the necessaries but stay near the boat. I won't look unless I hear you scream."

"Is that meant to be a joke?"

"Yes and no. I saw a careless tourist taken by a croc in Sandy Billabong last year. Revolting."

He looked away, as promised.

CHAPTER 29

ickey stood in the boat and poled us up the tributary's shallow winding channel. Green parrots zipped through the trees with metallic cries, flashing orange wing patches. Tiny red finches flocked *chip-chipping* loudly together. Bell-like calls rang from other birds hiding in the foliage and waterfowl muttered to themselves as they went about their business. The water was unmoving, clearer than on the river, dark with tannin. Shadowy fish passed beneath us. A four-foot-long snake swam by. At my gasp, Mickey snickered. "File snake's harmless, good bush tucker. My aunties catch him with their hands."

Mickey kept up his steady poling, stopping only once, when stinging insects showered me from low-hanging leaves. I swiped frantically at them. Mickey helped, then pinched one of my attackers in two fingers and showed it to me, a golden-bodied ant with a translucent green abdomen. "Eat it, it's good."

Eat a live bug? I took it as a dare and bit off the abdomen. The taste was citrusy and refreshing, bigger than I'd expected. Mickey collected the ones we hadn't brushed into the water and finished them himself. "Yum! Vitamin C."

Greenery narrowed the waterway until it blocked the view and I could touch leaves from where I crouched on the hard seat. Higher overhead, arching eucalyptus branches blocked air movement and trapped hot sun that filtered through. Their camphor-mint scent mingled with the smell of fishy mud. We followed a labyrinthine course, so I'd lost all sense of direction when we floated into a pool with green water and lily pads. It looked like a museum's Jurassic diorama. Shade from out-of-scale ferny, palmy plants made me feel cooler and disproportionately small. As idyllic as it appeared, this had to be a mistake, a dead end. The only outlet was the way we had come.

Mickey poled the several boat lengths across the pool and ran us aground on a patch of sand. "We're here. This is their billabong."

He took a bulging canvas bag from our cargo and stepped ashore. I clambered out onto the sand, strapped on my backpack and hurried after him on a jungly path. Mickey turned right. I had the sensation of being followed and spun around, but undergrowth hid everything. When I got to where I thought Mickey had turned, he'd disappeared. *Had* he taken the opening to the right, or the equally indistinct one on the left? What was the rustling I heard? I crashed on, slapping at another hail of green ants, and burst into a

Kristina Bak

clearing close on Mickey's heels.

A long-limbed woman squatting barefoot on a mat on the ground rose to her feet in one fluid motion. Her sleeveless dress draped her willowy body with natural elegance. Her skin was ebony; her eyes, the blackest I'd seen, divulged nothing. Her hair fell in long graying coils.

"G'day, Croc." Her voice was sharp.

"G'day, Yvonne."

"We mob been expecting Honey."

"Honey's busy."

"Busy how?"

"Dickie's come back."

"Dickie Morgan, huh! And who's this?" She looked at me the way she might at a strange dog, wondering if she should throw a bone or a rock.

"Not sure yet. Her name's Stevie. Your man around?"

"What kind of question is that? You bring his supplies?"

Mickey pulled the padded envelope from his carry bag. Yvonne sighed. "He's down the back. Come along."

My heart pounded in my ears. My perception strobed, then resolved in psychedelic detail, so I saw everything at once. Yvonne had been painting on a flat board, fine white lines webbed across earth colored symbols and patterns. Surrounding us were huts built off the ground on pole platforms, roofed with woven branches, canvas, corrugated tin; homely things, cooking pots and skillets, a grill over campfire-blackened stones.

My brain's signals to move weren't reaching my legs. My throat closed. Mickey urged me on, not unkindly. "You come this far, you can do it." I concentrated on my knees not buckling.

CHAPTER 30

*I*n a hammock slung between two trees behind a hut at the clearing's farthest edge a man worked on something he held in his lap. His scraggly white hair hid his face. He was shirtless, his shoulders powerful and muscled, but his ribs showed above his concave stomach. He glanced at us and his attention zeroed in on the padded envelope Mickey carried.

"Oy, Croc, not a moment too soon, man! I was running low." His mouth contracted around missing teeth, one eye socket was sunken and closed. Hearing my father's voice come from that defiled visage was like the cruelest ventriloquism. He held up a carved wooden figure, a delicate, long-billed water bird less than a foot tall. "I've done a dozen jabiru to send back with you. Working on this last one."

The quirk of his grin cut me with familiarity. He dropped the bird, snatched the envelope Mickey gave him, and sliced it open with his carving tool, dumping the bubble packs and plastic bottles into his lap, counting them, holding them up to his single eye to read labels. He wrested the lid off a bottle, spilling pills in his haste, popped one pill into his mouth and swallowed it without water. Yvonne scooped the rest back into the envelope and slipped out of reach with it. Mickey prodded me toward the hammock with his hand against my back.

"Your show."

The man took up less room in the hammock than he should, something was out of proportion. He squinted to get me into focus and my father was there in that keen blue eye. "I know you from somewhere." He sounded suspicious. This was never how I pictured our reunion.

"Daddy …" I choked on the word. "Daddy, it's Stevie."

He shifted in the hammock. I thought he'd get up and hug me. He sank back. Yvonne and Mickey were somewhere nearby, but I was aware of nothing but my father acting like a wounded animal searching for escape. "I'm not …" He started, then closed his eye.

"It's *me*, Daddy!" I raised my voice as though higher decibels could *make* him recognize me.

He scrabbled around himself, searched the pockets of his shorts, came up with nothing, finally gave up and looked warily at me. "You're not real. I've seen you here before, but so little and pretty. Those pills play silly buggers with my mind."

My dad raised his arms, to embrace me, I thought. I felt like I was walking on the moon, bounding to him gravity-free, but he fended me off with one strong hand on my chest, touched my chin with the other, talking under his breath, to himself more than to me. "You *are* real. Yes, yes, I see you now … there's something of your mother in your manner, in your face." Then, louder, faster, reproaching. "How did you find me? Is *she* here?"

He stopped dead. "No, don't look!"

I gasped and drew back, seeing where his legs should have been, the space they didn't take up in the hammock. My dad had no feet, no calves, no knees, his thighs ended in stubs. I couldn't hide my horror, horror reflected in my father's face. His voice went hollow.

"You weren't supposed to know, *not ever*. I wanted you to remember me whole, not like this, half a man. Let you think Sam Wales died a hero fighting the storm. I could've won, but the mast broke, the sea threw me overboard. The sharks took my legs, *my legs!* I didn't know I was alive myself for months, unconscious in Yvonne's camp on the beach. She saved me."

I remembered my nightmares, sharks rising to blood. I'd believed against logic it hadn't ended there; I'd never imagined this. Dad searched his pockets. Phlegmy and whining, he called out to Yvonne. She came with two pills and a cup of water this time. He lay back in the hammock. Yvonne stroked his forehead. "Hasn't slept for three nights. He'll be calmer when he wakes up."

We left my father sleeping. Mickey unloaded our cargo and Yvonne organized it in the huts. I knelt absorbed in Yvonne's painting, its lines and dots, dimensions beneath its surface. I may have appeared to be thinking, but I wasn't. I was doing thinking's opposite, my mind gone blank. I had the sense I was watched, not by Mickey or Yvonne, who looked carefully through me if their eyes turned in my direction; not by my dad, unconscious in his hammock. Sunset flared. Evening settled. The clearing's edge dematerialized into darkness, became defined by calling, chittering, splashing of things that crept and slithered and swam invisibly in the loud night.

Yvonne built a small wood fire that crackled beneath her grill. I expected exotic bush tucker. Perhaps on another day we would have had file snake, or kangaroo, or barramundi, but from the groceries Mickey had brought, Yvonne created lemon chicken, simmered with herbs and rice in an iron skillet. My mind didn't register hunger, but my body knew better. I salivated at the cooking smells. The three of us gathered, sitting cross-legged on woven reed mats, and Yvonne passed full bowls to Mickey and me.

Someone joined us, standing outside the firelight's radius. Yvonne put more sticks on the fire and I saw it was a boy, nearly a young man. A rough-haired yellowish dog leaned against his knees. Yvonne held out another bowl. "Take that to your father. Try to get him to eat some." Yvonne wasn't speaking to me. She was speaking to the shadow boy. My world convulsed, like living through an earthquake. He reached into the firelight to take the bowl and disappeared with it and the dog.

Mickey yawned loudly and made an unnecessary stir about getting to his feet. "Ta, Yvonne. You're a finer cook than Gav any day. Stevie, I've put your swag over there in that second house. Use the mozzie net when you turn in. I'm for some kip. We'll be leaving early tomorrow."

"Tomorrow? Micky, I …"

He left me with Yvonne. I hated her, the witch who'd held my dad prisoner all these years. I tried to keep the bitterness out of my voice. "That boy, who is he?" It was a pointless question. "I mean, what's his name?"

The dying flames reflected in Yvonne's eyes and the white shell necklace she wore. "That's Yiwun. He's a good boy, good to his mum and dad."

"He's lucky."

"Lucky?"

"He's grown up with his dad."

"Not the *right* dad, according to some, but we've taught him to respect the traditions. Your brother will stay his distance from you, like our old ones say he should."

My brother. That brought me to a full stop. *I have a brother.* I'd wondered sometimes what having a brother would be like, but my imaginings could never have brought me here. I hated Yiwun, too, for existing. Everything was Yvonne's fault. "Dad says you saved his life. I have to be grateful to you."

Yvonne twisted the shell necklace in her fingers and spoke into the fire. "Sometimes he is, too, when he remembers himself. It was better before the drugs, but I can't blame him. People think if you've got no legs they can't hurt. His legs went into a shark belly, but the leg-shaped pain stayed in him. A doctor in Brisbane buys our artwork. Me, he pays in money, but he started paying for your father's birds in pain pills. Now the doctor's paying *me* less every time, because we need more and more and they're expensive. If I take the pills away your father goes mental for them."

Her passivity disgusted me. "You have to do something!"

"Yiwun says he'll go to the city and kill the doctor. That won't help, they'll send him to prison and leave me alone with a crazy man. The biggest town Yiwun's seen is Jabiru.

I went to boarding school in Brisbane, so I know how hard a city can be."

"But, can't you take my dad to a different doctor?"

"I could. I could have Croc take him out of here. Then what? He's illegal. Immigration would catch him. Where could he go, a man like that? We've been exposed to the uranium. How much time do any of us have? We don't know. We need to spend it together."

Together. It was what I'd always wanted to be with my dad. Yvonne had been foolish to reveal to me the underbelly of their existence. If she wouldn't let me take my dad, I could bring immigration authorities here and force him to go home with me. I could report the doctor and stop the pharmaceuticals, or better, find the doctor, threaten to report him, and get control of the drugs myself. Dad would agree to anything then.

I would be Dad's *real* hero. He'd given up on liberation, been brainwashed by Yvonne into fearing the outside world. *I* would rescue him, take him home for high-tech prostheses, plastic surgery, rehab. He would be the man from my childhood, strong, vigorous and handsome.

I said goodnight and left Yvonne watching the embers. Mostly by feel, I found my swag, with Myrna's sleeping bag rolled out, on the shelter platform where Mickey had said it would be. I took off my shoes and stole on barefoot across the sandy clearing. I believed in my powers of persuasion; my dad would leave with me if we could talk alone. Above the clearing the sky sang with stars that echoed Yvonne's painting. From near the trees, out of the starlight, I saw their faint illumination rounding my dad's shape, made of shadow, sitting in his hammock. But another shadow, boy-shaped, sat beside him. The dog was nowhere to be seen, off on its own nighttime business.

Yiwun gave the hammock an occasional push with one foot, rocking it while he and my dad talked in a language I didn't know. Their conversation was desultory. The boy said something that made my dad chuckle, though they both sounded melancholy. I couldn't see Dad's disfigurement, could only hear the voice I'd longed for so desperately, my memory's soundtrack. At last I hear it in real time, except he's speaking in a foreign tongue and not to me.

I spied on them, uselessly. What my dad and I had shared in the first years of my life had been everything to me, a brief interval to him, half-forgotten. He'd moved on. I hadn't been deliberately disowned, I'd been *unfathered*. My jealous anguish as I watched him with Yiwun was too big to bear. I'd go mad trying to hold it. In finding him, I'd lost hope. I wanted to die, to end my pain right there. A venomous snake would do. They would find my corpse in the morning, crawling with ants. He would see what *he'd* lost in abandoning me. Let him suffer the guilt.

Something aglow invaded my hiding place. I stumbled deeper into the dark to shake it, but I couldn't. It stayed with me—*was* me! White light filled my palms. I hid them against my chest, sure I was already mad. The light passed inside from my hands to my heart. Now I couldn't see it, but I *felt* it. Improbably, it calmed me, but I couldn't take away my own pain, at least, not this kind of pain. I slunk away. This was a new and wretched reality, not the end of my life, after all.

Kristina Bak

CHAPTER 31

I slept dreamlessly, perhaps because no dream could be stranger than where I woke. The sky domed over the clearing was beginning to pearl. Performing the morning "necessaries" took courage here, where snakes not lurking around my ankles might drop from the trees. I dressed and rolled my sleeping swag. Yvonne was up boiling tea and putting damper to bake in a Dutch oven. I sat at her cooking fire, a pale column of astringent-smelling smoke between us. She looked aside, distracted from her tasks. I followed her glance and saw the dog come trotting. Behind him walked my dad.

Walked was an inadequate term for his tortuous advance. He'd strapped on two hand-carved and polished pegs, like a movie pirate's, his leg stumps resting in their cushioned tops. With his sinewy arms, he propelled himself forward on aluminum crutches. A woven carry bag dangled from one. A red bandana he'd tied over his missing eye accentuated the pirate impression. He'd combed his hair and wore a batik print shirt hanging loose over his shorts. My heart set up a pounding so hard my every bone and organ shook with it.

Yiwun came with a bamboo stool. Averting his face from me, he helped our father seat himself on it, then took off toward the billabong with his dog. Yvonne gave us sugary tea and damper and left us alone. Our lives' accounts to unfold and none of it mattered except that we were together, going on from where we were, not from where we'd been before. Dad tasted his tea and flinched at its heat. He turned his eye like a faceted sapphire on me. I covered my scar.

"Your mom?"

Did he want to hear she waited for him? I sorted the possible answers in my mind. "She's met someone, she seems happy."

He nodded at that as news about a stranger, which by now she practically was. "And what have you done?"

"I work in a stable, with horses."

"Good, honest labor."

"I'm almost done with school."

"That's essential, education. Yiwun was boarding at a mission, doing well, until the mine spill closed it. We're waiting to see what happens. Might be we'll shift east to where they still have schools." One leg jumped in its peg. He sucked in his breath and slopped tea onto his shirt front. A tear slid into a crevice on his cheek. The leg spasmed again. He grimaced and started the patting-his-pockets routine, coming up with nothing.

If my father refused to be rescued, to be what I'd always dreamed he would be when I found him, there was one thing I believed I could do for him. But did I want to? Didn't he deserve his suffering? Could I *reverse* my power, make it go the other way, intensify his torment? Was that why I'd come, to punish him? I'd learned the hard way satisfaction from inflicting pain didn't last, but cruelty could be like a drug, hoping a little more and a little more could be enough. My heart argued against it.

"Daddy." I savored the word's taste. "Daddy, I have to leave soon."

This time he held out his arms for real. I went to him and he hugged me awkwardly from his chair, but with such strength my breath rushed out of me. I pressed my palms flat on his back behind his heart, his body hot through his shirt. His pain invaded me, torture beyond anything I'd imagined, like rats gnawing my leg bones from the inside. Reflexively, light bloomed in the center of my brain, raced down my spine, out my arms through my hands and fingers, suffusing every nerve cell, his and mine.

I was there in his arms, yet I wasn't. I saw us from above, two dots in a clearing in the vast bushland, then I rose higher. Lost in Earth's spinning continents and seas and the turbulent stars I'd seen in the night, I was nowhere or everywhere, a second or a lifetime, light, energy.

My father released me and my consciousness flowed in to reinhabit my body. One of us must have cried out because Yvonne came quickly with Dad's pills. He rubbed his maimed thighs for phantom pain that was no longer there. "I … I don't need those. Not right now." Yvonne gave us both a wide-eyed look and retreated with them before he could change his mind.

Mickey joined us at the fire for his breakfast. "Best eat, Stevie. We won't be getting back to the store until teatime."

Mickey was right about Yvonne's cooking, her damper was lighter and tastier than Gav's. I sat close beside my dad's stool while we ate, but we had nothing to say that was more important than sitting near each other. Our worlds' intersection had been marked and crossed and was already becoming part of our divergent stories.

After breakfast, Yvonne brought out paintings and carvings carefully wrapped for delivery to their Brisbane doctor. Mickey wrote her receipts for each and they secured them in the boat. When they were done, Mickey called me and I stood to go.

"Wait, Stevie. I have something for you." From his bag, my dad drew the stilt-legged bird he'd been carving, the jabiru. He gave it to me. "Sorry there's a bit unfinished on its belly there, but more by feel. It blends with the wings to look at."

The wood was warm and smooth to my fingers, the unfinished part like a story to be continued. "Thank you, Daddy. I love it." *I love you* was what I wanted to say. Maybe what he wanted to say, too. "I'll come back."

He rubbed his empty hands together. "One way or another, we won't be *here*. Write to me. Send word to Yvonne, care of the Border Store. They'll find us."

"You can call me, or write to me at home, too. Wait a sec." With Mickey's marker, I printed my phone number and, in case he'd forgotten it, our island address on the back of a receipt.

He took the paper, held it to his eye. "Your mom's address? I can't do that, Stevie. Never."

"I'll be there, for if you change your mind."

I gathered my pack and swag and followed Mickey. In my last look back from the clearing's edge, Dad sat like a king on a flimsy bamboo throne, one hand raised to me in what I chose to take as a blessing, all he had remaining to offer me. Had I done all I could for him? His affliction with the drugs wouldn't be over, it wasn't that easy, but with his pain gone, he had a fighting chance. Having found him, what did *I* have? I was going home alone.

Yvonne waited by the boat. I struggled to find words to thank her for her hospitality, however imposed. It wasn't my place to thank her for rescuing Dad; he'd become more hers than mine. Anything I could say would be wrong. She salved my discomfiture by speaking first.

"Everybody needs to know their father. You did right to search him out. He's better for it, too, I think." With both hands, Yvonne lifted off her shell necklace, like a string of moons. With one graceful gesture, she looped the necklace over my head and settled it around my neck.

She turned to Mickey, not leaving room for my thanks. "Hey, Croc Man, you tell that Honey we mob want to see her next!"

They fell to joking in their own language. I could make out only "… Dickie Morgan." Yvonne waded into the billabong and shoved us off. As Mickey poled, her laughter faded behind us.

I'd grown used to the bush sounds, but we'd gone a few twists along the stream when we heard a new one. I recognized the didgeridoo, rhythm like heartbeats of giants, howls and yips, endless, circular.

Mickey explained. "That's Yiwun, saying goodbye."

CHAPTER 32

I was barely aware of the crocodiles on our trip down-river or being dive-bombed by Mickey's sea eagle friend. I felt torn in two. I sat with my arms wrapped around my belly to keep my guts from spilling out. In my mind, I was reliving every moment with my dad to guarantee it lodged in my memory forever. The one time I became hyper-alert was when, on a muddy bank, I glimpsed a large black and white stork with a long black bill and orange legs, like my dad's gift come alive.

Memory airbrushes blemishes, softens edges, fractures and yellows-over with time the way old oil paintings do. Without my phone, I hadn't been able to take Dad's photo.

I'd do my own verbal airbrushing when I told Mom, but I'd force myself to keep my personal memory unvarnished.

Mickey seemed lost in his own thoughts, too. His experience and memories were so different from mine, I had no way of understanding him.

When the border dock came in sight, more than half the day had passed. Richard Morgan waited there, lounged across the front seats of an old open-topped Jeep, his hat tipped over his face, boots propped, arms folded. Mickey called to him. By the time we pulled alongside, he was vertical. He gave me a hand ashore. He managed to look satiated and devastated at the same time, pleased with himself but shadowed around the eyes with sleeplessness or worry, or both. He looked at my chest. I prepared to be offended before he reached out and with one finger touched Yvonne's necklace. "You found what you came for?"

"I did."

"Good on'ya."

"Did you?"

"Brat! Close enough. We're going now. I can get us on a late Sydney flight, but we have to leave for Darwin straightaway."

"I can't, I need a shower, I stink. My things are at the motel."

"You'll smell better than half the mob in economy class and I've got your bag right here."

My bag was on the seat. I unzipped it. My phone was neatly packed on top of my clothes.

Morgan got in and started the Jeep. "Don't forget Myrna's swag. We'll drop it off at Jack's. Kiss Croc Man goodbye." Mickey passed me the swag and my backpack and climbed hastily back into the boat. Morgan laughed and waved to him. "Quint's coming to pick you up in time for tea, mate."

My stomach growled. "We haven't eaten since breakfast!"

"Meat pies in the cooler from Gav. He wishes you safe travels."

I'd exhausted my arguments. Other than my immense lust for a soapy shower, what reason did I have to go back to the Border Store except to thank Gav and Quint, and Gerry if he was around. Mickey could relay my message. I called down to him in the boat. "*Croc Man*, thank you! Will you tell Gerry and Quint and …"

Mickey beamed, what little of his face I could see beneath his hat and behind his glasses. "I'll tell them, Stevie. Don't forget us."

Perhaps we understood each other better than I suspected. I climbed into the Jeep's passenger seat, Morgan gunned the engine and we skidded out onto the road. We were well on our way when I remembered. "I didn't pay them, any of them."

"Don't you dare, they'd never forgive you."

The Jeep rode rough over the deteriorating highway, Morgan pushing it hard without regard for the condition of either. With one hand he flipped open the cooler on the floor behind him for a meat pie wrapped in foil he gave to me and a can of beer for himself. The pie was salty and greasy, the meat tough and unidentifiable, its juices dripping onto my khakis as I bolted it—pig, buffalo, crocodile, whatever it was. The detective seemed amused by my appetite.

"It's good I'm getting you out before you go altogether troppo on us. Never be fit for civilized company."

"Are you including yourself in that class?"

"Depends on how you measure it. Perhaps I need to redefine my terms."

"Whose Jeep is this?" He didn't answer right away. I thought he hadn't heard me over the engine noise and the wind from our speed buffeting our ears.

"Mine. I left in a bit of a rush last time, helicoptered. Quint's kept the Jeep for me till now."

"You're leaving in a rush this time, too."

"As may be. I dislike confrontation and I've annoyed Gerry. He's banished me from the borderlands again."

I'd had plenty of hints as to how "Dickie" might annoy people. I didn't ask for details. "Why didn't you warn me, about my dad?"

"I wasn't sure it was him. You don't know the name he goes by, do you?"

My meat pie threatened to come back up. He was right, Dad hadn't told me. Official Northern Territory sources said the man named Sam Wales was dead. I didn't know what to call him. He and Yvonne could disappear further into Arnhem Land, up a different creek, off a different river and unless they wanted me to find them, I never would.

"You tell me."

"That depends on the day and the need. Apparently he has a string of Yolngu names. He was *wakingu*, a person belonging nowhere and to no one, without relations to care for him and therefore nameless when Yvonne saved him. He's been gifted with names over time. Yvonne's people gave her grief when she had his child, so they went walkabout and usually go by 'white names' now, but those can change in a minute. The balanda bureaucracy's fallen apart since the mine closed. The traditional owners' council keeps track of people and if they don't want to expose them, they don't. Educated, creative people like Yvonne can live in either world. She's made her choice."

"But Gav and Quint and Mickey, they're here for the long term, right? My father said I could send him letters through them, through the Border Store."

We passed cone-shaped termite mounds taller than people, if there'd been any in sight. I waited for an answer Morgan was slow to give.

"Gav's living in dreamland and Quint's waiting for him to see the light. One more season and he'll catch on, there won't be any more happy tourists. Even backpackers know to avoid radioactive waste. Croc Man has his own ways and his own worries. He could be gone tomorrow. I wouldn't spend another day here myself if I were you, or me, for that matter, if I had any sense."

"Is that why you're driving so fast?"

"I want to catch that river crossing in daylight. I'm not in the mood to meet another croc. In the night you can see their eyes glimmer. Fantastic sight long as you're not in the water with them."

Its banks were cloaked in evening shadows when we got there, but I could see the river had subsided since we'd crossed it with Jack. Richard Morgan accelerated; water sprayed to either side, a funhouse ride without the fun. He pulled up on dry land looking pleased with himself and popped open another beer. "More pie, Stevie?" We were far from Darwin, but the river crossing marked a boundary between dreaming and awake. Eating Gav's meat pie stuffed with who-knows-what bush creature was suddenly inconceivable to me.

Night descended with its usual abruptness. The visible world shrank to what we could see by our headlight beams: an orange-colored dingo trotting by the roadside, poisonous invasive cane toads looking like animated cow pats the detective squashed grossly beneath his tires, a magnificent owl that flew straight toward us, lifting at the last moment to skim over our heads. Once we slewed to a stop for a fat black python so long it blocked two lanes. I watched, spellbound, as it took its own time to glide across and vanish. We picked up speed on the smoother stretches, braking and swerving a couple of times when kangaroos bounded from the darkness. The sultry night air smelled of eucalyptus and dust.

Nightlife in Darwin was in full swing when we arrived. Light, pandemonium, and drinkers spilled from pubs. I expected we'd stop at Jack and Myrna's. Instead, we went straight to the airport and left the Jeep in the parking lot.

"Jack can pick it up. We're out of time." Richard Morgan hurried me inside the terminal and did some quick work with credit cards, police ID, and my passport at the check-in counter.

This plane was smaller than the one we'd flown north on. I was glad our seats were four rows apart, though the privacy I wanted to check my calls was still in short supply. In my row, the window position was held by a man in a business suit who overflowed it by a good thirty pounds and smelled worse than I figured I did. In the aisle seat a teenaged girl, superbly styled, made up and perfumed, watched the safety instructions being shown on the seat back screen. She looked enthralled, which no one who had flown before would be at that particular programming. She appeared unfazed by my just-out-of-the-bush state. It had to be a Darwin thing. She tore herself from the riveting video seat belt demonstration.

"You going to Sydney? That's where I'm going, to be a model. Well, I'm going to work in a shop, too, but that'll be my day job."

Silly me, I thought modeling *was* a day job. Depends on what kind of modeling, I supposed. I wondered, briefly, what she was getting herself into. None of my business. The window man dominated the armrest on my left like an occupying army and the model-to-be gripped the one on my right with gorgeously manicured claws. Airborne I put on headphones for a movie and slept before the title rolled.

CHAPTER 33

We landed in Sydney and reclaimed the detective's city car from the parking garage. It was a decent Chinese hybrid littered with used cups and sticky fast-food wrappers. Too early to get into my hostel, we drove to a twenty-four-hour cafe in Newtown for predawn breakfast. It was a pitiless place for the sleep-deprived, every surface hard and glaring, an audio loop that could be titled Music-to-Eat-and-Get-Out-By flaunting the fact that there was slim choice of breakfast venues before 4:00 a.m. I washed as well as I could in the restroom, modest under the fish-eyed security camera recording whatever insomniacs got up to in there. My facial scabs were embellished now by fresh insect bites. My hair was flattened and tangled by three days of hat wearing and no way comb-able.

I took comfort that Richard Morgan fared worse, both eyes bruised-looking, his stubble gone from passably rakish to seedy, red capillaries fertilized by alcohol sprouting on his nose. His breath, gusting across the table with his words, wasn't great.

"We're finished, you know. As soon as it's daylight I'm dropping you at the hostel. I suggest you head home overseas before any more complications arise."

So he was playing smart-ass cop again, now that we were back in Sydney. He couldn't intimidate me anymore. "Did I not say thank you? Believe me, I appreciate your help, but I'll survive without a bodyguard now. And what do you mean, 'complications'?"

He made a face at the taste of his coffee. "As it happens, I don't know, but there's always something. Nothing really ends."

"Finding my dad, that's an end."

"I suppose it may seem that way."

Our breakfasts came, delivered by a jigging boy, out of his mind on something he'd taken to keep himself awake through the night shift. We plowed through the food. My omelet was as greasy as Gav's meat pies, but I had a better idea what might be in it.

We made halting progress driving to Balmain through the first commuters. Sun gilded the tops of buildings when we stopped at the curb in front of the hostel. Richard Morgan offered his hand. I took it and he clasped mine hard. "You're stubborn and brave—dicey combination. Take care of yourself."

"I could say the same of you, and some other things, but I won't."

He released me. "Thanks to you, I now have an undeserved reputation to maintain. I'll have to work."

I surprised us both planting a kiss on his cheek before I got out. "Thank Jack and Myrna for me."

The detective saluted. "Do ask in the unlikely event I can help again. Mind you, I already regret saying that." I closed the car door and he drove away looking like death. Alone and sleep-deprived on the sidewalk at sunrise again, I had a sense of déjà vu. I'd come full circle.

Part Four

Escape

CHAPTER 34

I splurged on a taxi from the island's ferry dock. On my flight north and east over the Pacific, home had been a beacon calling me. I couldn't tolerate delay. Fears yammered in my mind—my mom was glad I was gone; she hadn't missed me and loved James best now. I was ashamed of that last one. Couldn't I be more mature and high-minded? They didn't know to expect me. My weaker self wanted to catch them by surprise, no time to compose a scenario for my consumption. I needed raw truth, the way it had been when I barged into Dad's camp.

I'd never understood an ordinary life. Or did I mean normal? And did normal equate with good? That question was like a treadmill for me, I could go on with it for hours and never get anywhere. My mom was the most normal person I knew. If normalcy were contagious, I should have caught it by now. Was my worry that normal happiness with James would alienate her from me, the way Dad was alienated by his Australian family? I couldn't allow myself to be that selfish and besides, the circumstances were as different as they could be.

What would happen now? *Could* I be ordinary? Could I deliberately forget my pain-healing gift? That might be a blessing. No, forgotten it would be like a crocodile on the river, quiet as a log, until it wasn't. What do you do with something like this? Pain drove people to desperate acts; fear of pain made them crazy. What would happen if others found out what I could do? What would they demand of me? What if I failed them?

The taxi turned down Towhee Street. I had the driver let me off before our driveway. Behind a neighbor's madrona tree, I adjusted my smile and breathed. *Ready.* Why couldn't it be uncomplicated, the way other people's lives were: *Hi, Mom, I'm home, good to see you?* Over the last few days, I'd sent schmaltzy messages, pictures of a farewell trip with Fiona and Graham to Bondi Beach, the Sydney skyline, rainbow lorikeets, calming enough my mom hadn't asked for more. Most likely, she assumed I'd failed my quest.

Mom's delight at my return was tempered by too many past disappointments, but it was there in her eyes and so were her questions. James greeted me with warmth that seemed genuine and contrived a task at his house that couldn't wait until morning. He left the two of us wandering the backyard garden in the long summer twilight, so different from the tropics' sudden nightfall. The fragrance of lilies grew intense, their blooms ghostly.

I was glad our faces were hard to see in the gathering night, like the flowers. I'd plotted out nice ways to begin, what to avoid, lies I didn't call lies. She was on to me.

"Did you find him?"

"What do you think?"

"I think you'd best be straight with me for once in your life, Stevie Colleen. I didn't want you to go, I didn't want you hurt any more, but I know you uncovered something by how little you've told."

"Yes."

"Yes, what?"

"Yes, him."

"Alive?"

"Alive."

She shook her fists at the sky. "That bastard! I'm waiting, grieving, giving up hope. He abandoned me."

"Abandoned *us*, Mom, but it's not that simple."

"Oh, of course not. It's *complicated*. Isn't that what they say when they get caught? And now he's got you to make excuses for him."

I was glad she was angry. She could be angry for me, too, the way I hadn't been able to be when I saw him. "Mom, listen to me! I'm not saying it was right, what he did, but he had his reasons. For one thing, he thought he was protecting us from himself, from who he's become."

Arduous to me in the unearthing, the facts took only minutes to relate. I left the Sydney part for another time. When I'd finished, damp chill drove us inside. I went unwillingly, not wanting to see my mom's expression in the lamplight. She'd shed tears in the garden, her eyes were red and wet, but she looked younger. Whatever had held the hurt under her skin had let go. She brushed my hair from my face, let her fingers trace my scar. "Thank you, sweetheart. I'm going to bed now. I need to be alone."

That was it? No raging, no pouring a drink? No demanding more accounting on my part? How could everyone surprise me? My assumptions had proven wrong so often I should expect them to be by now. I couldn't think about it jet-lagged; it would have to wait until the rest of me caught up with my body.

Yvonne's shell necklace glowed on the dresser beside my old guardian angel nightlight. My clean nightgown lay in its drawer like a memory from another life. From habit I checked for messages before bed. I had one from Fiona and Graham, waving to me. I saved it to show Mom in the morning. I opened one other, from an unfamiliar generic address—a tattooed wolf's face, unsteady and distorted by the video angle, muscles beneath it flexing, an ephemeral message that erased itself in seconds. My heart lurched before my brain caught what it meant. Nate was out there, somewhere, thinking of me. Maybe Richard Morgan was right, nothing ever ends.

CHAPTER 35

Jupiter nudged my chest with his heavy, blazed fore-head. Pegasus, the palomino, nibbled an apple, tick-ling my hand with his velvety lips. Chestnut Penny, the bony swayback, shoved in snorting grassy breath. The pot-bellied miniature horse, Lilliput, and his inseparable Clydesdale companion, Lightning, who was like anything but, grazed the knee-deep timothy nearby, twitching their skin and flicking their tails at flies. Paint arched her neck over the fence from the next pasture, waving her ears like semaphores signaling for attention.

Bumping shoulders with the horses, I felt safe, an animal among animals, no matter Paint had nearly killed me. That had been my fault, flouting Sierra's warning, arrogant in my own power. I'd sworn not to repeat that arrogance, yet I had, with Raven. Sierra knew nothing about that. She'd given me one more chance, my old job caring for the horses, as long as I kept my distance from Paint. Starved and tortured before her rescue, the pinto had grown sleek. She was skittish; Sierra permitted no one alone with her. I knew she meant not even close, but Paint whickered, telling me it was time for reconciliation.

The horses had a prodigious wordless vocabulary. They understood and responded without deceit, the only beings I trusted with my secret. When we were alone I tested its limits. I touched their pain and channeled it from their arthritic skeletons and aging organs until they rested at ease. Only they and I knew. As long as I owned my secret, no one could make me do anything with it, or judge me for it.

The healthy and compliant younger horses—Star, Queenie, Belle, Pedro and Major—were with Sierra in the covered arena on the far side of the stables, earning their hay providing equine therapy for inner-city summer school kids. Here in the sunny hillside meadow with the old, retired horses, all was peaceful. Doves cooed in a maple tree, a crow cawed from the top of a cedar in the surrounding woods, a rabbit sat on its haunches nearby gobbling clover. Paint stamped a hoof. I pushed through the circle of old horses and approached her, calling endearments. She shifted impatiently. I wouldn't go through the fence. I'd only touch her, if she let me.

My pant legs swished in the grass. Paint turned her head to focus one blue eye on me. White showed around it, as it had the day she trampled my head. I offered my right hand to her, palm up. Her look softened, she faced me directly and lowered her nose over the fence rail. So close.

Kristina Bak

With a snort, Paint tossed her head. I spun around to see what had startled her. A girl climbed the rise from the stable office, long hair lifted by the breeze and backlit by the afternoon sun so it flared around her like an angel's halo. She edged around the horses. Winter Martin, not, definitely *not*, an angel. How dare my ex-best-friend trespass onto my happy place! She gave me one of her too-sincere-to-be-true smiles.

"Hey, Stevie!"

I waited for an explanation. Winter's smile died and she tried a new expression. This one, I gathered, was meant to project *contrite*. "Okay, I'm cool with you're not happy to see me, but I'm not all that happy to be here, either. It's community service, mandated, twelve hours and probation."

"What'd you do, murder somebody?"

"Funny. Nothing. I borrowed some earrings from that touristy shop near the ferry dock."

"Why? Your parents buy you anything you want."

"I didn't *want* them, I was going to put them back. It was a dare. They called it shoplifting."

"So, *here*, of all places?"

"None of the other kids from school will see me, not like picking up trash along the highway or something. Did you know they call you 'Horsegirl' now? Your hair looks good parted on the side. Way better than when you shaved it off. That was *not* a good look."

I covered my left cheek, where my hair curtained the scar, but Winter's short attention span hadn't changed. She rolled her eyes at the sight of my hands, un-manicured and reddened, probably the first she'd seen of a person who did physical work. The horses had gathered around us, curious.

Jupiter braced his legs and heedlessly unloosed a massive urine stream. Winter squealed when she bumped into Pegasus, who was sniffing her from behind. "Do they bite?"

I laughed. "Sure. See their big teeth? They kick, too."

Winter fronted up to me, hands on her hips. I smelled her coconut hair conditioner. "So I'm afraid of horses! I'm more afraid of creepy juvie guys on the community service crews. I chose this place because I knew you were here and I'd be safe with you."

"That's taking a lot for granted."

"Look, can we drop that episode with the hair lights?"

"Are you saying you're sorry?"

"You're the one who pulled mine out, with half my hair! I mean, yeah, sure, nobody wears those things now. It was a childish popularity game."

"A nasty one. You were a total bitch to me, you and your girl gang."

"They're not my gang." Winter's voice quavered. "They got me caught taking the earrings. You'd never have betrayed me like that."

Her display of vulnerability moved me, against my better judgement. I knew she planned to go to acting school. I could never detect when, if ever, she was authentic. I wondered if *she* could.

"You can help clean the stables." This time I was in charge, not drifting in Winter's wake.

Winter had dressed down in an old shirt and frayed denim shorts, but her creamy skin was perfect, her nails glossed ivory. In the empty stables, I gave her a push broom. She made ineffectual thrusts with it, while I applied another to vigorously sweeping out a stall.

"Have you seen a broom before, Winter? Shall I show you how to use that one or can you figure it out for yourself?"

She leaned on hers, watching me work. "You didn't used to be sarcastic. Remember how I helped you fit in at kindergarten when you came back, when you peed your pants in class? Eww, that was embarrassing."

I kept sweeping. "Came back?"

"From when you disappeared. We kids got in trouble if we talked about it. Nobody ever figured out where you'd been. They said you didn't know. It was like you were gone, then you were home. I asked you, when we were little, but you wouldn't say a word."

Gone? Paint's kick had robbed me of other things, but there'd already been a hole in my childhood memories. Could I trust Winter as an information source? She was self-involved and infuriating, but not stupid. I blasted the floor with the hose, making her move, and sent her to pretend to work at the opposite end of the building, so I wouldn't have to talk.

Winter left the minute her two hours were up. "Ten more to go. See you next week, Stevie."

I imagined Pegasus growing wings like his namesake and flying me into the sky, over the Olympic Mountains, away from having to see Winter, or listen to her. What did she *mean* about my having "disappeared?"

———

I sat on my bed staring at my tablet. I wished for Hero, wagging and doggie-smelling beside me. Instead, the clean scent of a neighbor's freshly mown lawn drifted in on the evening air that stirred my gauzy curtains. My finger hovered over my lit-up screen. The Internet search for my dad had been wasted energy. His life in Australia depended on his being officially dead. I had only found him by going into the *real* world. As for myself, a million times I'd been tempted to research "people who heal pain with their touch" to try finding someone else like me, but I'd been petrified by the online cruelty of my peers and other trolls. My resistance verged on full-blown phobia. No telling who might backtrack my digital footprints once I showed interest. Besides, this pain-healing might be a passing thing I would outgrow the way I'd outgrown lisping, or skipping everywhere when I was a kid.

But had I really "disappeared" the way Winter said? Afraid of the trail I'd leave, I'd never explored my online self. Afraid of what? Of being a freak and friendless? That came pretty close to describing my life since Nate left. What did I have to lose? I entered my name and hit the search icon.

I found the initial alert and, further in, my name on a list with other missing kids. How could there be so many? What Winter had claimed was true. As a five-year-old I'd been reported crawling under our back fence and disappearing without a trace one rainy spring evening. I'd reappeared at my grieving mother's door one night that fall, just as inexplicably, with a dog I called Hero. I ran across a celebratory article about my return in the local island media. It sounded lukewarm with the revelation no details would be forthcoming, due to my amnesia. The Seattle press hadn't bothered to report it. Making the information more elusive, my name had been spelled different ways. Apparently, *found* children make dull news feed if nothing grisly happened to them. There are always more lost children to report, more newsworthy horrors.

In the "before" poster I'm a fragile fairy-like child in a flower print dress and white cotton candy hair. In a blurry video clip dated six months later, my mom gives the evil eye to whoever is behind the camera, whisking a skinny kid in a knit hat, the prodigal me, into the house.

Those uncanny visions that had begun erupting into my consciousness less than a year ago—I hadn't had one since Australia—were they any weirder than this blackout in my memory? Not knowing, I needed facts.

Mom brought takeout for dinner. James was visiting his son in California, so she dropped all guise of domesticity, and her realtor persona, as she kicked off her shoes.

There'd been so much my mom wouldn't talk about, the unsaid took up as much room as the said in our conversations. Her arguments against my going to Australia had been as much about how it was better *not* to know some things, as about the dangers of the trip. Mom had listened to my account when I first got back and never spoke of it since.

We were in the kitchen. She was dishing some Afro-Asian fusion yam-noodle thing from takeaway containers into bowls when I lost patience with not-knowing.

"Mom, is it true I ran away when I was five?"

She froze, a forkful of noodles midair. "Have you remembered something?"

"I saw Winter today. She told me."

Mom finished dishing up the noodles and brought the

bowls to the table, setting them down with uncommon care. Her lipstick, half worn-off, crept into lines around her lips I hadn't noticed before. "You want chili sauce?"

"No." We both sat and watched our noodles cool. "Mom?"

She ran one finger around the rim of her water glass. "We never knew whether you'd run away, or ... I was watching a movie in my bedroom with Damien. Remember Damien?"

"Not really. Kind of, now that you mention him."

"It was 2009. Your dad had been gone two years. Damien moved in to help when I fractured my wrist and, uh, sort of stayed. You never liked him."

I shrugged. "You were watching a movie, and then?"

"Then, when I went to make sure you were asleep, you were ... you were gone, like that." Mom snapped her fingers. "Your Dorothy slippers were gone, the glass slider to the deck ajar. We looked everywhere outside. It was pouring rain. I thought you'd hidden in the garden shed—it was supposed to be your playhouse then—but we couldn't find you anywhere. Damien showed me a hole beneath the fence, behind the hedge. He said a dog had dug through there earlier from the other side. He'd put a rock to block it, but the rock had been moved. It was feasible you *could* have moved it yourself." Mom had spoken fast, words gushing out. She broke off.

"What? Go on!"

"That's all we know. The rain washed out any footprints, or tire tracks. The houses on the far side of the fence were under construction then. Nobody lived back there. No witnesses."

"And the police?"

"The police questioned Damien, over and over. They said

Kristina Bak

my giving him an alibi meant next to nothing. Perpetrators persuade innocent mothers or wives or girlfriends to do that all the time. I went unhinged. I made a thousand flyers and put them up all over the island and on the ferries, forced them on everyone I met, threw them into the water for people on boats. I posted on the Internet, knocked on doors, got my friends to search everywhere with me, in empty buildings, under bushes and piles of brush and driftwood. No trace. After weeks, the police gave up on Damien. He said he'd had it. He packed his clothes and left. No loss. I kept asking God, *Why me? Why you?* Then I stopped speaking to God. I'd go to work, try to ignore the gossip and pity. I'd come home and drink until I passed out and call it sleep." She stopped. "I shouldn't be telling you all this."

I'd been clutching the table edge. I let go and flexed my fingers. "I have a right to know. If it happened to me, I should remember it, but I don't—nothing. And I never asked where we got Hero. He just *was*."

"Hero? Oh, he came home with you, but I don't know if he was the dog who dug the hole. He *did* match Damien's claim."

Neither of us had eaten a bite. I couldn't. Mom looked at her noodles as though they were worms, took her bowl to the sink, and dumped them into the garbage disposal. "I need a drink."

Never a good idea. "Mom ..."

In the living room, she poured herself a straight double bourbon. "Don't preach, Stevie. This is too hard."

Too hard for her? My jaws hurt from biting back my question. "Why didn't you tell me before?"

"You had night terrors. Neither of us slept a full night

for weeks. You couldn't adjust to being home. The doctors said there was no physical damage, no sign of assault. They referred us to Gena."

"What? Gena knows all this and she kept it from me, too?" Of course, the whole island knew except me; I'd been walking around a blind fool all these years.

"She said it was post-traumatic stress. Asking you where you'd been made it worse. Your unconscious blocked your memory to protect you. I agreed to let you remember at your own pace and you never did. We decided it was kinder, safer, to leave it at that. We didn't talk about it and pretty soon everyone else had other things to worry about and forgot." Mom sank into her chair by the fireplace, cradling her glass.

My "hallucinations" might be memories. Mom didn't need to know about them. I suspected she was holding things back from me too, possibly a lot.

"Sweetheart, I …

"Don't, Mom. I'm going to bed."

I bent and hugged her, the aroma of her perfume mixing with the bourbon fumes. I wanted to be little, to crawl into her lap and press my ear between her breasts where I could hear her heartbeat.

In the morning, Mom looked frazzled. I'd slept badly, too, but I'd made up my mind.

"Mom, I'm not going back to high school."

Mom sighed, ran one hand over her eyes. "I wish I were surprised. You'll miss your best school year."

"I'd rather die than go back. Okay, not die, but the best of unbearable is still awful."

She was gearing up to argue with me. I headed her off. "I talked to Gena." That was true. A few days before, I'd run into her in the ice cream aisle at the grocery store. We'd debated the merits of salted caramel vanilla versus chocolate hazelnut marble. If Mom wanted to believe I'd gone for more counseling, I'd let her. We assumed client confidentiality by now, so she wouldn't ask Gena, and she'd never notice a bill that never came. She was busy enough trying to pay the many that did.

Mom decreed high school was negotiable, but education was not. My school let me go as gladly as I bailed, breaking out of a system where I'd never fit in, and the counselor helped me over the bureaucratic hurdles. She fast-tracked my application to a U-Dub early entrance, high school completion program, based on my pre-brain-injury standardized test scores. What she didn't know about my lost math skills wouldn't hurt her. I didn't look back with nostalgia.

Mom gave one of her sighs and signed for my tuition loan when my acceptance arrived. In our free time for the rest of the summer, when she wasn't with James, she and I did things I'd loved as a child—picnicking on the beach, feeding the ducks at Arrow Point Park, visiting the art museums in the city. Mom insisted I take driving lessons, too. When I aced my test on the first try, we went out for pizza, our rough edges smoother.

CHAPTER 36

*M*ost of my introductory classes for the university's fall term happened online, but I'd registered for Life Drawing 101 and for studio art I had to show up. I got as much buzz from the novelty of setting foot on the Seattle campus as I had landing in Australia. I bought the required art supplies at the bookstore and carried them proudly across the quad to the venerable twentieth-century art building. Digital and video art ruled on the main floors. I found life-drawing exiled to the basement along with painting and ceramics. The drawing studio was lit with bright LEDs in the ceiling to make up for its lack of windows. A dozen or so other aspiring artists were chatting together, setting up at easels clustered around a low platform. I chose an unclaimed one and clipped my 18x24 drawing pad to its board. I arranged the colored oil sticks we were to use for drawing and waited, excited, avoiding eye contact.

Our professor sliced a route straight through us from the back of the room, soundless and swift as an owl, while a nondescript woman followed him in and, ignoring us, methodically shucked off her clothes. She took a pose sitting, legs crossed, on a chair on the platform, the professor apparently oblivious to her as anything more than a functional object. A couple of tiresome male students made inane jokes, acting like the model might be deaf as well as naked. I joined the majority in shammed sophistication—she wasn't naked, she was *nude*. She was *a nude*, not a woman.

Without ceremony, the professor told us to begin. I certainly wasn't in high school anymore, but that wasn't what made my heart thump. His eyes, scanning the room, caught and held mine. He resembled my dad in his younger years. Some trick of his broad shoulders, blond hair, and easy grin grabbed me in a way that must have shown in my posture or my face. I looked away quickly, swung my focus to the model and the blank white paper on my easel, and made my first tentative mark.

I might study digital art someday, making precise holograms do and be whatever I programmed, but the process seemed cold. I had an appetite for human imperfection and my brain loved the challenge of interpreting what my eyes saw—not just the shape, but the person—drawing by hand, translating their wholeness onto my paper. I was fascinated by life-drawing. It was difficult, messy and unpredictable, thus the *life* part.

———

Our models came from the economic fringes, various ages and versions of the male-female motif, taking off their clothes for money to live. Sometimes their bodies, especially the older ones in long poses, held pains that distracted me. I couldn't help sensing them and I had to suppress the impulse to touch and try to ease them as I could the horses' miseries. I'd leave class with color jammed beneath my nails from controlling that urge by squeezing the oil sticks as I drew.

Early in our term, the professor came to stand at my easel in his critique rounds. "Relax! Let yourself *flow* with the lines." He mimed the looser gesture. "Your body has to feel it, groove with it."

I did my best to imitate him until he snatched the oil stick from my hand and drew firm swirling lines on my paper, his shoulders and hips swaying close beside mine. "There, start over! I want to see you doing *that.*" He tore the sheet from my drawing pad. He returned my oil stick, the heat from his fingers on it. Everyone had witnessed my humiliation. I wouldn't let that happen again.

By our fifth week, I'd earned an occasional non-disapproving nod to my work from our professor, if he noticed me at all. One morning I caught a model studying *me.* She was mid-twenties, voluptuous, pretty in an unconventional way, small features centered in a full-moon-shaped face, striking turquoise eyes, thick bobbed hair neon pink. I kept drawing, but her scrutiny disturbed me. I'd seen those eyes somewhere before.

At the break, she wrapped herself in a thin robe and came to me in bouncy steps. She was a head shorter, beaming as though we were old friends. She held out both hands. "Stevie, it *is* you! I checked the class list."

I recoiled. She'd broken through that consensual barrier shielding us from our nudes.

Her smile grew strained. "It's *Ruby*! You don't recognize me? I didn't think I'd changed *that* much." She tightened the cord of her robe.

"No, I…" I busied myself at my easel, to keep it between us.

She came around it to stand beside me and look at what I'd drawn. "Nice work!" *The room telescoped sickeningly to nothing but Ruby and me. I felt my hand clamped in hers, my stomach aching and empty, my feet freezing, my teeth chattering in fear. She was a round-faced teenager with frizzy brown hair, her turquoise eyes framed in hard-edged eyeliner, looking down at me, saying, "You're smart for a little kid."*

I swallowed my nausea, my imagination run amok. I told myself this wasn't real. The vision dissolved.

Ruby's forehead creased. "Stevie, are you okay?"

"My memory …"

"Yeah, it's been a long time. Hey, it's so great to see you! Let's get together after this."

"I can't. I have to be somewhere."

Ruby looked crestfallen, then she brightened. "Let's do it next time. We've got a lot to catch up on."

Ruby returned to the platform and dropped her robe. I'd lied to her. Perhaps there wouldn't be a "next time." Models came and went.

I hung with the older and cooler art students in a lounge outside the studios—scavenged chairs and tables, a disreputable sofa, an old microwave. The place perpetually smelled of someone's heated-up lunch. My ignorance appealed to those who liked an audience for their radical ideas. I listened well and disclosed nothing. My normalcy detector had yet to be recalibrated for this environment; I wouldn't have known what to find shocking. Our subterranean lair had an air of unreality. I liked it down there where it was always night, where the concrete walls and windowless rooms offered respite from the hectic campus above ground.

I'd cut my work with the horses to weekends and Wednesdays. Sometimes after class I stayed in the art lounge for hours, drawing in my sketchbook, loath to emerge and re-engage with the day. Late one Thursday afternoon I was the last person there, inking a comic I'd created, head down in concentration over orderly squares filled with my intricate, crosshatched images. A shadow fell across my page.

"Let's see the drawing." My professor had made one of his feather-footed approaches. He bent over me in a friendly way. I angled my sketchbook, hoping for his approval. He shook his head. "Oh, Stevie, Stevie, they're like you, beautiful, but too controlled." He sounded rueful; I'd disappointed him. "You need to break those boxes, *feel* more, think less." He lowered his voice. "I can help you with that. Come into the studio; let's do an experiment."

I looked into his limpid, earnest eyes. Had he praised me or criticized? His smile had been rare and hard-won in class. Here it was all for me. Did I hesitate? For a second or two, but this man's full regard overwhelmed my instinct to be prudent. Besides, everyone knew the campus was stippled and strafed by security cameras, from stationary surveillance cams to bug-sized drones. The lights were off in the studio. I waited just inside the door for him to turn them on. Instead he shut the door behind us. I backed against it, clutching my sketchbook and pen. I couldn't see his face in the dark.

"Shall I help you relax?" His breath blew hot against my

Kristina Bak

ear. I didn't answer, but I didn't resist, either. He smelled of the citrus cleanser we used to wash the oil colors off our hands. He stroked my shoulders, caressed my neck. Without meaning to, I leaned into him for more. He kissed my cheek, then my lips. "Breathe. Breathe, Stevie."

"I can't." My heart was beating too hard.

He laughed softly, then paused. "How old *are* you, anyhow?"

"Seventeen … and-a-half."

"You look older!" He thrust me away, as though I'd deliberately tricked him. He unlatched the door and checked to see if anyone was coming, then urged me out. "Go on, go!"

I crammed my sketchbook into my backpack and fled upstairs, my knees weak and rubbery. I emerged from the underworld, the sun's low angle edging each brick on the quad with gold, stretching students' silhouettes stork-legged over them.

I replayed that sequence in my mind all the way home on the ferry. Mom gave me inquisitive looks over the books we read at dinner; I averted my eyes, afraid she could read *me*. I didn't see the words in my novel. My professor was the last thing I thought about that night and the first when I woke in the morning. Not his face, or his voice—his lips on mine and how I'd wanted it to stop and to go on. The only other guy I'd kissed was Nate. He was a boy, my professor was a *man*. I'd spoiled our moment by telling the truth, but age didn't have to matter between us; no one else had to know and I'd be eighteen soon enough. I felt chosen and special, until the next class.

———

Ruby was our model, reclining, draped with red cloth that caught highlights and challenged us to find her body contours. I expected some private sign or signal from my professor, but nothing had changed. He made his rounds with corrections and criticism, saying "nice" at my portrayal of the cloth's folds. I knew my drawing was clumsy from the weak effort I was giving it; I took his word as a secret message to me.

After class, I put away my oil sticks and wiped my hands slowly, anticipating a moment with him, alone. Ruby spoiled that. I'd inadvertently given her time to dress. Here she came wearing her voluminous black raincoat, carrying a fringed bag, her pink hair and turquoise eyes her only embellishments. "Coffee? I'll buy."

On the far side of the studio, my professor sniggered at something an older student said over a drawing portfolio. No point in waiting. I hoped my leaving with Ruby sent a message to him that I didn't care, though I did. I crossed the quad with Ruby through Puget Sound rain, too light to use an umbrella, too heavy to stay dry without one, to an off-campus coffee shop.

Ruby sat forward, elbows propped on a table barely large enough for our two cups. "You *don't* remember me, do you?"

I shook my head. "You look ... I don't know. I feel like I should. We've met before?"

Ruby's giggling fit made her choke on her coffee. People

stared. "Sorry, sorry. Yes, we've met, when you were a little girl. I owe you, conceivably, my life."

I knew I'd forgotten a lot, but this was drastic. What could she be playing at, a hoax? "Who *are* you?"

"I could show you my ID. It wouldn't prove a thing. You're the only person in the world who'd know me as Ruby now."

"Show me."

The person I knew as Ruby pawed through her bag and came up with a Nevada driver's license, with a photo that looked sufficiently like her, as a blonde, to be convincing. The birth date made her nine years older than me.

"If that one doesn't meet your standards, I've got others. Here—California, Pennsylvania. Hawaii's a good one."

I read the name on this one aloud. "Marisol Louise Ingram. Is that who you are?" "Sometimes. When I found you, I was a fourteen-year-old runaway. Ruby sounded like a magical princess name. You know, the best way to change your life is change your name."

I *didn't* know that. "What do you mean, *found* me? Like a stray dog?"

"You and your little dog were both strays. I spotted *him* first. I'd had a dog, a tiny, tiny thing. My mom bought her as a fashion accessory. Her name was Sylvia. I loved her."

"Your mom?"

"The dog. When Mom realized her *accessory* had to eat and poop, she left her with the Humane Society. I told her *I'd* take care of Sylvia, I'd let her sleep with me, but Mom said I was irresponsible and I'd never walk her. I said how much do you need to walk a dog with toothpick legs four inches long? The last I saw of Sylvia was her tragic eyes staring from my mom's handbag at the shelter door."

"Is that why you ran away from home?"

"Ha! More like home ran away from me. Mom left."

"Where'd she go?"

"Where *do* moms go? We lived in Reno, lots of places to disappear to from there, Mexico, L.A., whatever. Dad was a zombified drunk. Who knows how long it took him to notice either of us being gone? After Mom left, I hitched a ride out of town with some guys. I thought I had nothing to lose ..." Ruby chewed a finger. All her nails were bitten ragged. "We'd sleep in the car, or camp with other kids on the road. That's how I met you. The two you were with seemed too young to be your parents. I caught on they stole you. You never said how."

I struck the table with my fist so hard our cups rattled. "That's crazy, you're making it up!"

"I'm not. I wish I didn't remember. Sometimes it's best not to."

"You sound like my *mom*."

"She's right." Ruby's phone dinged. "Listen, gotta run. There's a party at my place tonight. Come meet my other friends." She took a pen from her bag, scribbled an address and her number on a paper napkin, and left in a hurry, raincoat flapping like black wings. Ruby called me her friend, but she was a stranger to me, or was she? What was she was up to? I had to find out if she *did* know anything about my past. I would go to her party. I'd tell Mom I had a late class.

CHAPTER 37

At the address Ruby gave me, no one came when I rang the doorbell, but I heard party hubbub inside. I'd expected her to live somewhere cheap and rundown, not this prized hundred-year-old bungalow off Lake Union. I steeled myself to be social and went in. Not my scene, crushed among dancing, drinking, noisy people, but it was too late to run. Ruby pounced on me out of the rumpus like a cat on a bird. "Hey, you came!"

We shouted to hear each other over the music's loud techno beat. "Is this place yours?"

"*Dream on!*" Her expansive gesture took in the polished timber beams and columns, the deep wood-framed windows. "If I could afford this place, I wouldn't strip for grubby art students. No offense."

"None taken."

"Robert, IT brainiac, kayaks to work at Amazon across the lake, rents rooms to us artsy old friends. We provide him 'respite from the soulless tech-world' in exchange." Ruby laughed, took my hand, and pulled me further inside. "Come meet him. Honestly, we're family, not *blood*, but the best family *I've* known. There's nothing we wouldn't do for each other."

In the kitchen, party guests chatted and feasted on finger food. Ruby greeted several in passing who looked blandly technocratic enough to be the "IT brainiac" she'd promised. A broad-shouldered woman towered over the cooktop, stirring this, flipping that. She wore a ruffly apron over a mini-dress that exposed her athletic brown legs, and red platform sandals. My mouth watered to the smell of garlicky, buttery prawns that popped in her skillet. Ruby led me to her. "Robert, meet my friend Stevie!"

The person cooking dropped a lid that clanged like a cymbal and turned a ferocious look on us. She loomed through the savory miasma like a wrathful goddess. Iridescent green swept across her eyelids, scarlet over her chocolate-colored cheeks. Rhinestone earrings bobbled beneath her platinum beehive wig. She smiled. "Welcome, Stevie." Her voice was serene and girly.

I must have been staring, mouth agape. *This* was Robert? She tittered in undisguised amusement at my confusion. "I left Robert at work, honey, I'm Roberta tonight." The smoke alarm on the wall above the stove set up a shriek. *Roberta* turned to smother it with a kitchen towel and rescue the prawns.

Ruby and I covered our ears and escaped, elbowing through the crowd to the bar in the dining room. She poured two glasses of red wine, handed me one, and led me through French doors to a covered flagstone patio. We were alone outside in relative quiet, with the scent of potted lavender, rosemary, and rain.

Ruby sniffed her wine. "Mmm, good red. I should have snagged the bottle. Here's to us, being friends, all grown up!"

I lifted my glass politely. "I don't drink."

"I'll drink yours, too. It makes confession easier."

"Confession?"

"About the past, what you *say* you don't remember."

That was rich, Ruby seeing me through her own dishonest lens, dirtied by her corruption. I wasn't the one with fake IDs. "It's true, I *don't*."

"But I *do*." Ruby took a long gulp. "I've been ashamed of myself ever since."

I'd heard of imagining someone naked if they were making you feel uneasy, but that trick wouldn't work with Ruby. I'd seen her naked more than in clothes. *I* had nothing to be ashamed of, did I? "You said I saved your life."

"Yes, and I brought you back home."

Maybe that was true. Someone must have, but from where? If she'd been fourteen, I would have been, counting mentally on my fingers, yes, five. What could I have done? "You're saying we're even, I helped you, you helped me?"

"But it was a near thing."

Why was I bothering to be polite? "Cut the coyness, Ruby! Tell me what you mean."

Ruby drained her glass. "I would have sold you."

My breath caught so hard my chest hurt. *"Sold me?"* That happened to other kinds of women, abused homeless girls, not me. "Sold me!"

"Shhh." Ruby looked over her shoulder. We were still alone on the patio. "No excuse, but I was broke and starving. The only shoes I had were these preposterous high-heeled boots I hadn't taken off for days. My feet were so swollen, I was afraid I'd never get them on again if I did. What happens to a barefoot runaway girl with no money? I could hardly walk for the blisters. I was desperate. This is what I remember: You touched my feet and the pain went away."

Ruby glared into my eyes from beneath her shiny pink bangs, daring me to deny it. I tensed. If Ruby knew this, she knew too much about me. I refused to show any reaction, on guard. My mind tried to escape into triviality. Was Ruby wearing contacts or was that turquoise color real?

She went on. "So, I was amazed and grateful for about ten seconds, then I realized I could hire you out as a human painkiller."

There it was, the implied threat of exposure. She smiled, inappropriately, nervously, her teeth purplish from the wine.

"… but it dawned on me somebody older or bigger would turn me in or steal you from me. I had to make a one-time big sale. I lied to you so you'd cooperate; I promised I'd take you home. I started looking for the right person, the right opportunity." She rushed through the next part. "Long story short, we ended up with a scummy guy who tried to rape me. That's when you attacked him and we stole his car."

"What, I *attacked* …?" Not likely! Then I remembered I'd *attacked* Winter, too.

"Yep. Long enough for me to get free."

"And *we* stole a car?"

"I drove. Driving was the one worthwhile thing my dad taught me. By middle school I could drive him to buy booze if he was too far gone." Ruby took a sharp breath. "I can't *bear* now to think what might have happened to you out there alone! Obviously, I'd been about to make it a million times worse, but I couldn't after you saved me." She drummed her fingernails on her empty glass and took mine. "Well, say something! It's not *like* me to treat a lost little kid that way. I'd meant to be *your* savior when I took you from those others."

My words, any I could find, stuck in my throat.

Tears sprang into Ruby's eyes. "At least I brought you home."

I couldn't take any more. I left Ruby standing there, a glass in each hand.

She'd stirred up sounds and smells and images like a dust devil in the trash heap of my memory. They spooked me, though I couldn't see them clearly, or make them fit together.

In the last two weeks of the term I took care with my clothes. I outlined my eyes with kohl to look mature and mysterious. I cut my hair tapered on the sides and wore matte makeup to hide my scars.

I practiced channeling the unbidden energy in my hands into my drawings. I'd thought piling detail upon minute detail, every dimple, crease and fingernail, would bring my sketches to life, but it had left them overdone and inert. Now, I let those details go and let the feelings I sensed in the models emerge onto my paper, aching sadness in the tilt of a head, loneliness in the sag of the shoulders, defiance in the painful stiffness of a spine. My confidence and skill grew, and I often found one or two of my classmates watching me draw. Ruby didn't come back.

My professor kept his distance, offered me no more advice, none of the help and direction he constantly fed to others. He hurried out at the end of each class, while we were taking down our drawings, or engrossed himself in conference with someone else until I left. I lingered in the basement lounge, spying on him above my sketchbook through lowered lashes. Sometimes he would leave with the ceramics instructor, their man laughs echoing down the corridor. I stalked him, watched him buy a sandwich from a vendor's cart, but when I followed him downstairs, I found the studio doors locked. I did beautiful work; at the very least, I deserved acknowledgement and apology. He ignored me.

My anger ate at me like acid. He'd transgressed, then thrown me away like a dirty tissue and I wanted my accounting. On the last class day, I opened my portfolio for our final group review. When my turn came, with everyone watching, he was forced to praise me face-to-face, but it came too late. I'd thought it through. A creator's willingness to destroy demonstrates her confidence in her ability to make more and better, and I knew I could. I showed my contempt for the man's opinion. I ripped my best drawings in half, threw them at his feet, and walked out.

CHAPTER 38

I slouched on my bed that evening, angry with myself for feeling bummed. I'd made my point, stood up for myself, I should be happy and proud. I was proud enough, but with no one to share my pride, I wasn't happy. I was angry with *everyone* who'd ever made me happy for even twenty seconds, teaching me the difference between being joyful and just being alive. If I'd never been shown the difference, I wouldn't miss it. Now I missed happiness like my dad missed his leg—what *wasn't* there hurt more than what was.

I missed Nate, too. I'd thought we were soulmates, both of us different from other people. He'd started it, got what he wanted, then abandoned me. Were all males like that? Given a chance, I might have loved Waleed. I couldn't blame him for being dead, but he was gone, too. If only *someone* would stick with me!

I heard Mom's car pull into the driveway. I wanted to sulk until she came to ask me what was wrong. I would say "nothing," but aside from dubious Ruby, I had no one else to talk to and I was finding myself unpleasant company. I met Mom at the door and trailed her into her bedroom.

"You're late." I sounded more accusing than I'd meant to.

"What? Not very."

I relented. "I thought you'd be home earlier. I'm hungry."

"It's sweet you missed me, but the fridge is full of food. Let me get out of my coat and we'll find something for dinner. How was your last day of life drawing?"

"I'm pretty sure I'll get the best marks in class."

Mom smiled. "Congratulations, I'm proud of you. When can I see your drawings?"

"I'm *so* hungry right now."

Mom gave me a hug. "Me, too."

It was a leftovers omelette night. I toasted French bread a day from being too hard to slice. When we sat down to eat, whatever Mom had found in the fridge and stirred into the eggs tasted comforting. I opened a novel. The page-turner Mom had brought to read lay unopened beside her plate.

"Stevie?" The way she said it killed my appetite instantly. It announced an Important Subject. I wanted to eat dinner normally.

"Stevie, I have some news.

"Okay." I put my book face-down and crumbled toast onto my plate.

"I'm going to California for the weekend to meet James's son and his family. He's got two grandkids. I'll show you their pictures after dinner." She was babbling, her voice higher than usual. If this was calculated to make me join in her enthusiasm, it didn't. "I would have told you earlier, but you were so busy with your end-of-term projects and all. This was kind of a recent decision, the right timing."

"Right? Why now?" I tipped my chair on its back legs

the way Mom always complained would ruin it. She didn't seem to notice.

Mom blushed over a big bite of omelette, chewed and swallowed. Nothing was spoiling *her* appetite. "James and I are …"

"Getting *married*?" I was joking. *Ha-ha.*

"No, not getting married, not now. We're going to live together."

I sat forward; the chair legs banged down. "What? There's no space for another person here!"

"Not in this house, in his. You'll have a suite with your own bathroom and a walk-in closet. When I was his realtor, I wondered what he'd do with so many rooms. Isn't that funny?"

No, not funny at all. "I don't *want* to move. We've lived here forever."

"That's part of why I need to. I can't stand the echoes. All these years …" Mom looked around, as though our cozy kitchen were some stranger's place where she was surprised to find herself. "I stayed here waiting for your dad. I was like you, I could never believe he was dead. I tried to convince myself so I could convince you, so we could stop hoping for something impossible. Now, with the truth you've brought home, we're free."

"Oh." This sick sinking—was that freedom? I'd promised Dad he could find me here.

"We'll need to move all our personal things first, so I can stage the house for sale."

"You're *selling* our house?" I stood so fast my chair fell over. Mom twitched at the crash.

"It'll pay for your college. I've worried about how we'd

do that for a long time."

So, it was all about *me. Right.* I stormed out of the room.

———

Mom wasted no time. When she left for the airport with James Friday morning, she'd already begun packing to move. Big cardboard cartons sat around, some full and taped shut, others open like mouths waiting to swallow life as we'd known it. Two empty ones lurked in my room. I could almost hear them breathing. I was to have them filled for transport to my "suite" at James's house by Monday when Mom got back.

I stared out my window. Did anything last? By the fence with its tall shrubbery, I saw Hero's grave marked by dead flowers Mom had yet to clear. Hero's love had never failed me. How could I leave him? Someone digging in the garden might find his bones someday, his skull, and go *eew, a dead dog!* never knowing his nobility and faithfulness. I wrapped my sweater tighter around me and went outside into the not-quite-rain. I knelt on the wet grass by his grave.

A thud and clatter from Mom's garden shed startled me. Rats? Squirrels? They'd have to be awfully big to make a noise like that, knocking over a rake or a hoe. Raccoons, or a neighbor's cat accidentally trapped inside, more likely. I patted the ground over Hero. Maybe I could dig him up and take him with me. First I'd have to free whatever was in the shed.

Dad had built it as a playhouse for me—the last thing, besides his boat, he'd built in his garage workshop before he sailed. I'd never liked it, too big for me then, forbidding, its distance from the deck immense. I opened the door, cautious in case some creature made a dash for it. The small windows were shuttered. Nothing ran out of the dimness. Inside, the floor creaked beneath my feet. I stopped and the floor creaked again. A man-sized shape detached itself from the wall behind a folded patio umbrella. I shrieked, backed out and slammed the door shut, before I grasped what I had seen.

His voice was hoarse. "Stevie, are you alone?"

I cracked the door, doubting myself. "Nate?"

He poked through the umbrella's canvas folds, looking as fearful as the trapped creature I'd expected. "Shh …"

"What the *hell* are you doing in there?"

He was gaunt, almost unrecognizable, with a pointed goatee and shaved eyebrows, holding one arm protectively with the other. He winced and stumbled at the threshold.

I caught him. "Oh my God, you *are* real!"

Nate wouldn't come into the house until I convinced him it was empty. He perched on the edge of a kitchen stool darting looks at every sound, the furnace fan clicking on, a car passing in the street. He let me strip off his damp black hoodie. His right sleeve was torn and soaked with blood from a gash that crossed his upper arm. His pain staggered me.

"Ugh! Nate, what did this?"

"They shot me." He raised his eyes, ringed with bruise-colored shadows, meeting mine like a hurt little boy begging an explanation. I wanted one, too, but questions could wait.

I wasn't surprised my hands rose to his wound, his pain intense and throbbing. Fear invaded my body touching Nate's blood, like seizing a live electrical wire. I forced myself not to jerk away in the seconds before the jolt passed, taking the pain with it. Nate blinked, confusedly focused on my face. If he wondered why the pain had gone, he didn't say so.

The wound was raw-meat ugly. I cleaned it best I could with hydrogen peroxide and cotton balls Mom had kept stocked in the bathroom since I was a kid with scraped knees. "You might need stitches. I'll take you to the emergency clinic."

"No! They'll be hunting me."

"Who's *they*?"

"State police, FBI, NSA? All of them."

I shrank from Nate's sour breath and wild eyes. "You don't know what you're saying. That's impossible."

He tried to stand. I pushed him back down onto the stool.

"Stevie, people died! We're pledged to nonviolence, but all of a sudden they were shooting everywhere. Somebody shot a security guy and I picked up his gun. Another guy came at me. I didn't have a choice. It was him or me."

"What are you talking about?" He was delirious with shock. I tried to think where Mom kept her anti-anxiety meds.

"*Jesus Christ!*" Are you kidding? Don't you watch the news? We liberated this *humongous* factory farm east of the mountains. Global action against corporate torture and slavery."

"Wait, human trafficking, selling people?" That hit a nerve with me.

He shook his head with a horrid grin. "Not humans, pigs. We had a collaborator inside. He said no one else would come until the night shift change. We broke in and unchained the sows." His grin contorted into a scowl. "Then we realized they couldn't walk, couldn't stand up, most of them, their baby piglets squealing everywhere. It took forever to get them into the trucks. The security guards caught us and pulled their guns and everybody was firing at everybody else!"

"All that for *pigs*?" He had to be making an appalling joke, or, worse, he was insane.

"Listen! Do you know how factory farms raise your bacon? Turn sows into miserable meat machines?" His voice pitched higher, outraged. "Pigs are smart, like dolphins or elephants. They're faithful and affectionate as dogs. Would you eat your dog?"

My stomach roiled. "Don't say that, Nate!"

My reaction escalated his madness. Blood seeped through the dish towel I'd wrapped around his wound. He slipped off the stool, took a few jerky steps. "I ran for a truck to save the pigs, but somebody shot at me and I kept running, to our getaway car outside the gates. I didn't wait for anybody else. I should have, I … I saw myself brave, but when it came to it …" Nate's mouth opened in a horrified grimace, his eyes moving as though he watched his cowardice replay.

I bandaged his arm with gauze and tape and wrapped it in a fresh towel. He let me take off his shoes and tuck him in blankets on the sofa. He slept, so motionless I touched his chest to be sure he was breathing. I checked the headlines. Nate's raving was bad; seeing it was true was far, far worse. In video news, pigs caught in the crossfire, some still kicking weakly, sprawled beside human corpses; the farm manager, red-faced and spitting fury, swore death to the surviving perpetrators. A somber congressman reviled the terrorists who would be punished to the limits of the law.

When Nate stirred in the afternoon, I brought him a tray with a bowl of the creamy clam chowder Mom had left for me. He sat up. His right arm seemed stiff and he held it close to his body, but without any sign of pain.

"Where's your mom? What are all these boxes?"

"Mom's gone for the weekend with James, her boyfriend. Apparently we're moving in with him." I set the tray on his lap. "Here, you need to eat."

He spooned up the chowder greedily. "This is fantastic. Is there more?"

Mentioning the bacon bits in it would have spoiled the meal for him. He polished off seconds while I made coffee. Nate poured milk and sugar into his and guzzled it. I sat beside him on the rumpled blankets. He stank of fear and blood and something else I couldn't identify. His knees jiggled as he went on with his story.

"I drove through the mountains, the long way around because I didn't dare take the ferry—somebody might have seen the car near the pig farm. I ditched it in the woods before dawn. I made the last miles over the bridge and here on foot."

"But, Nate …"

"*Nate Wu* never left Asia. I'm still officially in Singapore, where my US passport is. I came as Albert Song from China, but Albert Song has to disappear. We have a safe house in Canada. I've got to get across the border. If anybody talks and connects Albert Song to Nate Wu …"

"Stop, stop!" I covered my face with my hands, trying to absorb what Nate had said, but he went on:

"Thank God, Mom and Dad are in Arizona for the winter. They don't know anything. I have to protect them."

My hands were wet with tears when I took them away and looked at Nate. "Protect them, but not me? *I* don't matter?" Of course not, I never had. Our "romance" had been my delusion. He touched my cheek. I felt sick with desire despite everything and I loathed myself for it.

He looked into my eyes. "My mom told me about your accident. I'm so sorry. I've missed you so much."

I couldn't look away. Should I whack him or cry? "Missed me, as if! *One* message in a *whole year*? *You* left."

"For the *Cause*, Stevie. It's bigger than you or me."

"The Fur People?" I spat the name.

Nate ignored my contempt. "That's not what we call ourselves, but yeah."

"Shooting people, stealing pigs? You'll go to prison forever."

"If it's war, we're the good guys. I'm not a deserter. I have to get back and prove I'm not a coward either."

Nate took my hand and squeezed it so tight it hurt.

"I have to get into Canada. Join us, Stevie. Come with me. You're kind. You love animals and … I need you. I love you, I always have. I was afraid to tell you."

The *L* word! This was crazy confusing. "And *now* you're telling me, now that you've *killed* someone, now that you're a fugitive? You want me to be part of that?"

Nate put his uninjured arm around me and pulled me to him. I realized that other smell was pigs. He kissed my scar with tenderness I craved.

I turned my head, my lips met his, so well-remembered and at the same time strange. What had he become, a bloodthirsty terrorist, a hero, a pure idealist walking his talk? I let myself rest in Nate's malodorous embrace. I was so tired of being alone.

CHAPTER 39

ate dozed, heavy against me. I slid out from under his weight. I cleaned up the kitchen and took the bloody cotton and towels outside to the bin. What interesting power I'd accrued! I could report my dad to the Aussie immigration authorities (whether or not they could find him); I could complain to the university about my professor (whether or not they could prove anything, his life would be made uncomfortable and his record deservedly besmirched); and now I could turn Nate in to the FBI (and no question on that one, he'd be in deep shit).

Did they all think I was a toy they could drop and walk away from and I'd just stay where I'd been left, or that I'd believe their lies and excuses? Raven had made that mistake, too, and look what happened to him! But, yes, *do* look at what happened. Maybe it was justice, but awful justice, and who made me the judge and jury? I'd never meant for Raven to die. I wouldn't think about Raven's fate. Everyone makes mistakes, sometimes horrendous ones, in the name of good intentions—Raven had, I had, now Nate had, too. His mistakes created repercussions on a bigger scale, but were they that different? My actions had landed on the side of the law, but Nate's were in service to a larger law.

I called Ruby and asked her to meet me at a fish and chips place on the waterfront that evening. "It's urgent, I need your help."

I shook Nate awake. "Come into the bathroom with me. We need to shave your beard and your head. Right now."

He couldn't lift his arm to do it himself, but I was an experienced head-shaver from those bitter high school days. He was too groggy to argue and I refused to explain.

"If I'm the only person you can trust, you have to trust me completely."

He sat uneasily on the edge of the tub while I worked. When I was finished, he looked like someone whose health, or lack of it, deserved sympathy. He didn't like my taking pictures of him. I told him I didn't see he had a choice.

"Right now, Nate, I'm the best chance you've got. You came to me. Don't fight my helping you. And take a shower while I'm gone. I'll leave you clean sweats."

Darkness had already fallen when I walked into the fried-fish-saturated atmosphere of the eatery on the harbor's city side. The place was badly lit, boisterous with happy hour beer drinkers and tourists. Ruby was there. I put on a grin that felt like it might split my face and joined her in the long "Order Here" queue, faking cheeriness. I surprised her with a hug and spoke into her hair.

"Hey, we're here for girls' Friday after-work gossip. Let's smile for the security cameras."

Ruby obliged with an expression that might have been

genuine pleasure. "Great! Hard day at the office?"

"You're good!"

"Don't all models want to act? What's going on?"

I yawned and covered my mouth. "All that ID you have? How did you get it?"

Ruby turned away as if she hadn't heard.

"Come on, *please*, I need some help. You said yourself you owe me." I jabbed her in the ribs, laughed at an untold joke, and stooped close to hear her reply.

Ruby surveyed the menu displayed high on the wall, reading our choices, her hand cupped over her chin and lips in concentration. "I've known Robert, Roberta, a long time."

I pointed to the halibut and chips and spoke close to her ear. "Passports?"

She shook her head and indicated the less expensive cod, then looked down, searching through her fringed bag. "Too risky these days. Birth certificates and driver's licenses."

"Canadian?" I could have been meaning the fish.

She nodded. "Better than US, I think."

We'd be next at the counter. I showed her my phone. We bent our heads over it to see the small images. "I'm sending you these photos. He needs a name, documents usable in British Columbia, like, right now." We *oohed* over some nonexistent cute kitties. "Delete these as soon as you can."

We both ordered fish and chips to go. I paid. We hugged outside, for continuity in the cameras there.

Ruby couldn't know how apropos her whispered goodbye was. "Tomorrow morning, eight-thirty, by the Pike Market pig."

Was she the one who'd, long ago, taught me about hiding in plain sight?

CHAPTER 40

*I*n the morning, Nate's wounded arm was pain-free, but red and swollen. I found some remnant antibiotics for him in the medicine cabinet. Expired meds were a bad idea, but we were caught in the consequences of a string of bad ideas and one led to another. As I applied a fresh bandage and improvised a sling from a scarf, I explained about Ruby and Roberta.

He snapped at me. "That's a terrible scheme!"

I snapped back. "It's our *only* scheme! You'll have documents in a new name. You can get a Canadian passport once you're over the border."

"If your *friends* don't turn me in first."

I bluffed through a twinge of doubt. "They won't, they can't. They're implicated now. Tell me your plan for the border crossing."

"When I'm ready."

Which meant he didn't have one, but I'd set my part in motion and it wasn't the first time I'd embarked on perilous action without a plan.

On the morning ferry, I was another raincoat-clad commuter consoling myself with my coffee and phone. Rain fell in sheets as we docked. Climbing the stairs from the waterfront to Pike Place, I hid under my umbrella. In the market I dodged stallholders unloading crates of fish and fruit and vegetables, bawling instructions and greetings to one another. I rubbed the bronze pig's nose for luck, like any other market visitor.

Ruby, in her black raincoat, hood covering her pink hair, appeared coming around a delivery van. As she strode past, her eyes flashed my way. I followed her at a plausibly deniable distance, up a block to First Avenue. There, a corner flower shop open to the sidewalk made an oasis of light and color in the gloom.

Ruby paused to sniff a bouquet of long-stemmed red-orange roses, checked the price, and went on across the street. No watcher could be surprised if the gaudy blooms stopped me, too. A small tan envelope lay on the shelf where a person might naturally put a hand while bending to inhale the roses' peppery sweetness, as Ruby had.

I shook out my umbrella in the entry, chilled from my walk home from the ferry. Nate called to me. He sounded excited. "About time you got back! I've got it, our way into Canada."

Before I was born, before Dad began building his boat, he and Mom were hikers. Nate had one of their old topographic maps of the North Cascades unfolded on the coffee table in the living room, among remnants of a toast and cereal breakfast.

"What are you doing?" I tossed my wet coat over a chair and sat beside him to take off my boots. "Why don't you look online?"

"Don't be dumb!"

I ignored that, another sign of his stress. He didn't mean to be cruel.

"I threw Albert Song's phone into the bay. Sooner or later they'll be on his tail. We have to go analog to be safe—*safer*. Look here." He tapped the map. "They patrol roads and towns close to the border, but they can't watch all the hiking trails through the woods."

I studied the squiggly lines in the national forest at the top of the map. "I don't see a trail that goes all the way over."

"So, a little bushwhacking on both sides, no big deal."

"What about cougars and bears?"

Nate's triumphant look lifted his face in unfamiliar

angles, like a freaky carnival caricature of the person I knew. "I kept the gun."

He couldn't have missed my revulsion. Nate carrying a gun, a gun he claimed had killed a man, was a different person than I'd known. It seemed once a man fired a gun, it was hard to put it down again and Nate with a gun didn't make me feel safer, especially crossing an international border. I fumbled for other reasonable arguments. "But this time of year? Won't there be snow?"

"These days, who knows? It's different every year. We dress warm, stick to the lower elevations as much as we can." He traced a line on the map with one finger. "It shows a ravine through the mountains here. We'll follow it. It won't be more than ten or twenty miles, depending how straight we can go."

"Ten or twenty miles? Nate, you're in no shape for that."

"They shot me in the arm, not my legs. Besides, it doesn't hurt anymore. We'll take your mom's car to Silver Lake. See? It's only about four hours north. We'll start from there. "

"My mom's car?" I was sounding like a confused parrot.

"Eventually they'll find it, but we'll be long gone in B.C. It's not like we're stealing it. This arm won't keep me from driving."

I liked how formulating his plan revived Nate. The details troubled me, but his eagerness to be away was infectious. "No, I'll drive. We can't let anyone see you. I have my license. And now, *presto!* you have one, too. You'll have to memorize your Canadian name, *Alphonse.*" I held out what Ruby had left me like a winning hand at cards. Nate's double-take hurt my feelings. "What, you didn't think I could pull this off? I told you I could get them. Aren't you pleased?"

He examined his new ID. "How did you …? Of course, I'm pleased. It's just, we need to leave right away, in case."

"In case you can't believe I was careful enough?"

Nate must have heard the tightening in my throat. "Stevie, there's no such thing as *careful enough*. That's what we thought we were being at the pig farm."

Those memories dulled his eyes. My helplessness against that kind of pain was my own failure. I wanted him to kiss me, to say he loved me, to say he believed in me. We were side-by-side, but he was far away.

Mom hadn't yet disturbed the layers of our lives accumulated on the shelves in the garage. Nate helped me search as well as he could. Behind a box of empty canning jars, we unearthed Dad's camping pack, complete with two lightweight sleeping bags smelling of mold. The pack looked cumbersome and old-fashioned, but by a miracle, mice hadn't nested in it. The hiking boots were a size too big; with thick socks they would work.

I raided Mom's moving cartons for her ski clothes. I'd give Nate my own winter anorak and take hers for myself. My wrists would stick out from the sleeves, but no matter, this wasn't a fashion show. We lunched on the leftover clam

Kristina Bak

chowder, thick and salty at the bottom of the pot, then foraged for trail food in the fridge and cupboards. We found cheese and crackers, almonds, chocolate bars, apples. I took the big flashlight Mom kept for when the power went out. We filled water bottles, rolled the sleeping bags and fit it all into the camping backpack.

Nate insisted he could carry it. "I said my arm doesn't hurt." He undid the sling. "See, I'm fine."

He needed to believe that. It wasn't the time to explain his pain was gone only because I'd taken it away. I couldn't make his wound heal faster. I gave him two more of the antibiotics, a higher dose than the label recommended. The pills past their expiration date were probably not so potent. I packed them and extra bandages. I looked around, anxious. "I feel like we're missing something."

Nate hefted the pack with his good arm, trying its weight. "Forget it. They'll have what we need at the safe house. Over the border we'll look like any other hikers. We can catch a bus from Chilliwack. It's not far. Let's go, let's go!"

I couldn't blame Nate for his impatience. This was life or death for him, or at least a free life or prison. And what would getting caught mean for me? I'd never looked good in orange. That was me trying to be ironic rather than frantic.

"One more minute." I ran to my room and pocketed the coyote fur patch from my dresser top, where it had stayed since I left for Australia.

———

Nate stretched out as well as he could in the rear seat. I hid him beneath an old Pendleton blanket and put our pack in the trunk before we pulled out of the garage. With the garage door closed behind us and the lights I'd left on glowing through the living room curtains, the house looked snug, like a good place to be. We headed north across the bridge off the island, Nate soon snoring in his blanket hideout. He didn't wake until we drove onto the ferry at Kingston. He kept hidden until we crossed the freeway on the other side to the smaller parallel state highway.

The afternoon was as dim and dismal as the morning had been. Rain diminished to drizzle. We stopped past Sedro Woolley, where the suburbs thinned, for Nate to move up front with me. He sat hunkered low as we went on, tracing and retracing trails on the topographic map with a penlight he'd taken from a kitchen drawer. The penlight quivered in his hand. "The camps and resorts around the lake should be closed for the season, nobody to see us. Slower! Watch out for that truck!"

"Cut it, Nate. I drove fine while you were under the blanket."

"Uh-huh, don't speed. We can't afford a traffic stop." I heard him swallow spasmodically.

The Nate in my heart was different from this Nate beside me. I wanted to talk to him about things important to me, our past, our futures, and he couldn't hear the simplest things I said. Having made a brave choice for himself, he seemed not to question that his choice held for me, too, with no need for discussion. He was terrified. His terror meant I had to be more confident. He'd been through so much more than I had and one of us had to stay calm. I blocked out his incessant comments on my driving and made myself think about other things, like, that in all the confusion of Nate's arrival and our hasty preparations to leave, I hadn't seen his tattoo. Exquisite to both of us when I drew it, it had to look amateur now. It *was* amateur, in the best sense of the word, done without expertise, but with love.

Nate broke into my thoughts with more directions. "Turn off at Deming, bear east to Maple Falls, then north."

Gray sky darkened toward sunset. The roads grew narrower and emptier, the towns marked on the map mere handfuls of houses and businesses. We passed fewer fields and farms, more stretches of forest.

Nate was right, we saw no people at all at the lake that lay like a liquid mirror. We drove on up its western shore to its northern tip. We weren't in a wilderness, but we might as well have been, boat docks and camp sites empty beneath the glowering trees. Nate was liking what he saw. "Yeah, yeah, farther, over there, turn, here!"

We parked and got out beneath an ancient cedar. Everything around us dripped from rain that had not quite stopped. Nate put on the anorak I gave him and raised the hood against the damp cold. My coat was tight on him, but plenty long. He peered into the dusky woods where a trail began. "It'll be steep at first. Our eyes will adjust."

I fastened the velcro on Mom's coat around my neck and wrestled Dad's pack from the trunk. I helped Nate ease the straps over his shoulders and fasten the belt around his hips. He shrugged to settle the burden. I'd done a good job with the pain, for better or worse. His voice was loud and elated in the surrounding silence. "By this time tomorrow we'll be in Canada."

"Wait." I held out the coyote fur patch, warm in my palm. "Remember this?"

Nate's gentle smile reminded me of who he'd been, who we'd both been a year ago. "You kept it!" He stroked the fur patch with his thumb.

I turned over his hand and closed his fingers around it. "Take it, Nate. You need it more than I do now. Coyotes are survivors. They thrive almost anywhere." I kissed him, long and lingering, not wanting the touch of our lips to end.

When it did, he grinned and moved quickly toward the trailhead. "Later, Babe. We'll have plenty of time for that soon. Onward!"

I watched the space grow between us. He started climbing, seeming certain I was close behind. I called to him. "You'll make it. We'll see each other again, somehow. I love you."

Nate froze in place. I turned and ran. The few yards to the car felt like a grueling uphill hike. Every time I lifted a foot I commanded my body to keep going. I was afraid if I looked back, I couldn't resist Nate's face, or that his expression might show he despised me. If he called to me, I didn't hear it. I got in, started the car, and peeled out onto the road before I could change my mind. In the rearview mirror, Nate waved *come back* or *goodbye*, the reflective strips on his sleeves red from the car's taillights.

I wondered if I was feeling what I should be, what a normal person would feel under the circumstances, then

I corrected myself: I was *normal* enough for me. I had no name for what pierced my heart, the sensation of endless free-fall in my stomach. Somewhere, sometime, I'd learned whatever I *felt* wouldn't change what was happening. This pain was bad; naming it wouldn't make it go away.

Trees raced past in my high beams as I sped toward home. I lowered the window and let the cold air batter my hair. I concentrated on watching out for deer leaping into my lane. I didn't dare land for long on any one thought, except that I'd done all I could to help Nate without losing myself. Loneliness wouldn't kill me. Letting myself need what other people couldn't give would hollow me out and leave me worse than nothing. I had a life to create, on my own terms now.

Acknowledgements

Stevie first became real to me five years ago. Since then, I've explored different directions she might choose from the beginning of her story before *Nowever* finally took shape. I'm deeply grateful to my fellow writers and readers whose critiques and companionship have demanded hard work and offered comfort along the way: Barbara Jones, Loretta Slepikas, Celeste Brody, Nancy Tyler, Ellen Perry Berkeley, Bob Sizoo, Elizabeth Kelly Stephenson, Jana Zvibleman, Jim Steinberg, John Kvapil (my rock), and Anna Bak-Kvapil (always an inspiration).

Thanks to all my Australian friends, teachers and guides, and in loving memory of Judy McBurney.

The intergenerational Not Your Average Book Club at Roundabout Books in Bend, Oregon, assured me of the intelligence, curiosity and compassion of young adult readers. I hope to live up to their standards.

Thanks also to Patricia, Claire, Kim and Melissa at Luminare Press, and to Willamette Writers.

Also by Kristina Bak:

From Here to Argentina:
A Tango Love Story

———

Visit Kristina Bak online:

www.KristinaBak.com

CPSIA information can be obtained
at www.ICGtesting.com
Printed in the USA
LVHW030214041019
633170LV00006B/169